Exposing the Forbidden

This exceptionally daring collection includes "Just Say No to Drug Hysteria," William S. Burroughs's bitingly critical essay on the hypocrisy in American anti-drug policies; "Private Rituals," Dorothy Allison's emotionally raw yet lyrical story about a young girl's sexual abuse; well-known pornographer John Preston's essay "How Dare You Even Think These Things?" about the writing of pornography; Hattie Gossett's wild and unequivocal poetry detailing the experience of urban black women; and "It's Only Art," Karen Finley's incantatory rant against government and religious censorship. Uncompromisingly truthful, unusually explicit, and unfailingly adventurous, *High Risk* is a literary event in the tradition of *The Olympia Reader*. It is a daring exploration of that cult of otherness" that gives us our deepest sense of who and what we believe.

HIGH RISK

AN ANTHOLOGY OF FORBIDDEN WRITINGS

EDITED BY

AMY SCHOLDER & IRA SILVERBERG

A PLUME BOOK

PLUME
Published by the Penguin Group
Penguin Books USA Inc., 375 Hudson Street,
New York, New York 10014, U.S.A.
Penguin Books Ltd, 27 Wrights Lane,
London W8 5TZ, England
Penguin Books Australia Ltd, Ringwood,
Victoria, Australia
Penguin Books Canada Ltd, 2801 John Street,
Markham, Ontario, Canada L3R 1B4
Penguin Books (N.Z.) Ltd, 182–190 Wairau Road,
Auckland 10, New Zealand

Penguin Books Ltd, Registered Offices:
Harmondsworth, Middlesex, England

Published by Plume, an imprint of New American Library,
a division of Penguin Books USA Inc.
Simultaneously published in a Dutton hardcover edition.

First Printing, March, 1991
10 9 8 7 6 5 4 3 2 1

For permissions, please turn to page 298.

 REGISTERED TRADEMARK—MARCA REGISTRADA

Library of Congress Cataloging-in-Publication Data

High risk : an anthology of forbidden writings / edited by Amy Scholder and Ira
Silverberg.
    p. cm.
  1. American literature—20th century. 2. Sex customs—Literary
collections. 3. Homosexuality—Literary collections. 4. Erotic literature,
American. 5. Homosexuality—United States. 6. Sex customs—United
States. I. Scholder, Amy. II. Silverberg, Ira.
PS509.E7H5 1991
810.8′03538′0904—dc20   90-47933
ISBN 0-452-26582-7   CIP

Printed in the United States of America
Set in Garamond Book
Designed by Leonard Telesca

PUBLISHER'S NOTE
The stories in this collection are works of fiction. Names, characters, places, and
incidents either are the product of the authors' imagination or are used
fictitiously, and any resemblance to actual persons, living or dead, events, or
locales is entirely coincidental.

HIGH
RISK

IN MEMORIAM

Carl Apfelschnitt

Cookie Mueller

Manuel Ramos Otero

To the memory of our dear friend
GREGORY KOLOVAKOS,
who inspired us to take on this project

Acknowledgments

We would like to thank all the artists and writers who submitted work to us during the various incarnations of this anthology. Without their support and inspiration, we might never have seen all this through.

We would also like to thank our agent, Peter Ginsberg; John Preston for all his anthological advice; Rex Ray and Kate Simon for help with our image; John Giorno; Hudson; Bo Huston; Eric Latzky; Scott Macaulay; Jeff Poole; Sarah Schulman; Patrice Silverstein; Barbara Smith; Charles Stockly; Gent Sturgeon; Betsy Sussler; Peter Topaz. And Carolyn Dinshaw and David Trinidad for help at home.

CONTENTS

**AMY SCHOLDER AND
IRA SILVERBERG**   xiii
INTRODUCTION

JOHN PRESTON   1
HOW DARE YOU EVEN THINK THESE THINGS?

MARY GAITSKILL   17
ACTION, ILLINOIS

GARY INDIANA   37
DREAMS INVOLVING WATER

PAT CALIFIA   55
POEMS

WILLIAM S. BURROUGHS   69
JUST SAY NO TO DRUG HYSTERIA

BOB FLANAGAN   81
BODY

DAVID TRINIDAD   89
EIGHTEEN TO TWENTY-ONE

ANA MARIA SIMO   93
HOW TO KILL HER

HATTIE GOSSETT   105
BRAS & RUBBERS IN THE GUTTERS

DENNIS COOPER   113
WRONG

KATHY ACKER   123
A YOUNG GIRL

ESSEX HEMPHILL   151
HEAVY BREATHING

DOROTHY ALLISON   169
PRIVATE RITUALS

WANDA COLEMAN   187
POEMS

MANUEL RAMOS OTERO   195
THE EXEMPLARY LIFE OF THE SLAVE AND THE MASTER

LYNNE TILLMAN   201
DIARY OF A MASOCHIST

TERENCE SELLERS   209
IS THERE LIFE AFTER SADOMASOCHISM?

JANE DELYNN   221
BUTCH

DODIE BELLAMY   233
DEAR DENNIS

ROBERT GLÜCK   253
WORKLOAD

KATE BORNSTEIN   259
TRANSSEXUAL LESBIAN PLAYWRIGHT TELLS ALL!

MICHAEL LASSELL   263
DREAMS IN BONDAGE

COOKIE MUELLER   267
THE ONE PERCENT

DAVID WOJNAROWICZ   275
BEING QUEER IN AMERICA: A JOURNAL OF DISINTEGRATION

KAREN FINLEY   287
IT'S ONLY ART

**AMY SCHOLDER AND
IRA SILVERBERG**

INTRODUCTION

HIGH RISK—

—all those activities, subjects, imaginings that challenge the limits imposed not only by society but by oneself. If sadomasochism is *about* anything, it's about transgression—of the limits we thought we had. If we've taken drugs for a *reason,* it's to go beyond consciousness—one we thought was fixed. If asserting an ethnic identity is an essential means of survival, it's because culture in American society is based on the fallacy of white supremacy.

Ira Silverberg:

In 1977, my sophomore year at the Bronx High School of Science, a friend handed me a dog-eared copy of William S. Burroughs' Naked Lunch. He claimed it had changed his life. That same day I was introduced to sniffing cocaine. I knew it would change my life. I was fifteen years old, already openly gay, and about to read a book that would considerably alter my perspective on life and literature.

My middle-class upbringing seemed to pale in comparison to the stimulation that awaited me. In retrospect, I see the synchronicity of my introduction to Burroughs and cocaine as a spiritual double whammy—especially for a fifteen-year-old. I began to read more Burroughs, along with the works of Sade, Genet, Céline, Selby, and others. Reading these books freed me. In their company suddenly I was safe. Safe to break the boundaries of my social and cultural background by exploring the extremes of my sexuality and my predisposition to substance abuse.

Within a few years, Burroughs would become an even more important part of my life. At the age of eighteen, I was one of his retinue; by nineteen, I was living in Lawrence, Kansas, as a full-fledged member of his family. When I returned to New York at age twenty-one, I had fully explored the depths of a new aesthetic introduced to me by William. I will always give him credit for teaching me how to read—by transcending the boundaries of literature and incorporating new values into my own life.

The Burroughsian aesthetic as such, however, is limited. Yet, in the context of this anthology, it is a pertinent example of the literature that emanates from a culture of otherness. The stories that are told by any disenfranchised group are the stories that define who we are and expose the society in which we live. My experience as a recovering intravenous cocaine and heroin addict has taught me this—not to disavow my past. The otherness of the junkie, the homosexual, the sadomasochist, the criminal, the prostitute, the marginalized—this is what the writing in High Risk *explores.*

High Risk is about exposure. The texts here seem naked. They make you feel naked when you read them. They stimulate, they emphasize, separately and collectively, that desire is as complex as the world in which we live. They do this without shame or righteousness. By their uncompromising truthfulness, these works capture ambivalence—

—in human nature: the startling truth that human nature is both attracted to and repulsed from its own natural extremes.

Ambivalence—in art: the great toll it takes on artists and writers fighting for freedom of expression under the strain of constant adversity.

Ambivalence—in sex: for some, the means through which the most intense connections are made; for others, sex is a commodity, an experiment, a game with rules that are ever changing. What are the consequences when someone comes to grips, through literature, with the hate and anger resulting from sexual violence that happened during childhood? What are the consequences when, later in life, sexual desires are satisfied by a new configuration of violence, one that is vertiginously close to the past?

Ambivalence.

How do experiences of altered states of consciousness affect us? And how are those perceptions transformed when expressed through language?

How are experiences actually shaped by the way in which language delineates thought?

Transgression—through literature: some writers have been challenging the established forms of literature used to express meaning, to tell a story; and, in this way, they challenge perceptions of the world and of ourselves. This is literature that transgresses physical and emotional boundaries.

How much can a body, can a mind take? Transgression.

As the dominant culture forces disenfranchisement on more people, and encourages homogeneity, the number of groups labeled "transgressive" grows exponentially: groups as diverse as HIV-positive women barred from abortion in their home states, to artists and arts organizations limited by the restrictive funding mechanisms of a repressive government. The community of others—transgressors—grows. And the literature that comes from these marginalized communities is the literature that by exposing our society, defines it. This is what *High Risk* reveals—a new definition of our society in a time of increasing oppression and censorship.

As a collection, *High Risk* defies the usual ways of categorizing literature. The work in this anthology emerges from rich and diverse histories, from aesthetic traditions that defy convention, that do not accede to hysterical social conformists. *High Risk* is a balanced anthology of lesbian, gay, and heterosexual writers from various ethnic backgrounds. What bonds these writers and the editors together is a continued belief in counterculture—that is, a cultural life and liveliness that is honest, thoroughly personal, and expressive of the conviction that there is nothing too dangerous or perverse in art or literature.

One reader might cringe while reading a story of lesbian sadomasochism; for another reader this might be the story that tells her that she is not alone. For someone else, her/his identification with a story on incest, rape, or prostitution might provide the strength to speak about her/his own experience. By breaking taboos of self-censorship within the aesthetic dimension, *High Risk* might provide the same gift of voice for a reader grappling with a corresponding personal issue.

It has been suggested that *High Risk* might encourage some to explore "high-risk" activities described in this anthology. We think not. There is an essential difference between imagery and live acts: self-revelation through literature explores risk, brutality, safety, and tenderness through truth and honesty. To the eye of the social conformist, this may seem a deadly, perilous, "high-risk" threat, but through the medium of art and literature we have the freedom of choice. And our *freedom to choose* to express fantasies must not be relinquished. The representation of the high-risk activity or the individual engaged in such does not dictate behavior to the free thinker.

Censorship affects not only the arts but also the rapid dissemination of information, particularly AIDS information. As the media and public officials continue to distinguish the risk level of *groups* as opposed to the risk level of *activities,* there are entire populations deprived of vital information and health care. The struggle against the violence that HIV and AIDS have unleashed has united diverse communities who have been thrown together in a corresponding struggle for empowerment and judicious representation. Misinformation, a dearth of educational materials, *any* form of censorship—this is a higher risk.

Amy Scholder:

High Risk is not an AIDS book, but of course, AIDS has impacted our lives, all representations, and how we read them. The premature deaths of some of this generation's most wild and creative artists and writers change everything. How to have sex, how to take drugs, how to form community when anti-sex fascists have used AIDS to isolate us from one another—these are the challenges faced by the contributors to this anthology, as well as all artists and writers, in the form and content of their work.

I've always wanted to believe that a certain kind of literature could open up the consciousness of its readers, as books did and do for me, as I search for alternative ways of thinking about my undivined future. I don't believe reading a book will change my life, or anyone's life, but rather that by opening up my imagination, some part of my inner self can be suddenly available to me. Revelation.

There is such enormous pressure to conform in this society, and those of us who reject these singular models of how to live, how to write, how to fuck, how to make art, are on the other side of the world. We have new stories and new ways of telling them. Here are some of the most challenging writers from the other side. I read them as visionaries, not as role models, because we don't need heroes. We need inspiration to envision the expression of all desire.

New York and San Francisco
July 1990

High Risk, Carl Apfelschnitt, 1989. Private Collection.

JOHN PRESTON

HOW DARE YOU EVEN THINK THESE THINGS?

THE FIRST STORY I remember writing was a medieval fantasy. A handsome lord rode through his domains examining the serfs who worked the land, stripped to the waist, their masculine beauty open to his evaluation. He was going to claim one of them for his bed, asserting his *droit du seigneur* to fulfill his lust.

I wrote the story on a ruled pad while sitting on the porch of our house and I still remember, over thirty years later, the sun's warmth on my groin as I scribbled out the tale of power and sex. I can't remember whether I fantasized myself as the lord or his peasants. I suspect it was probably both. I have always used my pornography to inquire into my own sexuality more than I have tried to capture a single point of view. Even then, pornography, for me, was exploration.

I left my work out on the table while I went to the kitchen to get a drink. When I came back to the porch, I found my grandmother reading my writing. She looked at me with fury and disgust. *"How dare you even think these things?"*

1

she yelled at me. Then she tore the small, amateurish manuscript to shreds.

No one in our house ever mentioned the incident afterward. I didn't write fiction again for years.

My mother gave me a great gift when I was in high school. I wrote an English term paper on conformity. It was the fifties and suburban America didn't appreciate rebelliousness. To make it worse, I had likened the price I had to pay for acceptance from my peers and my teachers to prostitution.

My instructor and the school administrators pointed to that word and accused me of writing pornography. They told my mother that she would have to come to the school and meet with them to discuss the disciplinary problem I was creating.

That afternoon, my mother sat in the principal's office and listened meekly as he ranted about my insubordination. I had been born when my mother was quite young. She was only in her early thirties at this time. She'd grown up in the same town that we lived in. She'd gone to the same school and had the same English teacher and had known the principal and guidance counselor during her own student days. My mother is a large woman, but she seemed as small as one of my classmates as she listened to them all agree about the dangers that I represented:

How dare he even have these thoughts?

To my surprise, and to the others' shock, my mother suddenly sat up straight in her chair, clutching her purse, and looked the rest of the adults in the eye, one by one. "You will not do to my son what you did to me. You will not tell him what to think."

She was the person most stunned by her own statement. She slumped back in her chair, exhausted. But she finished her speech: "My son will not be punished for what he's written. He's here to learn how to think, not what to think. You will do nothing to him. I've read his paper. I'm proud he could express himself so well."

Then she stood up and we went home. Once there, she went to bed with a cold compress on her head, a migraine pounding in her temples.

She would never tell me what had happened in her own school days, but it obviously had taken an enormous amount of strength for her to face the living demons of her adolescence. I learned then, from my mother's example, that courage could be costly. I also knew that I'd never been more proud of her.

When I look at pictures taken of me in my adolescence, I'm always stunned by how attractive I was. I didn't feel it. Some message I'd received told me I was repulsive; who I thought I was then had nothing to do with the photographic images I can hold in my hand today. I knew I was strange and that my strangeness was something others thought was despicable. It was, in fact, so abhorrent that I didn't even know its name.

Rumor told me that there were horrible men who loitered in bus stations. They were to be avoided at all times. Somehow I translated that gossip into something else: I should go to one of these places and find those men. They were waiting for me; they had something to tell me.

When I was no more than fifteen, I made up some excuse to go into Boston alone. I sat on a cold bench in the lobby of the Greyhound station and waited there until someone found me.

My escort proved to be a traveling salesman from Hartford who was out on the town after drinking too much champagne at a concert at Symphony Hall. He was tipsy enough to brazenly invite me up to his room at the Statler Hotel, on the other side of Park Square.

I remember—and I remember this *vividly*—sitting on the edge of his bed while he undressed, having only been able to take off my shoes and a single sock. "I've never done this before," I told him.

He sneered at me. Teenage boys who sold themselves in Park Square always claimed innocence, I'd learn later, hoping to drive up their price. But finally he listened to me carefully enough to realize I was telling the truth.

I have always been astonished by what happened after that: He proceeded to give me a complete sex education, including play-by-play illustrations of all the possible acts two men could perform. I sucked him; he sucked me. I fucked him; he fucked me. I ate his ass; he devoured mine. All through this action, he delivered a running commentary on how it should be done and with what discretion, and how to find my own partners.

Most of the talk was affirmative, but there were also very practical warnings. I was cautioned away from men who would offer a young man drugs that could turn into a trap. I was told how to identify syphilis chancres and other signs of disease that might threaten me. I was encouraged to use a condom if I had even the slightest doubts about the risk involved.

(He even had rubbers in his wallet and gave me a step-by-step demonstration on how to put one on, first illustrating the procedure on himself and then making me put a condom on my own cock, to show him I'd learned my lesson well enough.)

When I got older, I studied sexual health at a major university and eventually joined the staff of the school's program in human sexuality. I later worked for one of the largest and most prestigious sex information and education organizations in the country. I met with Masters and Johnson; I visited with staff from the Kinsey Institute; I shared meals with the leading sexologists of our times.

I have never heard such a brilliantly clear and helpful sex education lecture as the discourse that traveling salesman from Connecticut gave me on his bed in that hotel room. I have always thought it was one of the great blessings of my life.

I eventually found the written word about sex in the books by a man who wrote as Phil Andros. By the time I found those books, I already had the basic information down. Now I needed the mythologies of the world I was entering. I needed to know more about how others had built their lives around these facts; I needed to know the tales that would give them meaning; I had to learn to consider myself beautiful.

The kind of exciting and often hard sexuality Andros wrote about was what I wanted to experience, or, often, it reflected what I had actually gone through. I could only find his books in the sleaziest porn stores, but I used to scour their racks looking for his by-line.

Many years later, in the seventies, after I had started to write pornography myself, I discovered Phil Andros's real identity. He was Samuel Steward, once a protégé of Gertrude Stein's. I tracked down an address for him in Berkeley, California, and arranged to visit him.

Steward was in his sixties by the time I found him. We spent days together, just talking about his life and his experiences. I learned all about the charmed circle of writers and artists who had gathered around Stein and Alice B. Toklas. I also heard Steward's stories of handsome young sailors and street-smart laborers who'd inhabited his sexual world in Chicago, where he'd spent most of his adult years. With each story, Steward could usually bring out some memento as an illustration.

Steward had looked around at his life as a young man in the twenties and decided that the world was only going to give him loneliness in his old age. The silence within which he lived offered him no evidence of any other possibility. He defended himself against that isolation by compulsively cataloguing his adventures, not only by writing about them for his public but also by keeping an exhaustive journal and by accumulating an incredible collection of memorabilia. (His greatest prize was a lock of Rudolf Valentino's pubic hair, which sits, encased in glass, in a shrine at the foot of his bed.)

Steward felt he had written his pornography too soon.

No one would publish it but the smallest and, often, the trashiest companies. After a few years, he abandoned the work and retreated into his personal archives.

He hadn't seen that his pornography was changing the landscape in which it was happening. Many young men like myself were reading his adventures and were finding a mentor. Those once disdained, then out-of-print books had become collectors' items, passed hand to adoring hand by those of us who were the vanguard of gay writing, as it would come to be understood.

I wasn't the first young man to find him. I remember being enchanted by his description of one other—a porn star, as I recall—who would bicycle over the Bay Bridge from San Francisco to Berkeley to spend time with Sam and offer his adored body as an homage to the pioneer. Far from being abandoned, Steward was spending what he thought were to be his last lonely years receiving the adulation of a small but vital company of fans.

(Later, the cult that grew up around his writings would lead publishers to reissue most of his books. They were no longer hidden in cheap stores but were candidly displayed in the stacks of the new gay bookstores that were opening, bringing the written words of the gay experience to anxious readers.)

All this was the more astonishing to him because he had never expected to live this long; he'd had tremendous health problems. He described waking up every morning and pinching himself to see if he was still alive. He wouldn't plan for anything beyond that day, and, when each dawn arrived, he claimed it as a gift from the gods, something he hadn't expected to ever experience.

I knew that Steward had also been a tattoo artist at one time. I pleaded with him to come out of his retirement and mark me. I wanted put upon my own body a signal that the unspeakable was being uttered, that the things that should never be thought were coming true.

Sam arranged for the use of a friend's salon in San Francisco. We met in the storefront in the South of Market district. He drew on my chest the design he created for me: A quill dipping into an inkwell that became a pink triangle.

I spent a lot of time searching out the world of pornography. It wasn't the only literary country to which I journeyed, but it was always my favorite.

A few years ago, May Sarton was to be the guest of honor at a fund-raising dinner being held in Boston. I was asked if I would escort her to the function. Ms. Sarton was frightened of being in the city alone, especially after dark. She would be staying with old acquaintances in Cambridge. I agreed to pick her up and drive her across the Charles to the hotel where the function was being held.

There was a driving rainstorm that night and I got lost in the twisting streets of the university city, but I eventually found the correct address and had a lovely talk with the poet as we traveled down Memorial Drive. She'd seen some of my writing and liked what she'd read. We both had cats and we talked endlessly about them.

We got to the hotel and went into the cocktail reception being held for the honorees. A flock of lesbians surrounded Ms. Sarton with pure adoration.

That didn't surprise me; her reputation, especially among women readers, was very well established. What did startle me was that a group of gay men began to gather in line to greet me. I assumed, since we were all in our tuxedos for the big night, that these men wanted to meet me because of my essays, or perhaps some of the softer books I'd written, the ones that even May Sarton could admire. I thought they might have heard of me because of my reputation as an activist; the dinner was to benefit a political organization. But I was wrong.

One by one the men—the supposed elite of the new gay world—came up to me and confessed to me their most intimate secrets. I heard graphic descriptions about their sexual habits. I learned just where they read my pornography and just how long they could hold off having an orgasm while they did it. I realized that only a few years earlier, these men would never have dared say these things. They wouldn't have congregated together at a gay gathering. Only a few years earlier, they would have been invisible.

I listened to all of this come from the mouths of men who had won political office all through New England. It came from the mouths of men who owned large businesses. It came from the mouths of men who had used my books to explore the territory of their masturbatory fantasies with the help of the characters from my books. They knew Mr. Benson personally; they'd had sex with Pedro; they dreamed of the arrogant youths I'd found on the streets of Boston.

All the time I was smiling to myself. We were standing, after all, in the same hotel in which I'd lost my virginity with my Hartford salesman. It had been renovated and given a new name, but it was still the place where he'd taught me how to say the words of sex out loud. I wondered if he wouldn't be very proud of me now, listening to how much I'd passed on his lessons to these men.

> *Will someone please talk about our children? They are being deprived of sex and love. What will happen to a generation that lives without those miracles?*
>
> —COLLEEN DEWHURST

When AIDS struck, the first messages from the bureaucracies were demands for abstinence. I knew it was a disastrous strategy. Gay men who had grown up having to reclaim their bodies from the prohibitions of medicine and politics weren't going to listen to those "authorities."

But my sexual health training told me just how dangerous this epidemic was. Things did have to change. But it would have to be the role of the pornographer to retell the tales and transform the terrain of our fantasies.

I called together a group of pornographers and created with them a volume of safe-sex stories, trying to stake out new paths for our readers. Later, I found a man who was using his body to give strip shows around the country, interspersing his lewdness with lectures on how safe sex could be fun. I used him to write a book, a guide to the new land.

Some people have credited the massive outpouring of new erotica, of which my work was only a part, with saving lives. Gay pornography can do that. It has that tradition. I remembered that both Sam Steward and my traveling salesman had talked about the dangers of hepatitis (does anyone remember hepatitis?) and other sexually transmitted diseases. We could learn from their lessons. Pornography saved lives in other ways as well. It gave us words to communicate our feelings. It broke some of our most bitter isolation from one another. It created dreams and hope.

I'd thought that one of the rewards I'd get as a pornographer would be simple sex. It happened, not nearly as often as I wished it might, but those men did find me occasionally.

One of them lived in Boston, a hundred miles from my home in Maine. He would call me up and beg me to let him visit, or to at least see him when I went down to the city. He'd describe which of my pornographic books contained those adventures he wanted to have.

I finally agreed. We made a date. Then the tone of the conversations changed. He knew that I'd taken a test for HIV antibodies. He wanted to know my status.

What difference did it make? I asked. I had written the books on safe sex; he claimed to practice protection in his own encounters. We didn't have to know such things; our pornography could exist without risk.

But he pushed and shoved. The information I held was new to me, and it was tender, but I gave in to his insistence. I told him I was positive.

We were modern urban gay men, he assured me. That was no problem.

Our telephone courtship had been long-lasting and intense. When we met for dinner, it picked up immediately and we talked about our closest fantasies over good glasses of wine. But as the meal ended, and the time came to leave, supposedly for his apartment, he began to withdraw. It was so real that I actually thought the wall against which he sat was moving backward, away from me.

I said something blatant about my expectations. He proclaimed shock. Of course he hadn't meant that. This was just an escapade for him, a chance to meet a pornographer in the flesh. He had never intended to put his body on the line, not into my hands.

I sat there and realized what was happening. Put on the spot, he wasn't going to have sex with a contaminated pornographer. I told myself: This is how they're all going to act, if I tell them.

How dare I even think these things?

I had another dinner with a modern straight couple not long after my aborted assignation. I'd learned not to discuss my own infection. I talked instead about the work I was doing with people who were living with AIDS. In the conversation, the subject of their sexual longing came up. The woman in the couple screwed up her face in loathing: "How can they expect anyone to touch them that way?"

How dare I even think these things?

Public health officials are obsessed by "noncomplaint carriers," those people who have tested positive for HIV antibodies but who continue to show up in clinics with other sexually transmitted diseases. A calamity needs villains. The government officials see an army of Patient Zeroes descending on Maine to kill off innocent victims.

(Isn't that redundant, I ask: "Innocent victims"? How can a victim be guilty? I'm ignored.)

If people had decent sex education, they'd know how to protect themselves, I point out. We need to provide people with better information.

"We can't!" some of the bureaucrats respond. "That would be pornography!"

10

But if you don't, you're leaving people out there undefended.

"Gay men can provide their own educational materials," I'm told. Over eighty percent of the people who have contracted AIDS in the state of Maine have become infected through homosexual acts. The state doesn't fund any safe-sex material for the gay population.

But it's not just the state. This is the most common phone call I receive these days:

"Did you know that ___ was in the bars last night?"

"So?"

"He has AIDS!" (Or, "He's HIV positive!" Or, "I saw him at the clinic the other day!") "They shouldn't let him in. The bar owners have an obligation to protect us!"

"You have an obligation to protect yourself."

"He'll give all of us AIDS!"

"He's told me he's only having protected sex."

"But everyone should know that he's infected! No one should sleep with him."

Or me.

The lepers are defiling the temple! Cast them out!

How dare you even have these thoughts!

My body rebelled, before my spirits were healed, after I learned that I was HIV positive. I came down with a bacterial prostate infection, something that had nothing to do with my HIV infection.

"When was the last time you had an orgasm?" my doctor asked me.

"Days." Then I admitted: "Weeks."

She looked at me carefully and said, "I'd have a very hard time if I had to go that long without sex."

I didn't say anything.

Then she explained that the prostate contains a pool of fluids that become stagnant if they're not ejaculated during sex. They become a welcoming breeding ground for bacteria. I had to flush out my system. I had to have sex, of some kind.

Anne Rice describes pornography as a place where people visit; it's not a place where one lives. I've always loved that perspective, it helps me understand my role as a pornographer. I'm a tour guide helping strangers see the landscape of our erotic potential. "This isn't the time to stop writing pornography," she says. "This is the time when erotica is all the more important."

I sat in front of my VCR and watched erotic tapes, one after another, trying to get myself back into the now forbidden arena of pornography.

At first I could only jerk off in the most mechanical fashion. What was wrong with me? I had once claimed all of this for myself, and now I was a shunned outcast from a land I had helped to create.

But of course. My pornography had been full of details about the glory of men's cocks. I had pulled them out of their pants and I'd looked at them with adoring scrutiny. I'd taken images from aboriginal rites and declared men's semen to be the means through which lessons could be transferred.

With the news of my own infection, I was in such shock that the pornography I'd created became, in my own mind, the actually physical place where disease had passed into my body.

I had to work to climb back. First, I had to make my pornographic videotapes a place I could visit. Then I began to look at the devastation of my imagination, how much my own infection had altered the way I approached pornography.

I usually create pornography the way other people consume it. I sit at my machine and I write it until I'm so turned on I can't stand it, and then I rush to find a comfortable place where I can pull out my cock and then tease myself to an orgasm. Or else I find some fantasy so compelling that

I cannot ignore it. Those times, my dick is already so hard I usually can only type a page or two before I have to come, and sometimes I just shoot while I'm writing out the images.

Some of my pornography—not all of it but much of it—has been a retelling of actual events. As I saw the risk of the kinds of sex I once practiced become malevolent—and this happened before I understood that I myself was infected—my pornography moved to a more fantastic arena, one where pleasure remains without danger.

I created a world where proud men existed for one another's entertainment, where physical endurance was a norm but cruelty wasn't permitted. The Network was a place where no one was put at risk. It was the safe haven for my pornography during the epidemic.

I had left The Network when I learned of my infection. Slowly, over the weeks following that visit to my doctor, I rediscovered The Network's contours and fell in love once more with its citizens. They were moving, in my imagination, to an even more sacred place, one where they understood they were guardians of holy lands, where their duty was to keep the flames of erotic desire burning.

Readers want these explorations. The pornography I create sells well; it's talked about; there are new men on the phone wondering about the places I'm describing. But the rest of the world doesn't seem to want this material. Apparently trying to appear good and clean, book publishers move away from anything written about gay sex other than self-help manuals. A window opened in publishing during the time of gay liberation and sexual revolution. There were writers willing to promote our pornography as something important, and there was a time when publishers were willing to risk accepting that. Now the window is slamming shut. The pornographic word is being erased.

I ended one book I wrote about The Network with: "And the Master's Journals Will Be Continued." The editor had crossed out that line and had scrawled on the manuscript: "Not here they won't." It took three years to find another publisher willing to see a volume about The Network into the bookstores, and he's been fired by the conglomerate that has since bought the house.

The experimentation that had driven so much of the gay press is dying, or dead. Most gay periodicals that had once been journals of pornography, the places where I and my peers learned our craft, are now owned by one straight male businessman. Occasionally an editor at *Mandate* or one of the other magazines this man owns will try to create meaningful space in which a pornographer can work, but the lack of concern or care the publisher shows for this work is so intense that the effort never lasts.

And writers are abandoning this landscape as well. One editor has told me that over half of the manuscripts his publishing house receives—and it's been one of the major suppliers of gay literature over the past years—are set in the just recent past, obviously to justify sexual actions that couldn't happen safely today. Looking at our world and the way we are now, and looking at this world with its full erotic capability, is something too many writers have proved incapable of doing.

A writer like myself—one who can move across the boundary and live in a nonpornographic place—is put under great pressure to leave that world behind now. There are hints that I shouldn't continue to ruin my reputation, but the lure is often more subtle; the rewards for writing nonpornography during a time of AIDS aren't a mistake.

The ways that my road maps can reach people are being blocked; the words I write are written now without any real expectation that they can be published, or that they can be published in any form that isn't humiliating to me. While my pornographic books sell as well as any others I write, I'm paid a tenth as much for them. There's no way, now, to support oneself as a professional writer by creating pornography.

(And what will people think of my pornography now, anyway? Now that they find out I'm infected? *How dare he even think these things?*)

14

* * *

The avenues to writing about sex are closing. The boundary of what the world will accept as our pornographic vision is narrowing, at least in print.

Now I discover that we're reverting to an oral tradition, as though we must move the lines of our struggle back to some place from which we thought we'd escaped. The bookstores exist through which a reader can find a writer, but they become useless as fewer and fewer decently written pornographic works find their way through the new barriers and into print.

That doesn't mean people aren't looking for pornographic mentors. I now sit in my apartment in Portland and receive younger men who come to me and ask me to talk about what has gone on. They know about risks and infections, and they understand the need for caution, but they still want to know about the world of pornography.

I sit with them and tell them about the old days and show them the old books and magazines and answer their questions. "What was it like to go to a bathhouse?" "Did you really go to the Mineshaft?" "Was The Saint as glorious as they say?" "How does leather feel on your naked skin?" "Will those days ever return?"

And I see in their eyes the vision of pornography, and the hope that it will still be valued. *How dare they even think these things!*

MARY GAITSKILL

‖‖‖

ACTION, ILLINOIS

WHEN JUSTINE WAS TEN she read a poem about French Resisters during the Second World War in her children's classics book. In it, a French hero was crucified to a barn door with bayonets and tormented by SS men before a crowd of weeping French patriots. The poet dwelt on the hero's torment at voluptuous length before going on to describe the heroism of a small boy in the crowd who was given a gun by the evilly smirking SS captain and ordered to shoot the dying Resistance fighter, and who instead blasted the Nazi. This poem excited her even more than the cartoons that had induced her to make Richie tie her to the swing set. She kept the children's classic under her bed so she could read it at night with a flashlight and masturbate, imagining herself under a hot sun, crucified with bayonets.

They had moved from Michigan to Action, Illinois, Richie was no longer at her disposal, and she hadn't yet found anyone to take his place.

Action was a thriving industrial suburb outside Chicago, rife with malls and held together with wide "drives" that had no sidewalks but were instead flanked by an endless chain of muffler shops, donut stands, shoe barns, and their many retail cousins, all with huge concrete parking lots. Justine's father was a successful cardiologist who worked at the Action Medical Center, an interesting building that appeared to be made of plywood and concrete, where he was housed with a gynecologist, a dermatologist, two general practitioners, a pediatrician, and a psychiatrist. Her mother no longer had a job but did volunteer work at a center for emotionally disturbed children. Their house was a large wandering one-story with a flamingo worked into the aluminum of the front screen door.

They had moved there during the summer, when the sidewalks of the new neighborhood were active with lounging, bicycling, or roaming kids. When Justine ventured out onto the pavement, she was surrounded by three gum-chewing girls who looked as though they were trying to find something wrong with her. But suburban Michigan kids have almost the same laconic, nasally distorted speaking style that the kids of suburban Illinois had, and she was immediately accepted into the group. She spent most of her summer standing on the streets or hunched in front of someone's house with a small group of other girls. The sun turned her pale skin brown and her brown hair pale, and her blue eyes became hard and bright.

Justine was drawn to the most sexual of the girls in the neighborhood, Pam Donovan and Edie Barnard, who wore the tightest pants and tightest shirts over their tough little chests. Edie, the blond, was even sophisticated enough to wear pink powder and black mascara. Although all their friends described them as "cute," they were not pretty. They were skinny and sharp-boned, with sullen, suspicious eyes, thin, violently teased hair and faces that are generic to thousands of suburban little girls. But they were made beautiful by the ferocious eroticism that ran in their bodies like an illegal drug discharged from their eyes and lips.

In retrospect, it was strange to her that these girls, who harbored such power, were the most passive of the neighborhood gang. The three of them didn't like to play tag or

18

baseball or even ride bikes. They liked to sit on the small squares of concrete that were called "porches," sometimes getting up to walk around the block, getting whistled at and sprayed with stones by boys. They talked about boys with a nervous mix of fear, disgust, and attraction, about girls with malice or displays of alliance, about their mothers with contempt, and about their bodies, always about their bodies, with a range of emotions from protective, reverent secrecy to loathing.

There were race riots in Detroit that summer, and there was a lot of talk about that. Darcy Guido stood up to imitate Martin Luther King, tap dancing, rolling her eyes, and pulling her lower lip down and sticking her tongue up to make weird wet lips that looked like the genitals of an orangutan. The day the National Guard flew over their rooftops in helicopters, they stood in the streets and cheered. Even Pat Braiser's mother came out on her concrete slab and said, "That'll teach those animals to be decent!"

Justine sat quietly on the concrete during the first days of the riot, hearing distant Black people called animals and watching the genital-lipped eye-rolling clowning. Her memory of cold, silent Gemma rose up and stood mute, like a sign forbidding her to laugh at Darcy's joke, even when Pam, her best friend, nudged her and said, "Why don't you laugh?"

For days there were pictures of the riot on television. At dinner, Justine and her parents would sit at the table, eating and watching the dark figures run around on the screen like people in a foreign movie while flames flickered in the blackened buildings. Her father would speak on the reprehensibility of rioting and violence, smartly wielding his utensils, the very posture of his haunches expressing the rightness of his disapproval. Her mother would agree, adding praise for Martin Luther King. The people on the TV apparently felt the same way; after showing clips of rioting or angry Black spokespeople, they would console their viewers with old footage of Dr. King giving his famous dream speech. Justine became tired of seeing him, and of hearing him and of hearing him praised. She didn't see what was so great about him.

Then the riots were over and it was time to go to the Wonderland Mall for clothes. Justine loved Wonderland. It was dotted with shrubs and waste containers; there was a fountain with a rusting cube placed in the center of it. Muzak roiled around over everything, decorously muffling sound and movement. Huge square portals led into great tiled expanses lined with row upon dizzying row of racks hung with clothes. Signs that said "Junior Miss," "Cool Teen," or "Little Miss Go-Go" in fat round letters protruded from the tops of the racks, some of them illustrated by teenage cartoon girls with incredibly frail bodies, enormous staring eyes, tiny O-shaped mouths and large round heads with long straight swatches of brown or yellow hair.

Justine did real shopping with her mother, but what she loved best was to go with Mrs. Bernard and Edie and Pam. All the way to Wonderland, she and her friends would lie all over the back seat, giggling about pubic hair or how stupid somebody was while Mrs. Bernard, a strangely thin woman with a face that looked as if it were held in place with tacks talked to herself in a low, not unattractive mutter. (Edie said her mother had a mustache that she tore off with hot wax, but Justine didn't believe it.)

Once at the mall, the four of them would comb the grounds like a gang of cats, rifling the racks, plunging into dressing rooms, snacking savagely between shops. Mrs. Bernard would wander ahead, continually bushwacked by salespeople who thought her mutter was addressed to them, leaving the girls to stare and giggle, and to furtively admire the groups of tough older kids lounging on the public benches, smoking cigarettes and sneering. Sometimes glamorous older boys would follow them saying, "I'd like to pet your pussy" and other dirty things; this was exciting, like the poem about the crucified man, only queasier because it was real and in public. It was horrible to be in front of people having the same feeling that she had while masturbating and thinking about torture. She was sure that Edie and Pam didn't have feelings like that; probably they didn't even masturbate. They blushed and giggled and said, "You guys better stop it," but they swung their purses and arched their backs, their eyes half closed and their lips set in lewd, malicious smiles. Justine would imitate them, and when she did, sometimes a door would open and she'd step into a world where it was really very chic to walk around in public with wet underpants, giggling while strange boys in leather jackets and pointed shoes called you a slut. The world of Justine alone under the covers with her own smells, her fingers stuck in her wet crotch, was now the world of the mall filled with fat ugly people walking around eating and staring. It was a huge world without boundaries; the clothes and records and ice cream stores seemed like cardboard houses she could knock down, the waddling mothers and pimple-faced loners like dazed pedestrians she was passing on a motorcycle.

Once, at Sears, she was sullenly picking through the dressing rooms, trying to find a vacant stall, when she flipped back a scratchy yellow curtain and saw a strange person. She was about Justine's age and weird-looking, Justine thought ugly, with pale cold skin, a huge exposed forehead, and blue plastic glasses on her face. She was fully dressed and slumped on the floor in a position of utter passivity and defeat, right against the mirror, staring at herself with the lack of expression that comes from extreme mental pain. Their eyes met for seconds—the stranger's face faintly reflecting embarrassed humanity—and then Justine backed out. The sight of such mute, frozen pain was stunning and fascinating, like the sight of an animal with its legs hacked off. Justine had never seen such a naked expression on her parents' faces, let alone the face of a stranger. It made her feel queasiness and fear so intensely that she wanted to poke at the queasiness and fear so she could feel it all the more. To see and feel something so raw in the mall was obscene, much more obscene than the whispering boys. She went to get Edie and Pam.

"Come and see," she said, "there's a drooling retard in the dressing room."

Naturally they hurried back. Justine had imitated her deranged slump with embellishments of jaw and eyeballs, and they approached the dressing room with a sense of cruel illicit excitement, like men about to pay to see a woman strip. But when they got to the dressing room and flung the curtain back, there was no one there. They sighed with disappointment and turned to go and there was the girl again, standing up and peeping at them from behind the curtain of another dressing room. Her face was accusing and almost snotty. Edie and Pam knew it was her, but somehow they couldn't make fun of her, even though they would've liked to; her staring face made them feel caught.

"God, what a queer," said Pam as they left the dressing room.

They found Edie's mother eating candy necklaces at the coffee counter of Woolworth's and left.

When the first day of school arrived Justine had accumulated ten complete interchangeable outfits. And in spite of all the fussing, picking, and mutual encouragement from her friends in the purchase of them, she was afraid that when she walked into the classroom she would be ostracized for fashion reasons that would become horribly clear to her as she made her way to her desk through a blinding sheet of jeers. What if none of her neighborhood friends were in the class, or even if they were, what if they turned out to be hopeless retards so low down on the social scale that association with them condemned her forever?

She was so numbed with fear that she accepted, without retort, her mother's breakfast-table assurances that she looked "adorable" in her yellow and turquoise checked skirt and yellow knee socks.

The drive to school would've taken place in funereal silence if it hadn't been for maddening "Adventures in Good Music," which she hadn't the strength to object to, on the radio. She felt the whole magical summer—of huddling safely with her friends, talking trash and rejecting Black people in a blur of hot bright days and changeless squares and rectangles of the trusted landscape—had taken place in another world that would not help her in this terrible new place she was headed.

This was not true. The assigned classroom was filled with murderously aggressive boys and rigid girls with terrible animal eyes who threw spitballs, punched each other, snarled, whispered, and stared one another down. And shadowing all these gestures and movements were declarations of dominance, of territory, the swift blind play of power and weakness.

Justine saw right away that she'd be at home.

When they were let out on the asphalt playground that morning, she found Edie and Pam and they huddled together, chewing their gum and sending sharp stares of appraisal over their shoulders. They told one another who was cool and who was queer. By the afternoon recess, they had gathered three other girls about them, Debby, Dody, and Deidre. The D girls were all big and tough, charmed perhaps by Justine's sullen beauty and the sophisticated style of Edie and Pam.

Justine had made friends with Dody, the pretty one of the three. Her prettiness was of an unusual type in this time of anorexic cuties with ironed hair and white lipstick, she being a big raw-boned girl with large fleshy shoulders and hips, and large active hands and feet attached to long, confused arms and legs, multidirectional like rubber. Her eyes were extraordinary, huge and brown, shot with mad glowing strands of yellow and gold, which, in conjunction with the tawny mass of hair sprawling frantic and uncontrollable on her head, gave her the look of a restless, fitfull lioness. Her size and weight gave her no center; Justine's first retrospective image of her is of Dody, with arms and legs splayed, as though in the middle of a tornado, only laughing, open-mouthed and loud. The next image is an actual memory of the time Dody, to humorously display her hugeness and strength, picked up a scrawny fourth-grader by a fistful of her hair and swung her in a complete circle three times before letting the screaming creature fly. Justine remembers her strange vulnerability, her terror of thunderstorms and spiders, her moment of wide-eyed panic during a time she and Justine were making out in the mall restroom with two boys they'd met, when Justine had to hold her trembling paw. Ten years later, it had not surprised her to read in a chance paper that Dody LaRec, college junior, had become an unusual statistic, one of the few females to commit suicide with a bullet to the brain.

The others, Debby and Deidre, were not pretty, but they exuded an awful cynicism that impressed people and they knew a lot of incredibly dirty things—Deidre claiming, at the age of eleven, to have "done it." Besides, they were brutal. The six of them terrified the other kids as they patrolled the playground, looking for trouble. In gym class they were always on the top team, hand-picking the strongest, ablest girls to be on their side, often pitting themselves against the feeblest people, who they gleefully pounded. Parents were always calling to complain about them pulling down their son's pants or dropping someone's lunch in the toilet. Teachers cajoled, pleaded, and occasionally ranted, but they couldn't do anything and they knew it. Justine believed teachers to be secretly on their side as they trampled the weak and the uncool, people adults have to accept, and, as a result, become like.

There were only a small group of boys who weren't afraid of them, on account of their being so tough themselves. They weren't big boys—they were small, with sinewy racing-dog bodies—but their strength came out of their huge bawling mouths and their inhuman indifference to pain. They were always getting bashed with baseballs, splitting their skulls in rock fights, chipping their teeth, ripping open their elbows and knees, beating one another up as often as they beat retards and queers, but with more affection. When they weren't busy with any of these activities, they hung after Justine and her group on the playground, pushing them, pinching them, pulling up their skirts. Sometimes they'd stand quietly and talk about "The Man from Uncle," or what they'd done yesterday, Justine feeling that ghastly private torture feeling glowing through her lower trunk. She particularly liked little razor-faced Rickie Holland, who was beautiful, almost dainty, with hands that were such a contrast to his morbidly cruel personality. He was a loner within his little gang, almost protected by the other boys in some strange unconscious way, as if they knew that just a slight shift in their perception of him would render him a despised victim rather than a companion in crime. He seemed happiest when torturing small animals by himself, yet had had an inexplicable kind aspect that appeared randomly, and could lead him to risk rejection, like the time he protected a crippled girl who had been surrounded by the others. He was the first among them to smoke cigarettes, which, since drugs had not yet hit suburban playgrounds, was as chic as one could be. Justine had loved his sharp, expressionless face, his blank, lusterless eyes. There was nothing in that face anyone could hurt or even approach. Love would find nothing receiving it there, no claw hold in anything except perhaps that quirky kindness, which appeared for no reason and vanished again, too transient to support a reckless prepubescent love willing to crucify itself on the heartless surface of this boy, just to make an impression. He paid no attention to her.

At the beginning of October a new kid came to Justine's class. Her name was Cheryl Thomson. She was big and homely and she wore old plaid skirts that were obviously not from Sears or Wards. This would've been all right; some very cool kids—Dody being one of them, in fact—dressed this way. But they had a sloppy panache, a loose-limbed grace that made their flapping shirttails and shifting skirts seem sassy, and halting; thick-bodied Cheryl did not. She sat in her seat with her stubby hands in her lap, talking to people politely before class, a dull, dreamy look coating her gray eyes. Then the teacher came in and, in an innocent effort to help them get to know the new student, opened class by asking Cheryl questions meant to gently reveal her—for example, "What is your favorite food?" Cheryl did all right with that, but when asked about music, instead of saying "the Monkees" or "the Beatles" she answered "country music," causing a ripple of disbelief to alert the room. From that point on, every answer she gave confirmed her to be a hopeless alien in the world of primary-colored surfaces. She wanted to be a firefighter when she grew up! Her favorite TV show was "Andy of Mayberry"! She liked to go fishing! Every answer seemed to come out of some horrible complex individuality, some personal swamp reeking with vulnerable young humanity, nothing like the neat rec rooms they wanted to live in. The clarity and trust in her soft voice put their teeth on edge, made them squirm like a howling monster at the sound of human song, made them feel their own vulnerability like a knife.

In the lunchroom, everybody was talking about how queer she was. Her second day at school, somebody tripped her in the hall, the following week somebody put a tack on her seat. When she sat on it, she cried, and little Marla Jacob sneered, "God, what an emotional!" From that day on she was known as "Emotional," the worst insult imaginable.

Her presence changed the whole composition of the class, uniting everyone, even other unpopular kids, against her. Everything she said became another proof of her stupidity, her social failure. Every ugly and ridiculous thing introduced into any discussion—in the classroom, on the playground, at the mall—was "like Emotional." She was made to be, in other words, the focal point for every unacknowledged weakness and awkwardness in the blind hearts of her tormentors, the embodiment of the confused tender child who was not allowed to live in the tightly plotted landscape of Action, Illinois. In general she was taunted verbally, but there was also physical abuse—the occasional shower of orchestrated spitballs, the time she was surrounded by a dozen or so boys and girls who took off their belts and whipped at her bare legs and arms.

Emotional's reaction was by turns angry, hurt, and bewildered, but her most constant expression was one of helpless good nature. She was too even-tempered to remain angry or brooding; she always tried to reverse the tide against her, to make jokes, to not be a spoilsport, to be positive, to join in. Once Justine saw a smiling face drawn in marker on her notebook with the words "Happy-Go-Lucky" written underneath, and knew, sickeningly, that it was true, in spite of everything.

Of course, Justine took part in the Emotional pogrom. As with all the other little social massacres she'd taken part in, however, she was more a goader and abettor than an outright attacker. She was too small, for one thing, to be a real bully, and not really aggressive enough to be a ringleader. Besides, she was, in some secret way, too ambivalent. When she looked at the chalky, rigid face of some kid who was being shoved to and fro between Deidre and Debby, she felt deep excruciating enjoyment as well as equally deep discomfort that she deliberately provoked, like she'd chew a cold sore. These two feelings met and skewered her between them while she giggled and cajoled and incited her friends to riot, making her feel monstrously, corporeally alive, enlarged, overrunning the boundaries of herself, banging into the world like her memory of tornado-splayed Dody—yet unable to bear being in the world, turning in on herself like an insect run through with a needle.

These feelings were magnified by Emotional, who, in the space of a few months, became something other than human. Justine always joined in the teasing, even instigated it, yet the sight of Emotional's unhappy face brought darkness up from some thoughtless pit within her, made her turn away and frown when she should've been laughing. When she looked at Emotional, she looked into the face of her most private fantasy, the face of a victim crucified before a jeering crowd.

But for whatever reason, some subterranean bond was there, for, to Justine's discomfort, Emotional began showing up in her dreams. The most outstanding of these dreams featured her and Emotional in the front-line trenches of some war. There were other people in the trench, but there existed between her and the class queer some deep unspoken friendship that was mainly expressed in meaningful glances and, at one point, a fraught hand-clasping. The height of the dream was reached when Justine lay injured and paralyzed from an enemy blast, and Emotional ran to her side, ripping off a piece of her blouse to bind her wounds.

This nocturnal relationship was profoundly discomfiting to Justine and she was relieved when, on starting the seventh grade at the new junior high school, she found that Emotional wasn't there. Most of the kids were sorry to lose this entertaining outlet for their personalities, but Justine was happy to forget her, especially in view of the more interesting intrigues that took the place of torturing Emotional.

For example, Deidre, who had breasts and (it was rumored) hair between her legs, had begun seeing a boy from the eighth grade. He went to a different junior high school across town; she had met him while sitting beside the copper cube fountain in the mall, enjoying a cigarette alone. His name was Greg Mills. He had a concave torso, incredibly thin legs, narrow green eyes, lank ratlike hair, and red pimples that somehow added to his lurid charm. He wore a black vinyl windbreaker and spoke in monosyllables. Justine was secretly uncomfortable around him and wondered why, if he was so cool, he didn't have a girlfriend his own age.

Deidre described going with him and his friends to an empty housing development, breaking into one of the finished houses, and throwing a party amid the noise of their small but effective transistor radios, smoking, drinking, making out, and doing it, leaving ashes and rank stains on the bedspread of the display bedroom. It shocked and thrilled Justine to picture them sitting in the cold, deserted room with their jackets on, the cigarette smoke in their throats, the illicit taste of alcohol in their mouths. She imagined Deidre pulling her tight ski pants off, her bare bottom on the regulation bedspread, the naked mattress under-neath. She would be all gooseflesh and tiny leg hairs stand-ing upright, her feet clammy, her genitals hairy and unspeakable between her big thighs. Did Greg pull her legs apart and look at her or did he just stick his thing (report-edly hairy itself) inside her in the dark? Did he take off his pants and show *his* butt or did he just unzip? Justine would look at Greg and decide that either way was incredibly nasty and exciting. She admired Deidre tremendously.

Deidre began asking if they wanted to come with her sometime. "Not to some scuzzy development," said Jus-tine. "I don't wanna freeze my butt." Neither did anybody else, until one Saturday Deidre called Justine and Dody and told them Greg's parents had left for the day, that he was inviting over some really cute eighth-grade guys, and did they want to come? Justine's mother was at the Mental Health Center, so she told her father she was going to visit Dody and left.

Greg's house was exactly like Justine's and Dody's and everyone else's. Greg and Deidre were on the couch and there were two other boys, one of them with the large, empty, pretty eyes of a TV star. Justine saw, with a rush of excitement and fear, that they were drinking alcohol mixed with Coca-Cola. She didn't want to drink it, but she didn't want to say no in a prudish way, so when one of them offered it to her, she turned it into an occasion for sexual tension, saying, "Uh uh, I know what you guys are trying to do!" "Yeah," said Dody, taking her cue, "you wanna get us drunk and make us do things." She smiled in her fake innocence, fake sophistication, and real sexuality. Her gold eyes were half-lidded and glinting.

The boys liked this. "You'd better be good," said Greg. "We're babysitting you seventh-graders and if you don't do what we say, you're gonna get it."

The game was on. They sat on the couch moving closer and closer, the boys getting drunk, the girls getting giggly and excited. They teased and flirted and made fun of one another, the boys commanding the girls to do things, like

29

pick a piece of paper up off the floor. The girls would put up tremendous resistance and then do it, pouting and flouncing. There was a thick current of feeling coursing through the room, a wide band of glittering yellow-gold that swept them off the floor and into another sphere. At moments Justine stood back and looked at this process with wonder; most of the time she simply felt it move her. Greg and Deidre left the room, disappearing behind a closed door. The boys became rougher and more demanding; one of them told Dody to go make him a drink, and when she didn't move fast enough he grabbed her hair and pulled her toward the kitchen. "You leave my friend alone!" Justine yelled in the phony little-girl voice employed by sluts and whores the world over (and she an actual little girl!) as she leapt up to grab the boy's shirt, pummelling his back in the most ineffective way she could manage. There was a moment when she and Dody (who could've clobbered the kid) overpowered him, pinning him to the wall, greedily savaging him with pretend tickles until his friend leapt off the couch and the girls ran screaming as they were chased. They were cornered in a personal closet, Justine faint and nauseous with inexperience and desire.

"You guys are really gonna get it now," advised the blank-eyed boy. "You have to stay in here and wait while we decide what we're gonna do. You have to stand back to back with your hands behind you."

The boys left the room and they did as they were told, standing and telling each other how afraid they were in thrilled voices. "Do you think we should try and run for it?" asked Dody. "No, we'd better not," Justine said. "They'd really kill us then." Justine thought of her parents sitting at the table eating dinner, her mother daintily picking an errant morsel from her teeth, and for a minute she actually did feel afraid. What if she really was in another sphere and couldn't get back to the old one? Then she relaxed; but of course, it would be as simple as the times she lay in bed and, putting her hand between her legs,

became a victim nailed to a wall, and then, as her body
regained its tempo, became Justine once more.

The boys came back into the room. One of them said,
"Okay, LaRec, follow me." And Dody, sneering, saying,
"Oh, I'm really scared," followed him into the bathroom,
visible at the end of a short hall, leaving Justine to contem-
plate this large-eyed creature with chisled features, peachy
skin, and no human expression. Her heart pounded. She
wanted to sit down. He forbade her. He told her his friend
was "going to strip Dody and finger her." Her underwear
became hot and wet. She told him Dody was probably beating his friend's butt, but no sound of butt-beating emanated
from the bathroom. They stood silently, Justine's breath
getting smaller and shallower, every detail of the boy's
bored sideways-looking face becoming larger and more
maddening by the moment. She felt as if he were right next
to her, his breath on her skin, his smell up her nose. The
longer they stood, the more genuinely afraid she became.
The more afraid she became, the more bolted to the floor
she was, her armpits damp and itchy, her throat closed, her
pelvis inflamed and disconnected from her body, her head
disconnected from her neck. She heard Deidre laughing in
the bedroom.

The bathroom door opened and Dody paraded out with
her boy lurking and smirking behind. Her face was bright
red but every part of her body telegraphed pride.

"Come on," said Justine's boy, "your turn."

The bathroom was pink-tiled and green-rugged, the sink
decorated with large stylish shells and glass jars filled with red
and purple bubble-bath balls. The boy sat on the green toilet
and looked at her. "You hafta get over my lap," he said.

Justine thrust her hip out and tried to as though she were
making fun of him, but she didn't know how to do that
without her friends. The music from a ballpoint pen commercial was playing in her head, and she imagined huge-
eyed Cool Teens dancing to it. "I'm not gonna do that,"
she said.

31

"You hafta."

Back and forth they went. A knot of heat and tension sat between her legs, surrounded by white, icy space. He grabbed her hand and pulled her face down across his lap. She tried to appear graceful, feeling heavy and fat on his slim haunches. She looked at the toilet-cleaning brush in the corner as he pulled down her pants. Her breath held itself as his numb fingers pushed into her numb contracting body. He fingered her with strange mechanical movements. His hand felt far away even when it was inside her, as if he were doing something someone had told him to do and was pleased he'd succeeded in doing it, not because he liked it. His remoteness made him authoritarian and huge, like a robot in a comic book. It inflamed her. She thought of Richie whipping her at the swing set amid the red flames of her little cartoon hell. His fingers hurt her. She gripped his thighs—and, in contrast to his hand, felt him there, a quick boyish spirit in the warm feeling body of a young human. "It hurts," she said.

Perfunctorily, he stopped, took his finger out of her, automatically wiped it on her bare ass, and moved his hands so that she could stand. Probably his thighs were numb.

She walked out of the bathroom feeling like a busty blond on "The Man from Uncle" who giggles while someone makes jokes about her tits. Womanly, proud, languid, almost inert in the majesty of her dumb, fleshy body.

Then she and the D girls all went to Dody's house and had ice cream and vanilla wafers.

She never saw those particular boys again, but although she had occasion to make out a few times after that, the boys who kissed her and felt her tiny breasts never made her feel the way she had felt while standing in Greg Mills's house. The only person who provoked that feeling was a girl—a girl she didn't even like in particular! She was Rose Loris, a mousy, pretty thing with thin lips and eyebrows who wanted with fierce anemic intensity to be "in the group" and who was tolerated on the fringes because she was Debby's friend, although it was friendship based mainly on Rose's devotion to Debby, who was always standing Rose up at the mall.

This intent but drooping girl with the limp shoulders of a rag doll and the alert quizzical head of a bird, whose sleepy body seemed at odds with her straight, energetic spine, followed Justine around, wanting to be her friend. This annoyed or flattered Justine, depending on her mood. Rose was always saying weird things that she thought would sound cool, and this made Justine feel a discomfiting mix of embarrassment and the resurgence of the torture feeling. Still, she sometimes went to Rose's house to watch television and to sneak a look into Mr. Loris's incredible pornography collection.

One day they discovered, among Mr. Loris's many magazines, postcards, and books, a comic entitled *Dripping Delta Dykes,* about two huge fleshy rivals who, through a strange plot with many perplexing leaps and changes of locale, battled each other in their changing lingerie ensembles. On the kitchen table, in the boxing ring, on tropical isles, in hospital rooms (where they worked as nurses) they met and settled each other's hash, the brunette, after a lot of hair-pulling, arm-twisting, and tit-squeezing, generally trussing the blond up in a variety of spread-eagled poses so she could stick a number of different objects in her vagina.

Although Rose laughed and squealed, "Gross!" while perusing this comic, Justine noticed she kept coming back to it over and over. Rose's reaction irritated Justine; it provoked something in her, a tiny something, but a something with teeth and claws, something that got bigger and bigger with each of Rose's coy giggles. It made her want to slap or shove Rose. Instead she said, "Oh, God, this is no big deal, I've done this stuff with Debby. It's fun."

Rose's stunned face seemed to fractionally withdraw, and for a minute Justine was embarrassed at her lie. But then Rose drew near again, and Justine sensed something invisible come forward from her wide eyes and suddenly, as had happened in Greg Mills's house, she knew they had crossed a border together. Justine went on talking, saying that not only had she and Debby done the things depicted in the comic but that everybody did this, didn't Rose know?

She never knew if Rose believed this, but at the moment she also knew it didn't matter, that Rose was going to pretend she believed it even if she didn't. The torture feeling was roused and roaring as she wheedled and teased, moving closer and closer to the agitated, awkward kid until she was all but cornered against the wall, pulling her hair across her lips, Justine whispering that Rose was a baby, a goody-goody, that she didn't know anything. It took surprisingly little to get her in the basement bathroom, where they were least apt to be discovered.

It is with a mixture of incredulity, guilt, and conceit that she remembers that dreamy session in a cold damp toilet smelling of Lysol and bleach with the concrete walls of a police cell. She was incredulous at the docility of Rose; every cajolement or command elicited another trembling surrender and every surrender filled Justine with a boiling greed that pushed her further and further into the violation she'd started as a game. The occasional feeble resistance—Rose's pleading hand on the arm that rampaged down her pants—only magnified Justine's swelling arrogance and made her crave to rip away another layer of the hapless girl's humanity. Justine felt her eyes and face become shielded and impenetrable as Rose's became more exposed, she felt her personality filling the room like a gorging swine. Rose was unquestionably terrified and doubtless would've liked to stop, but she had been stripped of the territory on which one must stand to announce such decisions, as well as most of her clothes. For although Justine had only meant to cop a feel, within a few delirious moments Rose was placed on the closed lid of the toilet, her pants and panties in a wad on the floor. Her shirt was pulled up to reveal her tiny breast mounds, her legs splayed and tied to conveniently parallel towel racks with her own knee socks, her hands ritualistically bound behind her back with a measuring tape, her mouth stuffed with a half-used roll of toilet paper.

Justine stood and surveyed her victim with astonishment and contempt. She was shocked at the sight of the hairless genitals, which reminded her of a fallen baby bird, blind and naked, shivering on the sidewalk. It disgusted her to think she had something like that too, and she focused the fullness of her disgust on Rose. There were no more cajoling words, the mouse had been hypnotized, she was free to strike at leisure.

Fascinated by the meek, unprotected slit but too appalled to touch it, she plucked a yellowing toothbrush from its perch above the sink—pausing to glance at herself in the mirror as she did so—and stuck the narrow handle into her playmate's vagina. From the forgotten region of Rose's head came a truly pathetic sound; her face turned sideways and crumpled like an insect under a murdering wad of tissue, and tears ran from under her closed eyelids.

But it was not the tears that brought Justine to her senses, it was the stiff, horrified contraction of the violated genitals that she felt even through the ridiculous agent of the toothbrush, a resistance more adamant than any expressed so far. Suddenly she realized what she was doing, and could not bear to be in her own skin.

She left the sobbing child crouched on the cold concrete floor, pulling on her clothes with trembling fingers, while she bounded up the basement stairs and out the back door yelling, "I'm gonna tell everybody what I made you do!"

But she didn't. Out of some muddled combination of shame and barely acknowledged pity she kept it to herself, for her own frenzied, crotch-rubbing nocturnal contemplation.

Rose was absent from school for a week and then appeared like an injured animal dragging its crushed hind legs. No one remarked how her head, previously so busy and alert, had joined the collapse of her shoulders, or how her cheerful little spine had somehow crumpled. She avoided Justine and the gang, then tentatively approached and realized no one knew. She once accompanied Justine home from school in an abject silence that Justine was too embarrassed to break, except when they both mumbled "bye."

Although Justine told no one, the other girls sensed some new vulnerability in Rose, unconsciously recognized the loss of that nervous puppy spirit that had been her particular charm. They became aggressive and cruel with her; Debby was especially unkind. She walked home with Justine one more time and, at the corner where they would've said goodbye, blurted out an invitation to Justine to come play the game they had played before, in the bathroom. Justine snarled and turned away. Rose never came near the gang again. Since she was not in Justine's class, Justine only caught occasional glimpses of her in the halls, or on the periphery of the playground, wandering by herself or standing with a crowd of other mousy, unpopular girls.

This incident did not interfere with her other make-out activities, except in one way; after a squatting self-examination over a mirror, she vowed that while they could touch it all they wanted, she'd never allow anyone to look at that ugly thing between her legs. But she was only twelve, and knew nothing at all about her future, so one can't be too hard on her for breaking vows made at this time.

GARY INDIANA

DREAMS INVOLVING WATER

THREE BRIGHT HAMBURGER PATTIES in buns with chorus girl legs and flapping arms extruding from whorls of lettuce and glassy tomato slices dance and sing about burger toppings. The camera reverse zooms. The dancing hamburgers recede as the oblong proscenium of a television set shrinks into view. A red-canopied salad bar, emblazoned with the logo of a fast-food chain, crashes down on the TV.

Jesse cannot quite remember where he is. In the dim radioactive nightlight of the commercial, he could be in many places. He has an impression of heavy air, starchy sheets that rustle pleasantly against his legs, a logy recollection of a narrow room in the Gabrielli. He's woken with the taste of stale Bellinis in his mouth. The night clerk shakes him, he thinks, or perhaps only stands near the bed and calls him out of sleep: the cab he ordered last night is waiting. He sees that he nodded out, sordidly, with the phone knocked off the hook and all the lights on. Magical Venice. The water taxi to the airport, across a smelly lagoon in the bleary hour before dawn, costs something like eighty dollars. It's a trip for throwing money away, losing things and letting go of his normal circumspection. Jesse has been almost everyplace in the world without a dime, and he wonders now how he ever managed it.

There was another time in a different Venice room, one that had the same groggy underwater incoherence, its shutters closed to promote the spurious air conditioning. Despite the shutters, helixes of gray light spread circling webs against the wall. The desuetude and the silence make it impossible to know the time. Distant bells echo on the water, one set followed by another, devotions observed only by the invisible Venetians, the ones who really live here. A man he isn't in love with breathes aggressively against the adjacent pillow. He slaps Jesse's arm when it accidentally brushes his back. Anthony traveled with him to Venice and after that to Naples and finally to Rome. They slept together in the Santa Lucia and then in the Locarno, and in the little bar garden of the Locarno their friendship ended even though they didn't put that into words. Anthony goes upstairs. He packs and leaves the hotel while Jesse watches the flight of the evening swallows.

He continues ordering drinks, light Barcadis with Coke. He feels more relieved than he felt many years before in Rome when, after a week of sleeping in parks, money arrived at American Express. Anthony is a prickly companion, terrified by travel. He didn't bring enough money. Jesse's tried to assuage Anthony's nervousness by picking up the check as often as possible. Even so, Anthony keeps a written account of every lira he himself spends. In various hotel rooms, Jesse wakes to find Anthony, usually in his jockstrap, fretting over his budget book and silently forming the conviction that his money's disappearing because of Jesse: Jesse's insistence on this hotel, Jesse's choice of that restaurant. Jesse can easily read Anthony's mind. Anthony slipped into panic less than an hour after their plane landed in Milan. The sullen pig of a cab driver who dropped them at the rail station took him for something like fifty dollars. Things have moved too quickly for Anthony ever since. By the time they got to Rome, Jesse knew the next stage would be violence. Anthony's the type who either implodes or knocks the shit out of you. Since the Locarno is one of Jesse's numerous second homes, he feels calm enough to suggest various inexpensive ways in which Anthony could return to New York. They part without candor, keeping up a purely verbal civility. Jesse knows he will despise Anthony for a long time. After that he'll forget about him.

He now has the garden to himself. He watches the barman's white shirt moving through the mottled reflections in the plate glass and wonders why almost any bartender or waiter in a white shirt makes him think about sex. He ventures to say, aloud, "I am really so alone." The words just fade in the damp air. The swallows are changing into bats. The soft transition from twilight to evening has a hollow quality, a miasmic deadness. Jesse remembers that Rome is built on an enormous swamp. He studies the narrow street through the padlocked garden gate and wishes that anyone he knows except Anthony would turn up at the hotel. Few cars pass, even fewer people. The Locarno period is over for most of the people Jesse knows. In Jesse's head, Rome will always be a late-seventies city, pleasantly dead in the late eighties. The interesting aristocrat junkies have died, and the artists have moved away. He considers getting on a train to Paris.

He plays the cigarette game, telling himself he'll live ten years longer if he quits. Sometimes it works. Withdrawal is a delicious physical languor, a state of perpetual sleepiness full of real-seeming daydreams. He gazes at a leonine gargoyle spitting a cool stream of clear water into a marble scallop. His eyes follow a pointy ribbon of jade ivy up the garden wall. "I am really so alone," he says again, as if he's discovered magic words. The abrupt solitude makes him shy and hesitant to move. He speaks just enough Italian to be mistaken for an imbecile. Alone, he feels other people's eyes on him when he walks around to the Piazza del Popolo. Even familiar places turn strange when he becomes vulnerable to the glances of strangers. He feels an annoying surge of gratitude when the maître d' at Rosati greets him familiarly. He tells himself: don't feel awkward.

He picks a corner table. He remembers meals at Rosati with parties of fifteen and twenty, festive meals. He remembers being much younger, and excited by the world he moved around in. The familiarity of everything is reassuring and depressing. Jesse thinks he could go anywhere and never be surprised by anything. *Unless someone fell in love with me,* he thinks. *If someone who wasn't insane fell in love with me.*

He eats a large, heavy meal, laying off the wine because he feels the edge creeping up to his feet. Jesse is given to histrionic inner turmoil after a few drinks. He gets excited, aggrieved, stupid. He needs clarity, since he hasn't thought beyond the abandoned itinerary with Anthony. He knows if he drinks himself past a certain threshold, he'll start perceiving himself as an interesting person. So interesting that someone in this restaurant or in the street should get involved with his subjectivity. In Rome this would not be dangerous the way it would be in South America, but it would be obnoxious. Jesse has become economical about giving himself ugly memories.

He considers that in the years he's been coming to Rome, he's always handled his own luggage and never ordered room service at the Locarno. Midway in his reverie he recognizes the darkness around him as belonging to the Gramercy Park Hotel. If he switches on the light, he'll find his wallet and keys and a bottle of Perrier on the night table, beside a copy of *Winesburg, Ohio.* His slacks and underpants and a print shirt are heaped over his shoes on the floor. The dancing hamburgers have segued into Marlene Dietrich and Orson Welles on the TV.

Jesse thinks about dead people in the dark. He has the familiar thought that he's known a startling number of people who are now dead. Some people are a flicker of lightning, he thinks. He remembers people who've become nothing more than a single facial expression, a faint breath, a photograph, a momentary tug of the heart. Some aren't dead, but dying. He hates the way people fade even before they're gone.

He watches a soundless Janet Leigh being terrorized by hopheaded Mexicans in a motel room. Nearby, on the bed, a current issue of the *Advocate* lies folded open to the escort and massage ads. Jesse has circled some of the ads in pencil. He gropes for the switch of the bed lamp and settles the edge of the magazine on his chest. The Mexicans are approaching Janet Leigh, brandishing syringes full of dope. Jesse has narrowed the rent boy ads down to Hung Like a Horse, who gives his name as Ivan, purportedly "a Latino," and Nine Hard Inches, also known as Angelo. Ivan and Angelo have both tackled the composition of a personal ad with economy and directness. Jesse wonders if their services would correspond.

sometimes you're mistaken about things & it makes you crazy because you wake up with it & hear yourself rolling it over & over & it's terrible being alone when you think despair and death come so easily to the modern person the city too if you trap yourself peeling away all the layers of wishing for things when deep down what you wanted has been long lost & everything said & everything done is like darkness sliding into more darkness there's no hope or interest in the future it's just going to be worse & you'll get older & then die the world's full of lies & you get them coming and going

If anyone asked why he's living in the hotel, Jesse would say it's for the view. At night, looking out his windows and directly down, he sees the canopy of foliage over the wrought-iron fencing of the park, and the narrow street where taxis pull away from the hotel. He doesn't want a panorama. With the outside world reduced to this happy wedge of space, the specificity of the city and the year melts away. He loses the sense of where he is, staring out, and sometimes the sense of who he is, what life he's mired in, how much of it has passed, and how much of it is left. He's abandoned his East Village apartment, though he still pays his rent and utility bills. He goes there sometimes in the evening, to check on things, flip through the mail, play back messages.

there's something i have failed to piece together. i did not discover who i was until this knowledge had become useless. i terrorize myself with fantasies of doom and rejection. i've become strange in this element of strangeness, forlorn & superannuated by objects & voices & maybe dying of loneliness & discontent: however i arrange things i cannot find my way to any kind of life: not even delusion: not even a fantasy i can make myself crazy with, in the insufferable world of this town and the shitty people who fill it: the constant noise of voices constant fear constant violence

The park outside the window represents a flawless state of urban order. He can't go in, only property owners along the park have keys. Jesse remembers being in the park once, four years ago, on a Sunday: some structural work was underway, the park had been opened for one afternoon. Jesse has a memory of prams and pink balloons and some type of small orchestra. He feels rather glad they aren't there now. Instead there is the perfection of a place no one goes.

A California blond with perfect lips drives through a rainstorm to his girlfriend's house. Every time Jesse sees the commercial he imagines pressing his cock into the actor's mouth. He thinks the car being advertised is a piece of shit. Maybe the blond actor is a piece of shit, too. But he still buys the fantasy they're selling along with the car. He remembers things he forgot to buy during his afternoon shopping. He wanted candles. He's never burned candles in a hotel room, except in Third World countries, during power failures, and in the Grande-Bretagne in Athens, where candles are stocked in the bathrooms. He remembers outages in Bogotá and Quito and La Paz with nostalgia. He wishes New York would have frequent blackouts. Jesse recalls epic electrical storms in Cartagena, in Cuenca, in Malaysia. Though he avoids thinking about why he happened to be in some of those places, Jesse likes remembering the places.

And if he burned candles in a room at the Gramercy, Jesse could imagine being absolutely nowhere at all.

voices that sound the same as other voices: when you're on a bus for example or in a crowd and someone from some prehistoric moment of your childhood adolescence or even later on, we burn up so many lives in our lives, consuming friendships and loves like cars and houses, you turn expecting to see a familiar face aged with the traces of everything that's happened to it in all these years & it's the face of a complete stranger

The hotel in Istanbul used to be one of the palatial rest stops on the Grand Tour. Everything marble, everything scaled for Byzantine autocrats and British royalty. In the lobby are framed clippings under glass about Agatha Christie, who wrote some books there. The staff moves at a majestically relaxed pace. Objects are spaced at imperious distances from one another. The sense of place hangs in the air like soot. It absorbs and shrinks down every modern thing. It makes the American Express forms and Madonna records playing in the bar seem like piquant debris from another world. The paper currency fades and falls apart with the slightest moisture. Jesse thinks the coins are minted from recycled soda cans.

The hotel is wildly expensive for what it is. It does not feel like a haven of safety and graciousness.

Jesse's room overlooks the dining room terrace and a wide, two-tiered cement park where guests of the hotel sometimes drink tea in the evening. The park attracts local teenagers and a few old people, until two or three in the morning. At five every morning, when starry darkness still covers the immense valley to the left of the park, Jesse hears prayers yodeled by faraway priests. The town feels as if it's covered in fine dust. The streets are permeated by sunset colors and the odors of burning rubber and rotten food.

The room contains two single beds with hard mattresses and plain linen sheets, a gigantic oak armoire, and a pointlessly tiny writing table. The bathroom features lots of glistening, chipped white tile. The green oxidation smears around the bidet and bathtub drains disturb him. As if the putridity of the city could come seething up through the plumbing. Despite the epic dimensions of the room, it looks frugal and shabby. Its surfaces are too crisp and faded, like museum pieces under glass. He imagined Istanbul differently. He had heard that a certain erotic easiness prevailed, but he imagined that differently, too.

Every man under fifty he passes in the street offers him a stare of raw sexual appraisal. At first it quickens Jesse's interest. But the general condition of the town precludes going just anywhere with a stranger, and he doubts that just anyone can enter the hotel. The city looks like an immense hive that's been compressed in a vise. Jesse knows he can't develop the radar to move about in it fearlessly, so he sticks to large, well-lit streets. At night, even these sometimes dip without warning into hilly quadrants of pitch darkness. What little he feels adventurous enough to explore is enough for him. He came here on an impulse, to kill time in the kind of otherness that makes no demands and offers no long-term possibilities.

For Rent: 6'1", 185#, 27, cut meat w/huge nuts & beefy butt for the eating! Picturing a chunky, crude individual with mustache, IQ of 47, hair all over his meaty shoulders, doesn't know how ugly he is & thinks any queer would worship him because he can get it up for another man. Likes getting rimmed: nice. The type who says right away Do you have any porn, he wants to watch tapes while he fucks your butt. Really disgusting. Wants to drink a few beers first & be sucked & rimmed before sticking it in for two or three minutes. Asks for more money if he stays one minute over an hour.

One night in the dining room a waiter lays a heavy palm on Jesse's shoulder and asks him, almost inaudibly, if he'd like to go to a disco later. The waiter has beautiful skin, quick eyes, a sinuous smile. In New York, this man would be considered extremely handsome. Jesse imagines the waiter mounting him with ingenious skill. He doesn't want to go to a disco but says yes, then leaves for his room and falls asleep. Hours later, the phone rings. The waiter's voice mumbles incomprehensibly.

"No, I . . . the thing is, I'm too tired."

"Don't want disco?"

"No."

"May I come to the room?"

"All right."

The waiter taps on the door. When Jesse opens it, the man slips in and rushes to the alcove off the bathroom.

"I like you," he announces, unfastening the purple sash around his pants waist.

"I like you too," Jesse assures him, bewildered by the rapidity with which things are moving.

"In here," says the waiter, urgently motioning Jesse into the bathroom.

In the bathroom, the waiter lowers his pants, liberating a thick, hard prong that sticks straight out and a fat, tight scrotum.

"Please do not kiss me," he says, locking eyes with Jesse. Jesse can't tell if it's a command or a plea. He obligingly perches on the toilet seat rim and licks the man's penis and balls. He notices that the pubic hairs are clipped in a tidy triangle, to a quarter-inch length. He wonders if this is an Islamic custom or just some weird personal habit.

"Kiss," instructs the waiter, drawing a line with his thumbnail across his lower abdomen. Jesse dutifully kisses the salty-tasting area, just below the navel. The frenetic quality of the moment bothers him. A chasm is opening between the idea and the action. The waiter suddenly draws away, beckoning him over to the tub. He gestures for Jesse to lower his own pants and bend over the tub rim. Then, he searches for Jesse's hole with the hard, bobbing cock, without guiding it by hand, as if it'll naturally sink right in upon contact. After a few futile pokes he gives up, walks to the toilet, and settles himself open-legged on the seat.

Jesse steps between the waiter's legs and turns around facing the mirror above the sink. He lowers his ass. The waiter pulls him down closer, steering Jesse's hole toward his penis. This position is no good at all, and finally the waiter stands up, pushes Jesse to his knees, and sticks his cock into Jesse's mouth. Jesse gags, expelling the cock.

"Look," he says, "there are two beds in the other room. We really don't need to do this in the bathroom."

"People can see," says the waiter. "Close the windows."

Jesse walks out and draws the heavy drapes at the sides of the large windows. He hasn't noticed these drapes before, only the sheer white ones that can't be retracted. He now understands his room is wholly visible from the park. From the alcove the waiter tells him, "Lock the door."

"It's locked," Jesse says.

"No, lock it."

"It's locked, I tell you."

The waiter opens the door. He gives the outer hallway a nervous once-over and shuts the door. He's pulled up his pants. Now he removes them completely. He unbuttons the lower buttons of his shirt and pulls the shirt up around his nipples. He flounces down on the bed farthest from the window, with his knees raised and his legs spread. Jesse removes all his clothes. He kneels between the waiter's legs. He sucks the half-erect prick with grim concentration. Seconds pass. The waiter springs to his feet and pulls Jesse into the dog position at the edge of the mattress, stands behind him, spits into his fingers, greases his penis, and accurately shoves it in. He fucks Jesse's asshole for about thirty seconds. Jesse tightens his sphincters around the strong slippery meat. The waiter pulls himself free. He slips into his pants and shoes with insane haste.

"Can you give me some money?" he whispers.

"No," Jesse says.

"Cigarettes?"

Jesse takes out two for himself and hands over the pack.

"I'm going to get a drink," the waiter says.

"You're going for a drink."

"I'll come back," the waiter promises.

"All right."

"I'll come tomorrow," the waiter says.

"All right."

"I like you."

"I like you too."

He wonders what precise element of the situation has given the waiter so much anxiety. He doesn't think the waiter will return the following day. He regrets not offering money. Jesse calculates that the whole encounter has taken about seven minutes. He wonders about the dark roasted-walnut smell of the waiter's groin. He replays the scene many times in his head, touched and disappointed by it. Eventually he jerks off in the bathroom.

Uncut Latino. Rico: 24, 5'9", 158#, 30W, hung 9" thick, very friendly, 5 mins to Manht. 24 hours. Rico is a fraud like his accomplice Chico, potbellied not very clean & the cock's about 2–3 inches, stands there expecting you to give him a hard-on which he's never able to achieve, tries sort of pushing his limpness into you & then grunts a few times & he's out again. Some of these guys change their names from month to month, reword the ads, invent new bodies faces & cock sizes for themselves & show up with the same unsavory swindle. You can tell by checking the phone numbers against the old ads, for all they get ripping people off they're too cheap to change the numbers.

Slim's a vigorous & conscientious fuck, nine thick inches & he's cute, he'll get you into four or five positions whatever feels good & nice & slow sometimes he likes it. Tony from uptown, big frame, huge cock, pleasant face but nothing special: good if he's got poppers with him. Nice-tasting meat. European gymnast's half-Greek half-German, looks mainly German. Competent fuck, but mechanical, no initiative. Earns the money but it's no fun for either of you.

In front of the Blue Mosque, a small, ugly man with rotten teeth attempts to sell him a carpet. He says his name's Ghenghis as in Ghenghis Khan, that his brother owns a shop in the basement of the mosque. Jesse tells Ghenghis he doesn't need a carpet. Ghenghis says his brother also sells silver jewelry. Jesse says he doesn't need any silver jewelry, either. Ghenghis looks like trouble. Jesse has met a number of Ghenghises in his travels: not sharks, exactly, but smaller, parasitical fish who mistake themselves for sharks. Jesse knows if he doesn't get rid of this person he will end up separating Jesse from a lot of money. He will not use violence but intimidation and guilt. It's been so many days since Jesse spoke to anyone fluent in English that he equivocates at the crucial moment when a little hostility would send Ghenghis on the trail of a different tourist. They go into the mosque together and look at the vast floor of carpets, the columns, the windows. Ghenghis points out the abundance of blue tiles. Some restoration work is taking place. Many columns are draped with green scaffolding mesh. Ghenghis explains many details of the mosque that Jesse already knows about.

When they're outside retrieving their shoes, Ghenghis proposes showing Jesse around the area. Jesse again thinks he should ditch the guy. The area is, after all, world-famous, and Jesse knows what all the buildings are. Ghenghis also strikes him as a frightful bore, a bore with peasant cunning. Jesse calculates the amount of cash he can reasonably blow on a superfluous guided tour. He feels himself giving in. It's easier than detaching himself. He'll have someone to talk to, even if it's Ghenghis.

They trudge through the Topkapi and the Aya Sofya. The most important jewels of the Topkapi are out on loan, and the Aya Sofya hums with Japanese tourists. The streets are dense with bad air and traffic. Ghenghis takes Jesse through the cavernous cistern under the basilica. Water trickles and splutters down through the darkness, pooling to a meter's depth beneath the clay walkways, around dozens of arched columns. At the base of two columns deep in the cistern, they see chiseled heads of Medusa, one upside down, the other resting on a cheek. As they leave, loudspeakers blare "The Ride of the Valkyries."

Ghenghis proposes a trip to the Dolmabahçe Palace, in the same quarter as Jesse's hotel. Jesse thinks he's seen enough for one day, but he can't think of anything better to do. At the Dolmabahçe Palace, they wait on line for forty minutes until the mandatory guided tour takes them through. The air is cool here, by the water, and Jesse would like to sit under a tree, thinking his own thoughts. Ghenghis asks if Jesse minds taking the tour in Turkish, instead of waiting another twenty minutes for the English tour. Jesse doesn't care. They herd from room to room with twenty others. Sometimes Ghenghis explains what the rooms are, or translates the guide's monologue. Then he becomes, if not exactly thoughtful, absorbed in the grandeur of the decor. The sultans did many of their rooms in crystal. Crystal panels on the walls. Fat crystal banisters on the staircase.

During the tour, Ghenghis chats with another Turkish boy. The new boy has better teeth than Ghenghis and better clothes. He keeps a ring of car keys looped through his fingers and plays with them. Jesse wonders if Ghenghis is hustling this boy, but the boys seems too wary for that to happen. He's from a higher class and obviously thinks Ghenghis is amusing scum. Outside the palace Jesse asks the new boy if he's hungry. He's hoping to shake off Ghenghis. Ghenghis translates that the boy has to go home. He lives on the Asian side of the city. Jesse and Ghenghis go to Jesse's hotel in a cab. Jesse tries paying him for the tour.

"Not now, not now," Ghenghis says sharply, jabbing a finger toward the driver. Once they're out, Ghenghis tells him never to let a cab driver see his money. They walk up the road away from the hotel and go into the cement park. After some bickering Jesse gives him what he originally asked for. Ghenghis insists on an extra 60,000 lire. He says the tour lasted an extra two hours. Jesse points out that the Dolmabahçe Palace was Ghenghis's idea.

"You could have said no," Ghenghis replies. "Besides, we all need money, and you're rich."

Jesse sees no point in arguing. He supposes he is rich in comparison.

"And," Ghenghis says, after Jesse gives him the 60,000, "another twenty thousand for the tour tickets."

"Oh please," says Jesse, who paid for all the tour tickets. "Go fuck yourself."

"It's nothing to you, twenty thousand," Ghenghis responds smoothly.

"All the same, fuck off."

his voice sounds too sane, too ordinary. didn't ask what do you like, didn't talk dirty, didn't describe himself: probably he's really good. giant ants on the TV, radiation nightmare from the fifties. losing: time in your life, energy, friends, the will to continue, hopefulness. never meet anyone, nowhere to meet them. this one's name's tom. he just got home from the gym. 20, nice firm shape, dark eyes, black hair, a face good enough to eat. strips casually, gets on the bed in his briefs, lies on his back & lights a cigarette. i touch his cock through the briefs, he's already hard: substantial. where are you from. what do you do, i mean besides . . . play with his fingers, stroke his palm. it's hot outside. lick me, okay? he peels off his underpants and rubs his prick. pulls up his balls.

i lick down under his balls his ass rises slightly & he shifts his weight around until i can get my tongue into his asshole, spread his cheeks apart with my thumbs & suck his rectum & work gradually up across his balls & up & down his prick, a nice wide piece of work with a large sensitive head, nibble around the rim & flick the cordlike tissue just under it with the tip of my tongue, slide my mouth down over the whole thing, ease my head up & run my open lips down his cock bone & up the middle of the vein & then let him pump it in & out of my mouth kneeling on top of me he inches forward on his knees & then sits down on my mouth, his asshole centered on my tongue & i make love to his hole forcing my tongue deeper and deeper into him we stay like that for a long time & he leans back until he's lying down stretches out his legs & i kiss him everywhere

he's fucking me with my legs around his neck he pushes my legs away gripping my ankles until my knees are behind my head & my ass is sticking up & now he's lying

straight on top of me balanced on his toes like he's doing
pushups in & out of my ass pulling all the way out and
slamming himself back in on every stroke it hurts i love
him he turns me over & fucks me lying flat on top of me
his legs inside my legs pushing my legs wider & then slides
his legs over mine & pushes my legs closed fucking my hole
as if he wanted to make sure he's fucked it every way he
can think of & after that he carries me to the chair sits
down & arranges me with my back to his chest & slips his
cock back into my ass & fucks me for an hour so slow we're
hardly moving & he pulls it out just an inch or so and
slides it back up inside me & out again an inch & back in
as far as he can & every so often pulls out three or four
inches or five inches & holds it there like that for a long
time & slowly slowly pushes his hipbones forward just a
little just a little till it's all inside me again & then it's
almost imperceptible again for a long time & when i feel
like he's part of my own body he pushes his ass back draw-
ing out the whole nine inches except for his cockhead he
leaves inside & then slips the head out & pushes just the
head back in, lets it out with a pop & slips it in, just
the head five ten fifteen times & then it slides back inside
me the whole thing i feel his balls against my hole & him
breathing against my neck

He walks beyond the park into a narrow, winding bazaar
he explored on his first day in Istanbul. In a lane of vegetable and butcher stalls he finds a vendor selling freshly
killed fish and tinned food. He buys a half pound of Beluga
caviar, thirty-five dollars.

At the Pera Palas he walks into the kitchen off the dining
room. His presence violates some rigid hotel protocol and
immediately several waiters are clustered around him, ab-
surdly solicitous, as if he'd just been run over. Jesse asks
the best-looking one to open the caviar tin and bring it up
to his room.

In the room, closely observed, the waiter, who's introduced himself as Marco, looks beautiful as a movie star. His
hair is curly and brown, with red highlights. His features

are adorable, more rounded and Western than the sharper profiles around the hotel. He arranges the caviar on a bowl of ice on the table, turns to leave, asks Jesse a question Jesse can't understand, shrugs, moves closer to the door, pauses, turns, Jesse touches Marco's sleeve. Marco indicates he'd like to smoke a cigarette before returning to the kitchen.

They try to talk. Jesse has no Turkish words, Marco knows the phrases he needs for his job and nothing more. Marco sits down at the table. Jesse repositions his own chair so the table isn't between them. He glances at the caviar. He thinks it will go bad in the heat. He doesn't know how to make anything happen. He watches Marco smoke. He hooks Marco's right ankle with the toe of his sneaker and brings Marco's shoe to the chair cushion between his legs. Jesse unlaces the patent leather shoe and slides it off Marco's foot. It's a narrow, elegant foot with long, bony toes. Jesse grips it with both hands and massages it through the black rayon sock. The sock exudes an expanding odor of mildew and sweat. Marco closes his eyes.

"I come to you tonight," he says.

"Yes."

"I fuck you tonight," he elaborates.

"Yes, definitely."

The massaged foot moves to its shoe. Marco raises his other shoe and pulls it off. He pushes his left foot between Jesse's legs. Jesse massages the new foot. Marco presses the foot into Jesse's crotch and squeezes the hump of Jesse's erection with his toes. He lights another cigarette and watches Jesse carefully through clouds of smoke.

Jesse squeezes his thighs together around the foot, which Marco rubs up and down, clenching and unclenching his toes along the shape of Jesse's penis. Jesse comes. Marco replaces his shoe and stands up. He points to the caviar tin.

"Eat," he tells Jesse.

Jesse kisses him on the mouth. Marco wedges his tongue into Jesse's mouth. They stand locked together. Marco guides Jesse's hand to his crotch. Jesse feels a long, thick lump through the fabric. He kneels and kisses it, running his hands over Marco's buttocks.

He wakes again. Orson Welles is face down in a shiny black riverbed. Marlene Dietrich looks down at his corpse.

What does it matter, what you say about people. "What are you into?" "I like a lot of things." "When I saw the word 'master' in your ad, I wondered because I'm really not into pain." "No s&m. Okay, fine. But I'm definitely aggressive." "Well, so what kind of . . ." "I dig having a guy kneeling down in front of me worshiping my cock, taking my big cock down his throat, I like having him lick me, rim me . . ." "Okay, I think I'm probably a little tame for you. I like licking, I like sucking. But I can't stand having it rammed down my throat because I have this really severe gag reaction." "So tell me what you want." "I'm interested in, you know, getting fucked. And other things." "Like what?" "Anything you want." "That covers a lot of territory. I like water sports, I dig pissing on guys. I like bondage. I dig having my feet licked and a guy sucking my toes. I'm pretty broad-minded." "I'll do whatever you want, I just don't enjoy pain." "Well, I need to know stuff like that before I go to a place." "I wanna get fucked." "Fine, I dig fucking. I love fucking. The only thing is, if I'm going to fuck you in the ass you want to make sure you're clean up there." "You want me to douche." "I sort of require it, because the first sign of shit, man, that finishes the whole thing for me. It just turns me off completely. I'm not into shit at all." "I didn't say I was into shit, quite the contrary, really." "I'm making that a condition" "All right, fine." "I mean you can easily find somebody who's into that without any problem." "No, I mean fine, I'll douche."

how about if i bang you up against that window with your head hanging out? you've got a sweet little hole. nice fit. you like my cock? i could tell. ooh, yeah. how are we gonna make you come? you want me to like, open you up first? feel good? sit on that cock. come up a little more, you

can ride me better that way. oh yeah. you gonna come?
come all over my stomach, man. beautiful.

He saw people going away and people coming back. The
road to the cottage ran past the bay on one side and the
isthmus on the other, like the highway in Florida when they
went to Wakulla Springs. When he dreamed about that time
the road always looked as if it would dip down where the
two bodies of water met, at a point beyond the horizon.
People in the street were running. The pavement stretched
up the hill to the cathedral, flanked by low-rise offices and
grimy restaurant windows, turning hazy with smoke. Dozens of students were running, clapping sweater necks and
handkerchiefs to their mouths and noses. He felt the sting
of tear gas and clawing inside his throat. At the top of the
hill, another broad street curved up into the cathedral park.
Faraway the Virgin of Quito, several thousand tons of dull
aluminum, gleamed on a mountaintop. Below where he
stood, trim boys in green uniforms paraded on the grounds
of the military school. A satellite dish poked from a cluster
of stucco rooftops. He stood at the edge of the ocean and
heard water running in the bathtub. He read a paragraph of
Winesburg, Ohio. On the TV, crows ran under the spermy
arcs of water cannons. He stepped into the helicopter beside the river. The bells echoed across the water. They came
to a seafood joint with the best broiled mullet on the pen-
insula, if you scraped off the huge gob of butter in the middle. From far above, the little islands near the airport were
ringed with the white spokes of docks and boats. He always
wondered about these islands, who lived on them, how you
could find them if you rented a car and drove there. What
manner of life.

POEMS

Canada

it's another country,
she said in her letter
anything could happen
there are dark alleys here
nobody will know where you are
I want to take you into an alley and
fuck you until your ears bleed

nobody talks to me this way
in my own country

before I left
one friend expressed surprise
that I had to change my money
"don't they have dollars?"
she said

money is always ugly
even when it's new
it looks like something you should throw away
I hate the folded bills of
both countries
the state's arrogant ownership
of her body, my body

it's another country
she says
when I get off the plane

but it rains in Vancouver
like it rains in San Francisco
and the wind is wet and raw
you can wear your leather all the time
if you can cope with the boys
in caterpillar hats and pickup trucks
who point you out loudly
to their friends
"ugly dykes"
they shout as if it should be
a capital offense

maybe there is something ugly
about me if my presence makes
strangers threaten us
but I know there is nothing ugly
about you
you are enough to redeem this city
and I believe that
it was only after sodom and gomorrah
evicted all the queers that
the proud and unhospitable
cities of the plain
burned to the ground

we were on a bus
she sat behind me and
stuck her hand between
the seat and the wall
teased me with her fingertips
later we got a seat together
and her hands went beneath the newspaper on my lap
she tormented me for an hour
while I hissed at her to stop

at home she laughed at me, said
that bus was full of elderly Chinese people
who wouldn't have said a word even if
they knew I was not a boy

her son is 15, strange and intelligent
he is in a good school at last
the night he came home unexpectedly
the last night I was there
he talked loudly about
"your degenerate friends"
and being "the man of the house"
reminded her "you are a single working mother
not some adolescent pimply shopgirl
with a crush on a pop singer
and you have an obligation to me"
he was scared
we never made it to the alley

it is another country
this is another country

she moved to phoenix once
stayed long enough to
marry some faggot
who is probably dead by now
left before she could apply for a green card

because things did not work out between
her and the woman from arizona

what can I do what can I say
nothing I am ashamed
I don't believe in weddings but why
can't I give her my name,
take her name,
why can't we somehow hide one another
within the boundaries of our
separate citizenships

seven days spent
mostly in bed I barely knew
it was another country
until I had to leave

lust inspires a loyalty
inimical to the lines on the map
passionate outlaws
need their own territory
to desire is to be an exile
even a lesbian nation
would not give us passports

Jan when I remember
your tongue in my mouth
I come, standing up,
wherever I am

my clitoris is sulky
under my fingers,
but my vagina has not dried out
since I left you,
she is such a slut I can deceive her
into believing it is you
that pumps and fills me up

but really my body has become
another country
and I feel like an unemployed
illegal alien
how will I survive
where I do not belong
I belong with you

Gone

I called you one night
And you said,
"There's someone here.
I'll call you back in five or ten minutes."

I waited three hours, finally
Dialed your number,
And your son said
You were busy.
You could not come to the phone.
He sounded frightened.

Now I know damn well
There's only one person
Drops in on you just any old time
And he's not a friend.
He's a lot more important than that.
And you never turn him away.

I put down the phone
Remembering the last time
I fell in love with
A skinny dark-haired butch
From out of town

With crazy brown eyes
And a mean right arm.

She had a suicidal lover, 27 cats and
A golden retriever crammed into
A one-bedroom apartment in Queens, but
She swore she would find them all new homes
Before I moved in.

That was the year I
Single-handedly made a rate hike
For Ma Bell
Unnecessary.

One night when I called her
For a little phone sex,
Well, she was too busy.
She had to drive upstate
To the farm that had adopted her dog
And bring him home.
He just wasn't happy there.

I knew right then that
I couldn't live with her, but
That didn't mean I wasn't going to
Travel 3,000 miles to a city I hated
And make her sorry she had ever met me.
I had gotten that tired
Of living without my cunt.

I know now that
You can't come to the phone because
You are lying there turning blue,
Not really breathing,
And I thank God you listen to
That man's problems with his girlfriend

And tell him funny stories about
The good old days—

The bikers who took you in
When you were 15,
Making speed in a bathtub,
The last time you saw somebody
Get shanked in a bar,
Hiding dope in a condom
Shoved up your ass,
The johns who believed you really would
Stay all night long
For an extra forty bucks—

And whatever else you've done
To make him stay with you
And keep his favorite customer alive.

I wouldn't know what to do.

I know you will not tell me this
For weeks and weeks.
You won't exactly lie to me,
And honey I'll help you.
I won't ask.

No, I am not going to
Travel thousands of miles
To live with you.
But I know I will make myself
Go the distance for you
Even if it's all straight down.

I've always shared my lovers.
This time I feel like
Somebody is sharing you with me.

Is living without smack anything like
Living without your cunt?
On the whole, darlin',
I'd so much rather
You had a dog.

Heroin

you say,
tie yourself off—
it's like making somebody
hold their lips open
while you hurt them

you slap my arm
inside the elbow
places where the body bends
are always sexual

the needle tip is hair-fine
so sharp and you are
so deft it doesn't hurt at all
still I shudder

at the tiny feather of blood
distorted by the round
barrel of the syringe
it is the same color I see
when I close my eyes

it's like fucking,
you say,
having somebody at the end
of a needle
there is no way you're going to move

off of it
until I'm through

and you put the heroin
in my vein
and take blood and heroin out
and put it back in
it is indeed fascinating
I am tilting forward
feeling something warm hit me
in the stomach and come up
the back of my neck

it's better than coming
I don't think I ever want to come
this should not stop

I have always been
a clinical and somewhat cold
person
this is a clinical and somewhat cold
kind of drug
but somehow I don't feel bad about it
any more

the drug lays down along my bloodstream
like a strange animal
it takes over my heart
and makes it beat uncomfortably fast
it looks out through my eyes
seeking its own future

I feel as if there are two beings
inside my skin
they are not struggling with one another
but there is not quite enough room
for both of them
the one that is stronger begins to

systematically, not unkindly,
just because it is necessary,
kill off enough of what I was
to make room for itself
I like this a lot
I like it more when
we start having real sex and
there is no guilt or hesitation
just a ruthless joy

you wrap the narrow belt
you used to cinch up your own forearm
around my neck and
pull it tight as you
fuck me from behind
my face turns into a ceramic mask
I cannot breathe but
oh God I come I go
swimming fast underwater
like a crocodile after carrion or a mate

and I understand what you say about
how it makes you mean when you do a lot of it
it is the gift that heroin brings
to make you capable of doing
whatever you must
to get more of it

I know all this and of course I am not
addicted
but I am going to make sure
I can get my hands on
some more of this

the ancient reptile in me
smiles and continues to bask
in this tropical poisonous sun

We Really Should Stop This, You Know

I am not so much fun
Anymore;
Couldn't carry the role of ingenue
In a bucket, you say, laughing.

And I want to punch you.
I was never innocent, but
Thanks to you I know things
I wish I did not remember.

You don't like it
When I talk to the man myself,
Specifying quantities and
Give him the money
Instead of giving it to you
And letting you take care of it.

You keep asking me,
Where's the dope?
Until I finally say,
I hid it.
The look you give me is
Pure bile.

Well, fuck you,
This isn't like
Buying somebody a drink.
You don't leave your stash out
Where I might find it.

Finally I think I've made you wait
Long enough,
So I get out the little paper envelope
And hand it to you.
You are still in charge of

This part, so you relax,
Performing your junky ritual with
Your favorite razor blade, until
I ask you how to calculate my dose
So I won't O.D. when I do this
And you're not around.

Then you really flip.
You tell me it's a bad idea
For me to do this with other people.

Was it such a good idea
For me to do it with you?
Do you wait for me to turn up
Once every three months
So you can get high?
Is this our version of that famous
Lesbian fight about
Nonmonogamy?

Let me tell you what I don't like.

I don't like it when you
Take forever to cut up the brown powder
And cook it down and
Suck it up into the needle
And measure it, then take
Three times as much for yourself
As you give me.

I don't like it when you
Fuck me
After you've taken the needle
Out of my arm.

You talk too much
And spoil my rush.
All I really want to do

Is listen to the tides of blood
Wash around inside my body
Telling me everything is
Fine, fine, fine.

And I certainly don't want to
Eat you or fuck you
Because it will take forever
To make you come,
If you can come at all,
And by then the smack will have worn off
And there isn't any more.

I'm trying to remember
What the part is that I do like.
I think this shit likes me
A lot more than I like it.

Now you're hurt and angry because
I don't want to see you again
And the truth is,
I would love to see you,
As long as I knew you were holding.

So you tell me
Is this what you want?
I bet it was what you wanted
All along.

WILLIAM S. BURROUGHS

JUST SAY NO TO DRUG HYSTERIA

AN INTERESTING CASE OF mass hysteria is described in a book called *The Medical Detectives,* by Berton Roueché. The outbreak occurred at the Bay Harbor Elementary School in Dade County, Florida. A girl named Sandy, who was slightly ill with the flu, collapsed in the school cafeteria and was carried out on a stretcher as the next shift of students was coming in.

Sandy, it seems, was sort of a leader. In any case, the students started keeling over in droves. An officer from the Department of Public Health was dispatched to the scene. Fortunately, he recalled a similar case some years back from another high school, and quickly made a diagnosis of mass hysteria.

The remedy is very simple—get back to a calm, normal routine as expeditiously as possible. Get the children back to their classes. And that was the end of the outbreak. However, if the hysteria is not recognized and acted upon, it will go on and get worse and worse, as happened in the previous outbreak.

When hysteria is deliberately and systematically cultivated and fomented by a governing party, it can be relied upon to get worse and worse, to spread and deepen. Recent examples are Hitler's anti-Semitic hysteria and present-day drug hysteria. The remedy is simple—a calm, objective, common-sense approach.

Remember that during the nineteenth and early twentieth centuries—the "good old days," which conservatives so fondly evoke—opiates, cannabis tinctures, and cocaine were sold across the counter from sea to shining sea, and the United States did not founder as a result. There's no way to know exactly how many addicts there were, but my guess would be: surprisingly few. Many people simply *don't like these drugs.*

In England, before America persuaded the English government to adopt our own tried-and-failed, police-and-sanction approach, any addict could get heroin on prescription and fill his script on the National Health. As a result there was no black market, since no profit was involved. In 1957 there were about 500 addicts in the U.K., and two narcotics officers for metropolitan London. Now England presents the same dreary spectrum as the USA—thousands of addicts, hundreds of drug agents, some of them on the take, a flourishing black market, addicts dying from O.D.'s and contaminated heroin.

Obviously the sane, common-sense solution is maintenance for those who cannot or will not quit, and effective treatment for those who want to quit. The only treatment currently available is abrupt withdrawal, or withdrawal with substitute drugs. Withdrawal treatment dates back to early nineteenth-century British drug essayist Thomas De Quincey. Surely they could do better than that. Indeed, they *could,* but they show no signs of doing so.

Consider alternative therapy that is available: acupuncture, amorphine. Both therapies work because they stimulate the production of endorphins, the body's natural regulators and painkillers. The discovery and isolation of endorphins has been called the most crucial breakthrough toward the understanding and treatment of addiction since addiction was first recognized as a syndrome.

If you don't use it, you lose it. The addict is ingesting an artificial painkiller, so his body ceases to produce endorphins. If opiates are then withdrawn, he is left without the body's natural painkiller, and what would be normally minor discomfort becomes excruciatingly painful, until the body readjusts and produces endorphins. This is the basic mechanism of addiction, and explains why any agent that stimulates the production of endorphins will afford some relief from withdrawal symptoms.

De Quincey suggested that there may be a *constitutional* predisposition to the use of opium, and modern researchers speculate that addicts may be genetically deficient in insulin. I have heard from one addict who received an experimental injection of endorphins during heroin withdrawal. He reported that there was none of the usual euphoria experienced from an opiate injection, but rather "a shift of gears," and he was suddenly free from withdrawal symptoms. Researchers believe that endorphins, since they are a natural body substance, may not be addictive. Only widespread testing can answer this question.

Since endorphins were first extracted from animal brains, they are at present prohibitively expensive—$2,000 a treatment—just as cortisone was very expensive when it was first extracted. Synthesis has brought the price of cortisone within the reach of any patient who needs it. Is any of the *$7.9 billion* in Bush's latest War on Drugs plan marked for the synthesis and widespread testing of endorphins? I doubt if many of the congressmen who draft *"tough drug bills"* even know what endorphins are. And the same goes for the so-called drug experts who advise President Bush.

Billions for ineffectual enforcement.

Nothing for effective treatment.

I quote from a reading I have delivered to many receptive university audiences. This is an old number that is once again current and timely. It is called "MOB," for "My Own

Business," drawing a line between the Johnsons and the shits:

This planet could be a reasonably pleasant place to live, if everybody could just mind his own business and let others do the same. But a wise old black faggot said to me years ago: "Some people are shits, darling."

I was never able to forget it.

The mark of a hard-core shit is that he has to be RIGHT. He is incapable of minding his own business, because he has no business of his own to mind. He is a professional minder of other people's business.

An example of the genre is the late Henry J. Anslinger, former Commissioner of Narcotics. "The laws must reflect society's disapproval of the addict," he said—a disapproval that he took every opportunity to foment. Such people poison the air we breathe with the blight of their disapproval—Southern lawmen feeling their nigger notches, decent churchgoing women with pinched, mean, evil faces.

"Any form of maintenance is immoral," said Harry, thus rejecting the obvious solution to the so-called drug problem.

On the other hand, a Johnson minds his own business. He doesn't rush to the law if he smells pot or opium in the hall. Doesn't care about the call girl on the second floor, or the fags in the back room. But he will give help when help is needed. He won't stand by when someone is drowning or under physical attack, or when animals are being abused. He figures things like that are everybody's business.

Then along came Ronnie and Nancy, hand in hand, to tell us nobody has the *right* to mind his own business:

"Indifference is not an option. Only outspoken insistence that drug use will not be tolerated."

Everyone is obliged to become hysterical at the mere thought of drug use, just as office workers in Orwell's *1984* were obligated to scream curses, like Pavlov's frothing dogs, when the enemy leader appeared on screen. And they'd better scream loud and ugly.

William von Raab, former head of U.S. Customs, went

even further: "This is a war, and anyone who even *suggests* a tolerant attitude toward drug use should be considered a traitor."

Recollect during the Dexter Manley famous-athlete/cocaine-dealer flap, "Eyewitness News" was prowling the streets, sticking its mike in people's faces. One horrible biddy stated:

"Well, I think making the money they do, they should serve as an example."

She gets plenty of mike time.

And here a black cat, working on some underground cables, straightens up and says, "I think if someone uses drugs, it's his own bus—"

He didn't even get the word out before they jerked the mike away. Freedom of the press to select what they want to hear, and call it the voice of the people.

Urine tests! Our pioneer ancestors would piss in their graves at the thought of urine tests to decide whether a man is competent to do his job. *The measure of competence is performance.* When told that General Grant was a heavy drinker, Lincoln said: "Find out what brand of whiskey he drinks, and distribute it to my other generals."

Doctor William Halsted has been called the "Father of American surgery." A brilliant and innovative practitioner, he introduced antiseptic procedures at a time when, far from donning rubber gloves, surgeons did not even wash their hands, and the death rate from postoperative infection ran as high as 80 percent. Doctor Halsted was a lifelong morphine addict. But he could still hack it and hack it good, and he lost no patients because of his personal habit. In those "good old days," a man's personal habits were *personal* and *private*. Now even a citizen's blood and urine are subject to arbitrary seizure and search.

The world's greatest detective could not have survived a urine test. "Which is it this time, Holmes, cocaine or morphine?"

"Both, Watson—a speed ball."

It is disquieting to speculate what may lurk behind this colossal red herring of the War on Drugs—a war neither likely to, nor designed to, succeed. One thing is obvious: old, clean money and new, dirty money are shaking hands under the table. And the old tried-and-failed police approach will continue to escalate at the expense of any allocations for treatment and research. In politics, if something doesn't work, that is the best reason to go on doing it. If something looks like it might work, stay well away. Things like that could make waves, and the boys at the top, they don't like waves.

Anslinger's "missionary work," as he called it, has found fertile ground in Malaysia, where there is a mandatory death penalty for possession of a half ounce or more of heroin or morphine or seven or more ounces of cannabis. (No distinction between hard and soft drugs in Malaysia; it's all "Dadah.") Anyone suspected of trafficking can be held two years without trial. Urine tests are a prerequisite for entry to high schools and universities.

Mahathir Bin Mohamed, Prime Minister of Malaysia, has launched an all-out radio and TV campaign to create a *"drug-hating personality."* He is said to command widespread support for his drug policies. So did Hitler command widespread support for his anti-Semitic program. Just substitute the word "addict" for "Jew," and *Der Stümer* storms again. *Der Stümer* was Julius Streicher's anti-Semitic rag, designed to create a Jew-hating personality.

In order to get to the bottom line of any issue, ask yourself: "Cui bono?—Who profits?" According to Michele Sindona's account in Nick Tosches's book *Power on Earth,* the bulk of the world's dirty money is processed in Singapore and Kuala Lumpur, and the sums involved are *trillions of dollars.* Any liberalization of drug laws could precipitate a catastrophic collapse of the drug black market and cut off this salubrious flow of dirty money to the laundries of Malaysia. (Hanging small time pushers/addicts to protect huge Syndicate profits . . . does money come any dirtier?)

And I would be interested to examine the offshore bank

accounts of Malaysian officials involved in the fabulously profitable war against drug menace. But that is a job for an investigative reporter like Jack Anderson, a job he is not likely to undertake, since he seems to be in basic sympathy with Prime Minister Mohamed.

Interviewing Mohamed on the subject of drugs, Jack Anderson reports that he "spoke with real passion." (And so did Hitler speak with real passion.) In a column entitled "We Are Losing the War Against Drugs," Anderson speaks of thousands of "stupid and criminal Americans" who persist in using drugs . . . yes, criminal, by act of Congress. With the passage of the Harrison Narcotics Act in 1919, thousands of U.S. citizens—from frugal, hard-working, honest Chinese to old ladies with arthritis and old gentlemen with gout—were suddenly "criminals."

George Will relates the story of a Colombian woman who was detained at Customs until she shit out some cocaine in condoms. He goes on to say: "We should attack demand as well as supply. Life should be made as difficult for users as it was for that woman."

So thousands of suspected users are rounded up and forced to swallow castor oil in the hope of bringing illegal drugs to light. . . .

"Got one!"

"False alarm . . . just a tapeworm."

Fifty years ago, deep in the Ural Mountains of Lower Slobbovia, a thirteen-year-old prick, named Pavlik Morozov denounced his father to the local authorities as a counter-revolutionary kulak because he had a pig hidden in his basement. (A kulak is a subsistence farmer.) That was when Stalin was starving out the kulaks to make way for collective farms, which didn't work. Stalin levied an outrageous produce tax, knowing that the farmers would hide their crops, then sent out patrols to search and seize concealed produce and farm animals. At least three million people starved to death in the winters of 1932 and 1933, and that's a conservative estimate.

Little Pavliki was hacked to stroganoff by the outraged neighbors—good job and all. *Thus perish all talking assholes.*

"His name must not die!" sobbed Maxim Gorky, his hearty voice contracted by painful emotion. So Pavliki became a folk hero. Got a street in Moscow named after him, and a statue to commemorate his heroic act. He should have been sculpted with the head of a rat. And the village of Gerasimovka is a fucking shrine, drawing legions of youthful pilgrims to the home of Pavlik Morozov.

"Dirty little Stukach."

That's Ruski for "rat"—a word designed to be *spat* out.

It is happening here. *Lawrence Journal-World,* October 29, 1986: "Girl, 10, Reports Mother's Drug Use." It was the fourth time that a California girl had turned in her parents for alleged drug abuse since August 13. And Reagan's Attorney General Ed Meese said that management has the obligation and responsibility for surveillance of problem areas in the workplace, such as locker rooms and, above all, toilets, *and the toilets in the nearby taverns,* to prevent drug abuse.

I am an old-fashioned man: I don't like informers. It looks like Meese and Reagan, and now Bush, intend to turn the United States into a nation of mainstream rats.

Well, as Mohamed says, one has to give up a measure of freedom to achieve a blessed drug-free state, at which point the narcs will wither away. Sure, like the KGB withered away in Russia.

In April 1987, I was privileged to attend a debate between Timothy Leary and Peter Bensinger, former head of the Drug Enforcement Administration (DEA), and at that time one of Reagan's self-styled drug experts. The debate was held at the Johnson County Community College in Kansas City, Kansas, in the heartland of America.

It was a massacre. Bensinger was lying, and the audience was fully aware of his blatant falsifications. Pausing for applause after some assault on logic and common sense, he received instead a chorus of boos. Fully 90 percent of the audience supported Leary, who won the debate hands down.

Lying comes as natural as breathing to a politician, and as necessary to his political survival. One mark of a liar is his refusal to answer any direct question. When asked if the billions a year spent on enforcement of unworkable, unenforceable laws would not be better spent on research and treatment, Bensinger replied that the Defense Department spends more in a week than the DEA spends in a year.

"Boo! Boo! Boo!"

Asked about the English system of allowing addicts heroin on prescription, he said: "They went right out and exchanged it for stronger street dope."

What could they find on the street stronger than 100 percent pure pharmaceutical heroin?

"Well, uh, cocaine." (Which can also be obtained on prescription in England.)

Lies . . . Lies . . . Lies. The Lie Decade.

Here is a passage from my work in progress, *Ghost of Chance:*

The Board had lost interest in the Museum of Lost Species, some members even suggesting that the Museum was a figment of the late captain's drug-clouded mind, perpetuated by the superstitious villagers. In any case, there were more pressing matters: international dissent on an unprecedented scale. Their computers estimated that dissent would become acute in the next fifty to a hundred years. They had to think at least that far ahead.

To distract from the problems of overpopulation, depletion of resources, deforestation and pandemic pollution of water, land, and sky, they have inaugurated a war against drugs. This will provide a pretext to set up an international police apparatus designed to suppress dissidence on a worldwide level. The international apparatus will be called ANA: Anti-Narcotics Association. Ana means "I" in Arabic, so ANA can be shortened to "I," or "Eye."

Propaganda will follow the tried-and-true methods used by Adolf Hitler. Just substitute the word "addict" for "Jew." Same song, different verse—DOPE FIENDS covered with sores, reeking of sulfurous evil.

If it works, don't fix it, and it is working. Kids turning in their parents, and here is a California Reader writing in the Ann Landers column suggesting we take a lesson from Communist China: shoot all the drug dealers and all the addicts. . . . "Then we'll all be much happier."

"One kook."

"Yes, but . . . there are plenty who see through our plan right now."

The Texas member looks up from his crossword puzzle.

"We should worry? We got the Moron Majority."

"It's not a majority."

"Who ever needed a majority? Ten percent plus the police and the military is all it ever took. Besides, we've got the media hook, line, and blinkers. Any big-circulation daily even hinting that the war against drugs is a red whale? Anyone asking why more money isn't going into research and treatment? Any investigative reporters looking into money laundering in Malaysia? Or the offshore bank accounts of Mahathir Bin Mohamed? Anyone saying that the traffickers hanged in Malaysia are not exactly kingpins? There is no limit to what the media will swallow and shit out on their editorial pages."

Unfortunately, my own most "paranoid" fantasies in recent years have not even come close to the actual menace now posed by antidrug hysteria, if current polls are even approximately accurate. According to a survey conducted recently by the *Washington Post* and ABC News, 62 percent of Americans would be willing to give up "a few freedoms we have in this country" to significantly reduce illegal drug use; 55 percent said they favored mandatory drug tests for *all* Americans; 67 percent said all high school students should be regularly tested for drugs; 52 percent said they would agree to let police search homes of suspected drug dealers without a court order, even if houses "of people like you were sometimes searched by mistake"; 67 percent favored allowing police to stop cars at random and search for drugs, "even if it means that the cars of people like you are sometimes stopped and searched"; and fully *83 percent* favored encouraging people to report drug *users* to police, "even if it means telling police about a *family member* who uses drugs."

President Bush said in his television address not long ago: "Our outrage against drugs unites us as a nation!"

A nation of what? *Snoops and informers?*

Take a look at the knee-jerk, hard-core shits who react so predictably to the mere mention of drugs with fear, hate, and loathing. Haven't we seen these same people before in various contexts? Storm troopers, lynch mobs, queer-bashers, Paki-bashers, racists—are these the people who are going to revitalize a "drug-free America"?

The emphasis on police action rather than treatment has persisted and accelerated. The addict seeking treatment today will find long waiting lists and often prohibitive costs. And the treatment is old-fashioned withdrawal, with a very high incidence of relapse. In all the television and newspaper talk about drugs, I have yet to hear a mention of the possible role of endorphins in such therapy, or any other innovative medical approach.

The dominant policy of police enforcement has nothing but escalating addiction rates (and ballooning appropriations) to recommend it. Americans used to pride themselves on doing a good job, and doing it right. Hysteria never solved any problem. If something clearly and demonstrably does not work, why go on doing it? It's downright un-American.

My advice to the young is: Just Say No to Drug Hysteria!

BODY

I HAVE UNRULY HAIR. When I wake up in the morning it's all bunched up into a stupid point at the top of my head. It never does what I want it to. Some of it goes this way, and some of it goes that way. My mother used to say you have to train your hair, the way her brothers did, spending hours in front of the mirror with gobs of Brylcreem and a stiff brush to force it into the right direction. But I didn't know the right direction, and besides, I didn't want to train my hair. I wanted my hair to be free. One summer Sheree ordered my entire body shaved, including my head. I was surprised at what a nicely shaped head I had, although to look at me I'm sure people thought I was going through some kind of chemotherapy.

Before the Beatles caught on my dad had a flat-top and the rest of us had butch haircuts, which is ironic since, as far as my family goes, that was and still is my name: Butch. The story is my dad's sister, Helen, married a dwarf. I had dreams about this dwarf chasing me up and down the stairs, but that was impossible since Uncle Foster couldn't walk. Helen had to carry him around like a little doll. When I was born Foster took one look at my puny and sickly body and must have been struck with a sudden wave of empathy. "Butch! His name is Butch," he insisted. And out of fear or pity no one disagreed with him. Besides, they must have figured I'd need all the help I could get. So my name is Butch. Butch: the archetypal bully on the block. Butch: the tough-looking woman in men's clothes. Butch, as in "he's butch": which means he's got nerves of steel, and he can take it without flinching, whatever "it" is.

A hammer falls from the sky and cracks my head. I slip while climbing on the bathroom sink and BOOM! My mother whirls around from the front seat of the car and slaps my face for mouthing off, accidentally bloodying my nose, which I milk for all the sympathy it's worth. Mr. Comedian: I make some nasty jokes about my aunt while she's on the phone and BOOM! More blood and more sympathy. "Butch," she says, "you just never know when to stop."

Sheree gives me a hard crack right in front of our friends, because I'm testy with her and totally unsubmissive. It straightens me out all right, and makes my penis stiff, too, but our friends don't talk to us for months, even though they know the kind of relationship we have. And Jim of all people should know better because he's the one who put this ring in my nose to begin with. He knows what it means. I'm like a prize bull and sometimes I've got to be smacked in the snout when I get off the beaten path. This nose ring is a symbol that my body belongs to Sheree to do with as she wishes. When we split up I stopped wearing it, not only because it lost its meaning, but also because I got tired of being stared at and pointed at by strangers. My earrings are innocuous enough, but I notice that people still don't look me in the eye. I can see their gaze fixed onto my earlobe as we talk. The first time my mother saw my earrings she heaved a resigned sigh and said, "Oh, Butch, what's next, a ring through your nose?" Oh, Mom, I thought to myself, what you don't know won't hurt you. She has enough to worry about and feel guilty about when it comes to my body, so I keep my mouth shut about the juicy stuff.

There's an image from my childhood that I can't get out of my head. It's a Porky Pig cartoon, one of the older ones where Porky's character isn't quite developed yet. With his tiny vest and his fat naked ass he looks particularly obscene. He's obsessed with food, as always. While the other kids play, he dreams of chickens, watermelons, and corn on the cob. He swipes one of his mother's freshly baked pies and swallows it whole. At the dinner table, while his family says grace, he ties everyone's spaghetti together and consumes it all in one continuous slurp. At night he has a dream. He's strapped to a chair, in the clutches of a mad scientist who crams his mouth full of food with an elaborate array of machinery: automatic soup spoon twirlers, banana openers, ice cream cone emptiers, and sandwich makers, and a juke-box pie dispenser. Porky's left an obese blubbery mess, but he still hasn't learned his lesson. As soon as he's set free he grabs a chicken leg, shoves it into his mouth, and explodes. And then he wakes up, just in time for breakfast, which he proceeds to scarf down with his two fat fists like there was no tomorrow.

My mouth was always open, like a baby bird screeching its lungs out. My mouth: open wide for the doctors with no clue as to what's wrong with me. My mouth full of bleach (an accident). My mouth full of medicine: "Take this. It'll make you feel better." My mouth full of phlegm, con-stantly. My mouth, with the body of Jesus melting over my tongue. My mouth pressed against Sheree's cunt as she crouches over me, letting loose with all her piss, which I obediently swallow, not spilling a single drop. Some guy's penis in my mouth because Sheree wants to see me suck him off, but he's not hard and I'm not hard, and it's all so unfulfilling. My mouth, screaming at Sheree because she's always so depressed, oblivious to what she has—which is me—and I still have enough ego to know, in spite of my submissive and masochistic nature, that I'm a pretty good catch: I cook; I clean; I do the laundry; I run errands; I build shelves; I solve problems; I'm passionate; I'm artistic; I'm creative; I'm sexy; I'm obedient; I'm loyal; I'm funny; I'm witty; I'm smart; I sing songs; I write poems; I fuck; I make her come: I make her smile; I make her laugh—but I can't, I never have, and I never will make her happy.

She's choking me. She's striding my penis, she's got the bathrobe cord wrapped around my neck and she's choking me. Something we picked up from the movie *In the Realm of the Senses*. My face is a deep red-purple, like the head of my dick. That's all I am: a head connected to a cock, like a stick horse she rides all around the room, on the ceiling, in the clouds. I'm dizzy and about to faint. I'm either going to die or I'm going to come. I come. In the movie, a true story, the man is choked to death, and the woman cuts off his penis as a token of their undying love. "What if I accidentally kill you?" she says. "How could I ever face your parents?"

Death is always with me. It's in my lungs. I'm a factory of mucus as thick as pudding. The faucet is always on and it drips this gooey mess like "flubber" in the *Absent Minded Professor*. Like The Blob and just as deadly. I have a physical therapist who, for an hour each day, slaps my chest with her hands to dislodge the plugs of mucus, like shaking apples off a tree. Sometimes I just swallow it, but usually I explode into these body-racking coughs, spitting the loose phlegm into paper Dixie cups, sometimes two cups per treatment. I'm a human Foster's Freeze machine making sundaes of sickness. It got so bad they put a vacuum tube down my throat to suck it out, colonies of bacteria living in this thick mucus slime, so resilient they render ordinary antibiotics useless. So I had a catheter installed in my chest for repeated doses of intravenous drugs. It's gone now, but I still have a scar, one of the few nonsymbolic, non-self-inflicted scars.

I have this barrel chest that makes me look deformed. What happens is air flows into my lungs, but because of all the obstructions it can't get out, so my chest keeps expanding, like some giant balloon, which I imagine will pop someday, sending me splat against the wall. When I was a baby there was so much fluid within my chest cavity they had to draw it out with long needles. Hence my attraction to piercing. Notice my lovely nipple rings. And hey, since most of my medical needs are paid for by the government, I get all my needles for free! Thank you, California taxpayers.

Looking as frail as I do made me an easy target. Kids called me Casper. "Hey, Casper, don't you ever go to the beach?" (Thank you, California assholes.) On the way to school one day three of them jumped out from in front of a parked car and started punching me in the stomach. I thanked them for it. I said, "Please hit me harder. I deserve to be hit." I begged them to hit me more, not because I was into it (that came much later), but because I instinctively thought if I could make them believe that I was totally crazy, and if they still had a shred of decency about them, they might just take pity on me, or at least be so weirded out that they would leave me alone. So we made a date to meet after school where they could punch me some more, but that was the last I saw of them.

In those days I had more problems with my stomach than I ever did with my lungs. Another aspect of my disease is a lack of certain pancreatic enzymes, so I can't digest food properly, and I get these awful stomachaches. From the beginning that was the center of my existence and the focus of all my pain. It was why I couldn't gain weight. It was the excuse for missing school. It's the reason I started masturbating. "Don't do that," my mother said, on one of those sick days, with the pain so bad that only my rubbing against the sheets could soothe it, my entire body thrusting in an effort to throw off the hurt. And suddenly there was this thing down there, throbbing, the way moments earlier my stomach had throbbed, but different—this was pure pleasure. And as my penis swelled, the pain of my stomach retreated and felt far away, muffled as if it were buried somewhere deep in the mattress below me. "Don't do that," my mother said. "Only babies do that."

I get these raging hard-ons but they don't go anywhere because I have a steel ring through the tip of my penis that's padlocked to another ring in the perineum (that no-man's land between the asshole and the balls). When I get a hard-on the head of my penis pulls at the padlock and it hurts like hell. The harder it gets, the more it hurts; the more it hurts, the harder it gets . . . you get the picture. It's like a pornographic painting by M. C. Escher. I have to wear a tight girdle at night to keep my penis and its assorted hardware contained, otherwise I'll be awakened every hour on the hour by these excruciating nocturnal erections, something I like to call my "Alarm Cock." But what gets me the most excited is the knowledge that Sheree holds the key to the whole contraption. She is the owner of my penis and the guardian of my sexuality. And that's a good thing, because left to my own devices, who knows what I'd do. Take, for example, this journal entry dated "Saturday, August 18, 1979," one year before Sheree and I met:

I've been in quite a mood again. It started when I remembered that Mistress Laura said there'd be a party in September and there was a chance that she might pierce my nipples. Anyway I'm into it now: sleeping tied up on a bare mattress with no blankets, sheets, or pillow. Submerging myself in a tub of ice cold water—that was great! Peaceful and hypnotic. But just now I had an accident. I nailed the head of my dick to a board, the way I saw it done in a magazine the other day. I got so excited by the magazine that I had to try it myself. But while trying to drive the nail in a little farther I missed and just (I thought) tapped the tip of my poor dick. It didn't hurt (the nail was handling that job) but shit! It started swelling up immediately. I thought it would never stop and imagined it bursting and that being the end of me and sex the way I know it. I pulled the nail out as quick as I could, using alcohol swabs to stop the bleeding. The penis bleeds an enormous amount. Just one little pin prick and it looks like a murder has taken place. Imagine what a nail hole is like. So now there's a big black knot on the end of my dick. All I can do is hope it goes away. I'm amazingly calm. I've had accidents before and they always seem to turn out all right. After extracting the nail and stopping the blood and putting ice on my throbbing knot I tied myself up—on my stomach, wrists attached to ankles (don't ask how; it's too complicated). I got excited and jacked off. When I looked down—shit! The whole towel and mattress were soaked with blood. There were spatterings of blood far away from the towel even, which made me think for a second—more than a second—that I had really fucked myself up and was coming blood. I stayed calm, though, and methodically cleaned everything up, just like Tony Perkins, my blood swirling down the drain like Janet Leigh's. After that I pissed in the sink—thank God it came out yellow and not red like I was afraid it might.

I'm still not through. I'm going to try and keep this mood going for two more weeks, when I plan on seeing Mistress Laura again. And two weeks after that, maybe she'll put a nice pair of rings through my nipples. I'm excited again just thinking about it. But I have to slow down now. I've got to stretch this out for a long time. I'm going to make it a lifestyle, and not just a mood.

DAVID TRINIDAD

EIGHTEEN TO TWENTY-ONE

I

He said his name was Nick; later I learned
he'd crossed the country on stolen credit
cards—I found the receipts in the guest house
I rented for only three months. Over
a period of two weeks, he threatened
to tell my parents I was gay, blackmailed
me, tied me up, crawled through a window and
waited under my bed, and raped me at
knifepoint without lubricant. A neighbor
heard screams and called my parents, who arrived
with a loaded gun in my mother's purse.
But Nick was gone. I moved back home, began
therapy, and learned that the burning in
my rectum was gonorrhea, not nerves.

II

Our first date, Dick bought me dinner and played
"Moon River" (at my request) on his grand
piano. Soon after that, he moved to
San Diego, but drove up every weekend to see me. We'd sleep at his "uncle's"
quaint cottage in Benedict Canyon—part
of Jean Harlow's old estate. One night, Dick
spit out my cum in the bathroom sink; I
didn't ask why. The next morning, over
steak and eggs at Dupar's, Dick asked me to
think about San Diego, said he'd put
me through school. I liked him because he looked
like Sonny Bono, but sipped my coffee
and glanced away. Still, Dick picked up the bill.

III

More than anything, I wanted Charlie
to notice me. I spent one summer in
and around his swimming pool, talking to
his roommates, Rudy and Ned. All three of
them were from New York; I loved their stories
about the bars and baths, Fire Island, docks
after dark. I watched for Charlie, played board
games with Rudy and Ned, crashed on the couch.
Occasionally, Charlie came home without a trick and I slipped into his bed
and slept next to him. Once, he rolled over
and kissed me—bourbon on his breath—and we
had sex at last. I was disappointed,
though: his dick was so small it didn't hurt.

IV

I made a list in my blue notebook: *Nick,
Dick, Charlie, Kevin, Howard, Tom* . . . Kevin
had been the boyfriend of an overweight
girl I knew in high school. I spotted him
at a birthday bash—on a yacht—for an
eccentric blonde "starlet" who called herself
Countess Kerushka. Kevin and I left
together, ended up thrashing around
on his waterbed while his mother, who'd
just had a breakdown, slept in the next room.
Howard was Kevin's best friend. We went for
a drive one night, ended up parking. His
lips felt like sandpaper, and I couldn't
cum—but I added his name to the list.

V

Tom used spit for lubricant and fucked me
on the floor of his Volkswagen van while
his ex-lover (also named Tom) drove and
watched (I was sure) in the rearview mirror.
Another of his exes, Geraldo,
once cornered me in Tom's bathroom, kissed me
and asked: "What does he see in you?" At a
gay students' potluck, I refilled my wine
glass and watched Tom flirt with several other
men in the room. Outside, I paced, chain-smoked,
kicked a dent in his van and, when he came
looking for me, slugged him as hard as I
could. It was the end of the affair, but
only the beginning of my drinking.

VI

I ordered another wine cooler and
stared at his tight white pants—the outline of
his cock hung halfway down his thigh. After
a few more drinks, I asked him to dance to
"The First Time Ever I Saw Your Face." He
pressed himself against me and wrapped his arms
around my neck. I followed him to his
apartment but, once in bed, lost interest.
I told him I was hung up on someone.
As I got dressed, he said: "If you love him,
you should go to him." Instead, I drove back
to the bar, drank more, and picked up a blond
bodybuilder who, once we were in bed,
whispered "Give me your tongue"—which turned
   me off.

VII

As one young guy screwed another young guy
on the screen, the man sitting a couple
seats to my right—who'd been staring at me
for the longest time—slid over. He stared
a little longer, then leaned against me
and held a bottle of poppers to my
nose. When it wore off, he was rubbing my
crotch. Slowly, he unzipped my pants, pulled back
my underwear, lowered his head, licked some
pre-cum from the tip of my dick, and then
went down on it. As he sucked, he held the
bottle up. I took it, twisted the cap
off and sniffed, then looked up at the two guys
on the screen, then up at the black ceiling.

ANA MARIA SIMO

HOW TO KILL HER

To Harriet Hirshorn

1

BETSY PAINTED HER LAST nail. She turned off the bedroom light and her nails became a deep red wound in the dark. A few minutes later she was walking on the snowbanks of Avenue C, protecting her lips against the bitter wind with an ugly Indian scarf stolen the night before from a restaurant coat-rack. She liked the scarf because it was shiny, like the metal studs on her leather bracelet, like her unnaturally red hair and perfect teeth.

McSorley's, on East Seventh, was thick with smoke and stale beer like all cheap bars. But to this was added a rancid layer, wafting from the sweaty underwear and unwashed scalps of its college male customers. A line of such males, goosing, pushing, and fondling each other like football players after a big win, snaked out of the front door and onto the sidewalk, waiting to be seated. Sandwiched here and there between the beefy columns, a few bored and ge-nerically blond young females could be seen. On Saturday nights, the future Wall Street executives would throw up against the walls and doorways of neighboring buildings.

Sunday afternoons, the greenish, dried-out puddles, with their promise of great fun to be had inside, would freshly excite the new boys on line.

Betsy worked the Saturday night line. She was implacably thorough and in a couple of hours, exactly between ten and midnight, she would make at least $200. Once, the night before spring break 1987, she made $325. Her blow jobs and hand jobs were clean and to the point: Betsy always delivered and she would do so inside her car, parked across the street, under the hulking egg-shaped shadow of the Ukrainian Orthodox Church.

None of her clients ever lost his place on the line because everything was over so quickly. In between clients, she cleaned her hands with a towelette and, whenever her mouth had worked, she rinsed it with undiluted Listerine.

Betsy neither liked nor disliked these men. She viewed them with the same remoteness with which people who are not animal lovers view cats and dogs. She did object, however, to some of the odors they left in her car. She kept two potent air fresheners on the dashboard and would open the doors for a minute or two after each of them was gone.

She was extremely accurate at calculating when each one was ready to come—she would get her mouth out of the way and catch the sticky substance with a hand towel.

"It's like playing softball," she once told Maura.

Once in a while, out of daring or boredom, she would miscalculate and the white stuff would end up in her mouth. She would quickly spit it out on the towel and precipitously end the session to rinse her mouth with mouthwash. She always made a mental note of the unpredictable comers and enjoyed the challenge of their return visits. The "accident," as she would call it, had never happened twice with the same client.

Betsy always referred to them with the neutral word "client." To her, the world was not divided into two sexes; there was only one sex: female. The rest were clients, actual or potential, curiously asexual but sexually needy creatures. Betsy was not dealing sex from her car, but hygiene and medicine and exercise for certain limp and underutilized parts of her clients' bodies.

She could not understand how any woman could fall in love with one of them. She could understand fucking them, even if she personally found it not worth her effort. But falling in love? She felt sorry for the women on the line. With their little wan smiles, they looked like lost tourists in an unfriendly city, hoping to find a nice person who would show them the way back to the train station. She never hustled a man standing next to a woman. Once, she didn't see the woman in the shadows, the humiliated look on her face. She was still on line, waiting, when they came back, and Betsy almost told her to go home and forget the asshole. Instead, she just looked at her in the eyes and smiled. The woman stared back with hatred. Betsy kept smiling and drove away with only $75 in her pocket—she didn't feel like working any more that night.

When she got home, Maura's voice was on her answering machine: "I think I've killed her," Maura said, then hung up.

2

Maura put down the receiver and the phone cord came off.

"You're fucking never home!" she said, letting Betsy's phone ring twenty times. She was sitting on her toilet seat, naked except for a pair of shorts. The bathroom light was on, bouncing harshly against the white tiles. She was sweating.

"Where are you?"

Maura had always wondered how Betsy made a living: in the seven years she had known her, Betsy had never held a job. Every few months, she suspected that Betsy was a call girl. She imagined her having two, maybe three steady clients, preferably old men, who she would see once a week for a large sum of money.

Maura could accept Betsy having a maximum of three steady tricks without it affecting their friendship. More than that seemed problematic because it was not financially efficient and maybe pointed to some kind of unpleasant lack of control on Betsy's part. If there were only three a week, Betsy would have to charge each at least $100, maybe even $150.

What can she possibly do to be worth so much money?

Maura could not imagine Betsy having conventional sex with these or any other men.

Maybe she whips them.

Maura noticed that her toenails needed to be trimmed. She took a pair of scissors from the bathroom cabinet, but her hands started to shake and she was afraid she would hurt herself. She dialed Betsy's number again and again.

She knew that Betsy could whip people. Once, during their brief affair, she had asked Betsy to spank her with Laurie's tiny horsewhip. Betsy had done it until her arm hurt and Maura's ass turned purple—a darker shade than Betsy's hair. Maura wanted to find out what pleasure she had given Laurie when she had whipped her, at her request. She found out nothing. After this failure, Maura hid the tiny whip at the bottom of her laundry bin. And Laurie, already opaque in her memory, became totally dark, unreadable. Laurie would not answer Maura's annual phone call and letter, so she could not be brought back from the ex-lover's grave to explain.

"This fucking thing sucks," Betsy said, throwing the tiny whip across the room. Not knowing had never bothered her.

Maura tried Betsy's number again and got a busy signal. Her whole body was shaking now. The phone kept slipping off her cold hands. Was she home? Was someone else leaving a message on her machine?

"It's an emergency!" she told the operator, tightening the receiver to her ear with both hands. The operator clicked switches trying to bump off the intruder from Betsy's line. Maura looked down and she suddenly saw Elsa there, at her feet, her brown hair loose and full, her eyes closed, her dark lips open, her cheeks flushed, sleeping maybe, except that there was a tiny pool of blood where her right ear, small and delicate, touched the white tiles.

3

Betsy kicked Maura's door open. A fine line of light filtered under the bathroom door. She hesitated before it. Was Maura lying in the tub, with slashed bloody wrists, fingers stiff, still clutching a razor blade? Betsy opened the door slowly. Maura was crouching in a corner, her eyes shut. The phone was on the floor. The bathtub was filled with dirty laundry, but no water.

"Open your eyes," Betsy said, picking up a pair of blood-stained panties from the tub and dropping them back in.

"Is anyone else here with us?" Maura asked, her eyes still shut, her black hair falling wildly over her face.

Betsy sat on the side of the tub and lit a cigarette.

"Is there anything on the floor?" Maura's lips were quivering and words came out of her mouth almost in hiccups.

"You haven't killed her," Betsy said, putting out the cigarette under the faucet.

Maura opened her eyes.

"What do you think is happening to me?"

But Betsy was already at the door.

"Next time you see the fucking bitch on your bathroom floor, remember she's not really there."

Betsy slammed shut the front door behind her so hard that the bathroom walls shook.

"She's having a good time, asshole!" Betsy blasted from the stairs. Maura ran after her but it was too late: Betsy was back on the street. Maura double-locked her front door, frightened. She knew she couldn't call Betsy the next time.

4

The flower shop was like a battlefield after a carnage, the aroma of crushed stems littering the ground as thick as gunpowder. A few yellow gladioli nobody wanted remained in their filthy vases. The morning light coming through the glass window quivered between sunshine and freezing drizzle. A very old man emerged from the bowels of this vegetable Verdun, this rotten Antietam. He was as filthy as the gladioli vases and he stank.

Maura asked to see the roses. The old man disappeared into the back of the store. His odor lingered and she held her breath. He reappeared holding twelve dark-red roses. Each had the long, strong stem, the firm, tight, elegant head Maura had read about. She let her breath out in an explosion that swept away the dust from the counter. But the roses didn't move; they were heavy with meaning, and human breath was too unimportant to them. Maura felt humble—a worm. She didn't dare touch them. They were inhumanly perfect, almost sacred, and they made her want to cry.

Years ago, she had taken white or pale-pink gladioli to the Virgin on the first Friday of the month. The nuns demanded them, even if it meant that some of the children would go without lunch that day. Maura never went hungry, because her grandmother fasted on that and many other days so she could eat. Her grandmother would always go with her to buy the Virgin's flowers. The amount of money passing from her hands to the florists' always made Maura's heart beat wildly, as if she were sinning. Flowers were expensive and died quickly. While her grandmother fished pennies and nickels from the purse attached with a safety pin to her bra, Maura would try to understand how could she possibly feel sinful when the flowers were for the Virgin Mary.

But these dark-red roses were infidel swords dripping blood, sexual and tumultuous. When placed inside an elegant silver-gray box, they became the right hand of a young Apollo Maura had once seen—the hand, cool marble creating the illusion not of flesh, not of human meat that decays, but of the immortal essence of flesh.

The red roses made Christianity look sad and petty this morning at the flower shop. Maura's tears disappeared now under her scarf, their salty smell distracting her for a moment from the old man's stench. She was not crying for herself or Elsa or anything in their small, physical world— she cried because she had no adequate words or emotions for the red roses. She was a tiny vase that could not contain them.

She paid and carefully put the box under her right arm. The street was windy but the drizzle had stopped. She now had to find a careful and reliable stranger to bring Elsa the roses. It was to be an anonymous gift.

Walking now toward the East River with the flower box, Maura imagined hitting Elsa on the mouth, drawing blood on her fist, while telling her that she loved her. That was not easy or cheap—killing Elsa, killing herself. There was no reward. Would Elsa then see how gratuitous, and true, Maura's love was?

Elsa would open the box and put the flowers in an ugly green vase in her bedroom. But the roses were too beautiful—they would invade the bedroom. Elsa wouldn't know at all what the roses meant for Christianity. She wasn't interested in plants or love or religion. She wouldn't sit transfixed in front of the roses. But the roses would. They would sit in the middle of the room, amused by the mystery of Elsa's unawareness of Elsa.

5

How could a superhuman emotion, such as that which Maura felt for Elsa, go unrewarded? Maura would have given Elsa anything she asked—for example, the keys to her apartment, which she had denied all her lovers—but Elsa had never asked for anything. She didn't need to. She already had Maura, unwanted.

When she was in seventh grade, Maura had read *Anna Karenina* because it was her mother's favorite book, and her mother had told her that a long time ago people used to be the way Maura now was with Elsa. Novels of separation were written then where lovers, apart ten or even twenty years, would never forget each other and would be reunited at the end, in life or death, when they were too old for their sin to matter. Had people really been like that or was it only the novels that had changed?

For the past three months Maura had thought about Elsa every day, several times a day. Each time that Elsa came to her mind Maura was frightened and each time she would think of Anna Karenina.

Maura was afraid that she would never be happy again, but if someone had asked her to mention when had she been perfectly happy for more than a few days at a time, she would have been unable to answer. Although Maura had not gotten Elsa to be her lover, which was the source of her present unhappiness, she had not been happy for any extended period of time with those who had agreed to it— let alone eagerly wanted to—be her lovers.

"They were not Elsa. That's why," Maura answers. "With Elsa even unhappiness would have been happiness."

The "M" in Maura's name stands for miserable masochist mule, smelly macaque, mawkish masher—as in O. Henry's "It was Soapy's design to assume the role of the despicable and execrated 'masher.' " If she can't have Elsa, she doesn't want anyone or anything else. Maura, who is terrified of death, doesn't want to live.

And now, sitting at a café on St. Mark's Place, looking out the window at the happy couples walking east—women and women, men and men, women and men—she closes her eyes and wishes for a miracle to happen, for an angel or a rotten beam to fall from the ceiling and crush her head, putting away her pain. Like Anna Karenina, she wishes for an act of mercy. She doesn't know it, but she has just stopped loving Elsa. Like a hungry dog in a dog kennel, her desire for an act of mercy has become stronger than her longing for Elsa.

6

Once before in her life, Maura was this lonely and unhappy, and she turned to men. She would run out of her tiny room in the Bowery and roam the side streets, her heart beating, her fingers cold in an anxious sweat, her eyes unable to rest. She would fuck men in hotel rooms on East Houston or in Chinatown. The warm, furtive human flesh appeased her for a while. The anonymous weight smothering her slight frame against the bed was particularly comforting, like a teddy bear, a blanket, a pair of felt slippers.

She smiled and nodded, but never talked to them, never saw them a second time. She would rip up the little pieces of paper they would give her with their phone numbers and throw them in the mud-thick Bowery gutter as soon as they turned their backs. Sometimes she would stay alone in the hotel rooms after they had left, enjoying a half hour of calm on the stained, cigarette-burnt bed sheets of the Bowery Arms, the Prince, the Bedford. But she was twenty-two then and suffering for the first time from a woman.

All these years, Maura had thought that something like that would never again happen to her. But now she felt the same pain on her neck, her chest, her right ankle—a pain that seemed to flow with her blood and go into her bone marrow and her hair follicles, a pain on the tips of her hair, on her eyebrows. And she thought again about men.

A man walking his dog across the street saw the dark-haired woman at the window open her mouth as if to scream, but no sound came out.

Soon after, Maura realized that she wasn't longing for a

man but for a lesbian whore who, for a fee, would fuck her and hold her while she cried, understanding all, expecting nothing in return.

"I need a lesbian whore with a heart of gold," she said. But there was none.

7

Two things Maura does not allow herself: masturbate to Elsa and think about The Other Woman.

It's three in the morning and Maura can't sleep. Lit by the street lamps, the snowfall is creating an aurora borealis inside her bedroom. Maura jumps out of bed, runs, runs, slams her head against the kitchen wall in the dark, once, twice. She falls to the ground, unconscious.

She comes back and sees Elsa's clenched fist going up Jeannie's cunt from the rear and coming out, slow and wet, and going up again.

"I know what you're doing, bitch," Maura whispers.

But Elsa can't hear her. And if she could hear, she wouldn't listen. And if she listened by mistake, or because Maura is now screaming so loud that the whole building, the whole street shakes under the snowstorm, if she was forced to listen now, Elsa would blush and her blushing would immediately turn Maura into a mangy rat who has peed in her cage, a cannibal, a Haitian zombie, a smelly dark, old woman with flaccid tits, a small mammal with leprosy. Missionaries have always subdued the inferior races by blushing—that is their weapon.

Maura crawls back from the kitchen into her bedroom, crawls back cockroach-style into her bed and the walls and bed sheets are blushing and lowering their sensuous eyelids, covering their pale blue eyes in embarrassment before her savagery—so late at night, so unprovoked, so filthy the blood trail, a tiny drop dotted line from kitchen to bedroom to bed, to mark the crawling.

The short, dark creature Maura stuffs bed sheets in her mouth and gags.

"Oh, God!"

In a spasm, she kicks her alarm clock onto the floor, against her will.

She's afraid she'll shit in bed.

"Mother of God: I hate hating, I hate being hateful, I'm afraid I'll get cancer. It's not her fault. It's fate. Sacred Heart of Jesus, make me humble, compassionate, accepting, help me not be unclean!"

Maura drops on her knees to the floor, from the bed, hurting her knees. She promises the Virgin Mary that she'll walk on her knees on a trail of uncooked rice from her bed to the kitchen and back until her knees bleed, if she helps her forget.

"Mother of God, I wouldn't mind this as much if I could imagine fucking Jeannie myself, but I can't—she's got no cunt and no brains."

Not to be able to sleep because of a cuntless, brainless Other Woman made Maura so violently angry that her head and neck went through the bed's wooden headboard grill and she spent the rest of the night trying to free herself.

BRAS & RUBBERS
IN THE GUTTERS:
its enough to have my mother turnin over in her grave!

Special thanks to clovrrr chango

fiercely free 40s

for years she had been planning that when she reached her fiercely free 40s she would launch a new phase of development. somehow she knew her monogamous phase would be completed by then and she would be ready to have free and casual sex with a variety of men. she would live alone of course. and she would only deal with men who were self-sufficient enough to make their own 24-0-7 arrangements for laundry and housecleaning and to take turns picking up the tab.

all during her middle and late 30s she looked forward to enjoying this sexual freedom and variety. there would be young ones—especially early 20ish. and maybe a couple in their 50s or 60s. and definitely several 30ish ones. in her fiercely free 40s she wouldnt care what race or class the men were since she had found that men of no race or class had a premium on being cool. nor would she care whether a man seemed to be a likely candidate for building a lasting relationship. she would have all the lasting relationships and emotional bonding she needed with her women friends, who were better at these things anyway. with men she would just have sex.

she figured that free and casual sex would be one of the few real joys in life by the time she made 40 and had accepted the reality of herself as a struggling woman whose lack of money and power didnt necessarily have to inhibit her sense of fun. and what could be more fun than sex? especially when she no longer had any illusions about sex being a prelude to picket fences and color-coordinated washers and dryers and walking off into the sunset with the one and only man of her dreams who would remain faithful to her and her alone for ever and ever amen bring up the violin background music please.

so what happened? well at the dawn of her fiercely free 40s she thought she had made a good beginning when the nineteen-year-old boy seduced her. yes *he* seduced *her*. she couldnt believe it. she had been busy telling him he was too young and probably didnt even know what to do for a grown sophisticated woman like her when she suddenly realized she was getting ready to blow the opening act of her new phase of development. so she took a chance. and was she ever surprised at what this boy could do! he could give lots of older dudes lessons. after that promising beginning guess what happened?

well first there was hepatitis. then there was a big increase in the number of sexually motivated murders of women by men. then there were new strands of venereal disease that defied penicillin. and then there was aids. yes aids. she soon figured out that aids did not exclusively strike white gay males with blue cross coverage or black hetero male dope shooters with medicaid despite the media blitz that presented primarily these men and their sexual partners as victims of this terrifying disease. she never believed that. she knew there was too much cross-fucking going on for that story to hold water. then when she read the news about hetero nondopeshooting aids victims in central africa and the usa and about lesbian aids victims about people who got aids from blood transfusions or infected medical needles she knew. aids was everywhere. anybody could get it. nobody was safe.

oh no oh no! she cried as she saw her dreams of mature sexual variety and spice being flushed down the drain. oh no! but what was she to do? with whom could she safely screw? how could she lay down and spread her legs with abandon when she didnt know what kind of disease she might get up with? or if she would ever get up at all. how could she enjoy casual sex with strangers when she never knew who might be the mad macho machete murderer or who might have what disease. if she met a handsome stranger could she search his pockets or backpack to see if he was carrying a machete or gun? could she ask him if he was into female brutality? could she believe him if he assured her he wasnt? could she tell him she would love to get together for some afternoon dalliances but could he first accompany her to the clinic to get tested for vd and hepatitis and aids? briefly she considered rubbers. she had always hated rubbers because they diminished pleasure. besides they often broke. plus she found it next to impossible to get men to use them. forget dental dams.

so instead of enjoying fiercely free sex during her 40s she learned about celibacy. after long days of having her nerves worked at work she spent her free time taking long hot baths or going for walks or having drinks and dinner with the girlfriends or at a meeting or a party or taking an african dance class or doing carpentry or reading or listening to jazz or talking on the phone or sleeping late or going on trips. all this was fine. but no sex.

and so our story ends with our hero facing another brutal truth. there would be little or no sex for her to look forward to during her fiercely free 40s nor in the foreseeable future. and so one more illusion—the illusion of sex and sexual freedom—was lifted from her eyes.

boys game—she asked for it

the boys have this game they play called she asked for it. heres how it goes. a boy is accused of sexually brutalizing and grotesquely murdering a woman. he doesnt deny he did it. he merely says she asked for it. then the lawyer boys and police boys and reporter boys all back him up by revealing many things about the dead woman to prove she asked for it. like they will say she was a tramp anyway— everybody had had her. or she let him pick her up in a bar. or she played all kinds of freaky sex games with him in the park. or she was too demanding. or she suddenly decided she didnt want to be bothered with him no more. she asked for it. and whats a po boy to do when she asks for it? why hes got to give it to her thats what! after all he cant be expected to exercise any self-control once his dick gets hard. everybody knows that. once his dick gets hard his mind gets soft. he might do anything—even rape and murder. cuz she asked for it.

however the lawyer/police/reporter boys dont always extend this game of male privilege equally to all the rape-murder boys who plead she asked for it. consider how the latin son of a building super who sexually brutalized and grotesquely murdered an upper-class white woman on the upper west side in new york city was denied his male right to play she asked for it. he wasnt allowed to drag the reputation of this upper-class white woman through the mud on the front pages of the newspapers and on the tv news. no. el latino had to go directly to jail for life—do no pass go.

on the other hand the white preppie boy who sexually brutalized and grotesquely murdered a white woman of his same social class in central park was granted full permission to play she asked for it all over the front pages of the newspapers and on the morning and nightly tv news. he was allowed to talk about this dead woman like she wasnt nothin. and since she was dead and only the two of them knew what really happened nobody could argue with what this boy said. and the lawyer/police/reporter boys knocked themselves out letting us know all the ways in which this woman had asked for it. and since the white boy most certainly didnt get life in jail we know that the chances of him meeting up with the latino boy on the penitentiary cafeteria line are slim indeed.

and we know that the lawyer/police/reporter boys helped this white boy win another round in that age-old game of she asked for it. after all they are clear about the fact that white boys are still running the world and therefore have the greatest right to be protected from these dangerous women who refuse to stay in their places and submit— these women who go around asking for it all the time. even if the women are upper-class and white. everybody knows it takes at least 1000 women to equal the worth of one man. especially if he is white. right?

aint nobodys bidness if i do?

are all human beings equally endowed with an inalienable right to enjoy soul-satisfying sex?

do i have a right to enjoy any kind of sex with anybody anytime and anywhere?

do i have a right to let someone tie me up and beat me and titillate my clitoris with a lighted cigarette?

do children have sexual rights?

do i have a right to earn my living as a prostitute?

do i have a right to look at pornographic pictures?

did your parents tell you that it is nasty to touch yourself down there?

do fat/old/physically or mentally challenged people have a right to wear bikinis or shorts or see-thru shirts or tight pants?

do you tell your children that it is nasty to touch themselves down there?

do i have a right to sell pornographic pictures?

do i have a right to refuse to rent/sell/lease my property to you if you enjoy a kind of sex i dont approve of?

do i have a right to pose for pornographic pictures?

do women have an equal right with men to be topless in public?

do i have a right to buy the services of a prostitute?

do i have a right to deny my lover/spouse the right to sex if i am tired and dont feel like being bothered?

does my lover/spouse then have a right to kick my ass?

do i have the right to sing the masochistic blues?

if you find your lover/spouse exercising her/his sexual rights in bed with someone else what are your rights?

welfare clients

is it true that welfare clients lay around all day and watch tv and listen to loud music on those big radios and drink cheap booze and use drugs and eat greasy food and fuck fuck fuck?

what is the difference between a welfare client and a foreign-aid client?

could you raise 6 kids with the nyc welfare allowance of $754 per month? (Food = $247; rent = $308; all other essentials = $199.)

what is the difference between government subsidies to welfare clients and government subsidies to the defense industry?

how much money does the government lose annually on the thousands of $200 wrenches and $75 thumbtacks it buys from defense industry contractors?

is it true that welfare clients make no productive contribution to society?

how come the government cant find any $3 wrenches or 10-for-$2 thumbtacks like the ones that are sold in my neighborhood?

do people become welfare clients because they are too lazy to get up in the morning and go to work like normal honest redblooded americans?

how come welfare clients live in slums and foreign-aid clients live in palaces?

how come there arent enough jobs for everybody who wants to work?

how many welfare clients have you heard of who own 3000 pairs of shoes or a nuclear bomb or a fleet of rolls-royces?

what is wrong with having a lifestyle that allows you to
fuck fuck fuck all day long?

the homeless/does economics take precedence over sexuality?

do homeless people have sex?

would you be concerned about the number of orgasms
you were capable of having if you were a homeless
female?

if you were a homeless man would you be concerned
about how long or how fat your dick was or if it stayed
hard long enough to suit your partner?

are all homeless people heterosexual?

do homeless people masturbate? do any of them have oral
sex or anal sex? are any of them into s&m or role playing?

if you lived in a doorway or in a subterranean tunnel
beneath grand central station, if your bedroom was a
warm grating during winter or a park bench during
summer where would you have sex?

can homeless women get birth control devices or
abortions?

would you have sex with a homeless person?

if you were homeless would you be so busy worrying
about where and how to eat and sleep that you wouldnt
have time to think about getting a little bit?

are you sure?

DENNIS COOPER

WRONG

WHEN MIKE SAW A pretty face he liked to mess it up, or give it drugs until it wore out by itself. Take Keith who used to play pool at the Ninth Circle. His crooked smile really lights up the place. That's what Mike heard but it bored him. "Too obvious."

Keith was a kiss up. Mike fucked him hard then they snorted some dope. Keith was face first in the toilet bowl when Mike walked in. Keith had said, "Knock me around." But first Mike wanted him "dead." Not in the classic sense. "Passed out."

Mike dragged Keith down the hall by his hair. He shit in Keith's mouth. He laid a whip on Keith's ass. It was a grass skirt once Mike dropped the belt. Mike kicked Keith's skull in before he came to. Brains or whatever it was gushed out. "That's that."

José was Keith's friend. Now that Keith wasn't around he moved in. Mike said okay *if* they'd fist-fuck. José's requirement was drugs: speed, coke, pot, the occasional six-pack. "Oh, and respect, of course."

"Great stuff," José whispered. Mike shrugged. "Too

fem," he thought, putting a match to José's pipe. José had hitchhiked from Dallas. He had a high-pitched voice, wore a gold crucifix on a chain. "Typical Mexican shit."

José slipped on a dress. Pink satin, ankle length, blue sash. He put on makeup. "Mamacita!" Mike fisted "her" on the window ledge. "She" dangled over the edge. Mike shook "her" off his wrist. "She" fell four stories, broke "her" neck.

Steve had blond hair, gloomy eyes and chapped lips. "He should be dead," Mike thought. He liked the kid's skin, especially on his ass. Sick white crisscrossed with gray stretch marks. Mike liked how lost it became in pants, like the bones in an old lady's face.

Mike knocked a few of Steve's teeth out. He'd called Mike "a dumb fuck." That night Mike kicked in Steve's ribs and tied him up for the night. They fell asleep around four. By morning Steve was cold, eyes open, blue face. Mike dressed and took off.

He walked home. He thought of offing himself. "After death, what's left?" he mumbled. He meant "to do." Once you've killed someone life's shit. It's a few rules and you've already broken the best. He had a beer at the Ninth Circle.

He picked Will up on the street. "Snort this." Mike tore Will's shorts off and slapped his ass. "Shit in my mouth," Mike said. Will did. It changed the way Mike perceived him. Will was a real person, not just a fuck. Mike let him hang out.

Will's body came into focus. It wasn't bad: underweight, blue eyes, a five o'clock shadow. Beauty had nothing to do with it. Mike could see what he was looking at. But he got used to the sight. One night he strangled Will to be safe.

The night was rough: wind, rain, chill. Mike walked from Will's place on West Tenth to Battery Park, chains clinking each step. He stared out at the Hudson. He put a handgun to his head. "Fuck this shit." His body splashed in the river, drifted off.

Morning came. Cops kicked Will's door in, found his corpse. Will's friends got wind of it, phoned each other up.

Down river tourists were standing around on a dock looking bored. One girl pulled down on her mom's skirt and
pointed out. "What's that?"

George looked out at the Hudson. He saw a dead body.
He shot the rest of his roll of film then milled around with
the other tourists. Guides led them back to the bus. It was
abuzz with the idea of death, in grim or joking tones. George
listened, his feelings somewhere between the two.

The World Trade Center was not what he'd hoped. It
wasn't like he could fall off. Big slabs of glass between him
and his death. No matter where he turned his thoughts were
obvious. The city looked like a toy, a space-age forest, a
silvery tray full of hypodermics. He wanted one fresh perception but . . .

Wall Street was packed with gray business suits. Seeing
the trading floor he thought first of a beehive, then of the
heart attacks those guys would get. It was like watching a
film about some other time and place, very far back and
relegated to books.

George took his clothes off. He lay on the bed. "Where
you from?" It was his roommate, a Southerner if he could
judge by the accent. "West." "Of what?" the man asked.
"This," and George turned his back. The Texan shook his
head. "Not worth it," he thought.

That night George walked through the West Village. "I'm
tired of sleeping with *that,*" a man sneered as they crossed
paths. The guy was chatting to some friend of his but he
eyed George's ass. Hearing this, George felt as cold as the
statue he'd touched at the Met last night. A boy was playing
the lute when art froze him stiff.

The Ninth Circle was packed. Hustlers in blue jean vests,
businessmen in all the usual suits. George leaned against the
bar lighting a cigarette. "What's up pal?" It was his roommate's voice. "Not much," George thought, but they talked.

Lights out. Dan's cock was minuscule so George agreed
to be fucked. Dan spread the asscheeks and sniffed. George
did his best to relax. He thought of ovens with roasts cook-

ing in them. He knew his ass smelled more rancid than them but maybe that was the point.

George thought of home. It was a white stucco, one story. His room was paneled in oak. He never aired it out. It reeked of B.O., smoke and unlaundered sheets. The smell was clinically bad but he loved the idea that he'd had such an impact on something outside himself.

George didn't want to be held while he slept. He never got enough rest as it was. No lover could comprehend that. To them a hug was an integral act. George felt pinned down by one, too pressed to squeeze back. "Don't." Dan sighed and moved off.

George dreamt in bursts. Little picturesque plots. Casts of peripherals refocused, brought to the fore in a world he'd backed into unknowingly. He saw himself floating dead in the Hudson; Dan held a knife to his throat in an alley; the room caught fire and he went up in smoke.

Dan thought of love as defined by books, cobwebbed and hidden from view by the past. Too bad a love like that didn't actually exist. In the twentieth century one had to fake it. He put his cheek on the boy's ass and seemed to sleep. He couldn't tell if he was or not. Then he did.

George sat on a park bench feeding some birds what was left of his sandwich. He drew a handful of postcards from one jacket pocket. They were all cityscapes, what friends and folks would expect. Bums limped by begging for change. Their clothes were falling off. George turned his palms up. "Die," he said under his breath.

"Dear Philippe, New York makes sense. I fit right in. I'm sitting under a bunch of trees. They'd be great if bums weren't dying all over the place. Everything you said was right. I'm going back to the hotel now to take a nap. Anyway, George."

"Dear Dad, The trip's going great. We're in New York for the weekend, then up to Boston, then the ride back to L.A. The man I'm sharing a room with reminds me of you.

He's nice, from the South. Don't touch a thing in my room. I'll be home in two weeks. Love, George."

"Dear Sally, I thought about you today as I walked forty blocks to a pretty park. My legs are used to it. They sell marijuana in stores here. I bought a baggie for ten bucks. I'm smoking it as I write. Out of room. Be seeing you in a while. Love, George."

"Dear Santa Claus, For Christmas I want a penthouse in New York, one in L.A. and one someplace in Europe. I've been a good boy, plus . . ." George ripped the card in half. "Duh," he said, giggling at himself.

"Dear Dennis, I think I miss you most of all. What's-her-name said that to Ray Bolger, right? Yesterday I saw the top of what's on this card. Today I'm off on my own. Tonight I'll hit the bars. Hope you're great. See you, George."

George headed toward the hotel. His calves ached. Times Square was spooky; too many junkies out, pissed eyes way back in their heads. The hotel lobby felt homey. Dan was out. George kicked his shoes off, snoozed a bit.

The Ninth Circle was packed. George downed three beers in no time. One man was cute but his haircut resembled a toup. Another stood in an overhead light, too sure of its effect. His expression was "perfect." Between them George would have chosen the latter, depending on who else showed up.

Fred's loft was spacious, underfurnished. Track lighting bleached out its lesser points. George got the grand tour. "This is the bed, of course. This is a painting by Lichtenstein. Amusing, yes? And these are the torture devices I mentioned." George saw a long table lined with spiked dildos, all lengths of whips, three branding irons, sundry shit.

To George it looked like a game. Whether it wound up that way or not was beside the point. Handcuffs clicked shut in the small of his back. Electrical tape sealed his lips. Black leather shorts made him feel sort of animalesque.

George fantasized that his father was hugging him. He didn't know why. It had something to do with a gesture that couldn't be downgraded or reinterpreted, made into some half-assed joke. Someone who made him feel this all important must be intrigued at least.

It started out with a spanking. Slaps to the face, which George wasn't so wild about. His asshole swallowed in something's enormity simply enough. More slaps. Fred's breaths grew worse, a kind of storm knocking down every civilized word in its path.

George was hit on the head. "Shit!" Again. This time he felt his nose skid across one cheek. His forehead caved in. One eye went black. Teeth sputtered out of his mouth and rained down on his chest. He died at some point in that.

George was across the loft watching himself kick. The sight was slightly blurred like the particulars in a dream sequence. He saw a club strike his face. It was unrecognizable. His arms and legs slammed the tabletop like giant, crudely made gavels.

George had a lump in his throat. He wondered why, if he was still alive, he should feel shit for that too garish wreck of himself. "But that's the beauty of dead kids," he thought. "Everything they ever did seems incredibly moving in retrospect."

He watched until his old body was such a loss that each indignity was simply more of the same. So he looked down at his current form. He was a hologram, more or less. "Too much!" he thought. He tried to walk. It was a snap, like bounding over the moon.

So this was death. "Hey, not bad," he thought. He inhaled slowly and slid without incident through the steel door. Descending the stairs was exactly like falling down them, liberated and discombobulating, a drug hallucination without the teeth grinding.

He walked west, sometimes right down the middle of streets, cars plowing through him. He strolled through shoppers, amused by the idea that he was just part of the air to them, at best a breeze they'd write off to earth's natural forces.

Seeing a husband and wife, the male of which he'd have been quite attracted to during his life, he followed them up a rickety staircase, through their front door. Jeff, as the wife called him, hit the head. George watched him shit, loved the dumb look on his face but was driven back into the street by the subsequent stench.

Now what? He took a leisurely stroll to the river, down Christopher Street. The piers were decrepit. One was completely decapitated. A few rotten pylons stuck out of the water. George felt an odd emotional attachment to them.

He sat on a bench. The sun felt terrific. He warmed slightly like fog just before it burned off. He thought of movies he'd loved where the ghosts of dead men were big jokes, mere plot twists, a sort of stab in the dark.

Who would have thought it was true? All those old ladies in New England mansions were far more sane than their distended eyes would have had one believe. "One," he muttered. He'd always hated when people used "one" in conversation. But it was the right term for him now.

He stared out at the brownish river. It was the first time he'd thought about water's solidity. If he were to hurl himself in, would he break into millions of molecules? Or would he, like Jesus Christ, land on his feet? "Interesting prospect," he thought, but he couldn't chance it.

He walked slowly up West Street past several leather bars he would have liked to check into, but he was tired. Sure, he could crash out wherever he liked, see whichever cute rock star nude, fly to London for nothing. But he'd get bored of the voyeur bit before he knew it. Then what?

George thought of things that had haunted him during his life: A staircase which, after turning a corner, led to a brick wall. B&W photos of great buildings destined to be dusty heaps. A human face which had turned into just one more mudslide from heaven.

The hotel loomed in the distance. Its neon sign blinked out "Vacancy." "An appropriate place for myself or what's left of me," George thought. He headed for its rococo, checking the faces of hapless pedestrians for his reflection. But they stared straight ahead, not realizing.

George passed through the door of Room 531. Dan lay on the single bed nearest the window, writing a postcard, probably to the wife he'd been complaining about on the previous night. His face seemed peaceful but maybe it was the light: low, grayish.

George liked Dan, though "liked" was too clear a word. "Something" had drawn George to him. It had to do with Dan's fatherliness, George thought. That was a much bigger turn-on than tight jeans on tanned, overexercised guys. His ideal man was a little bushed around the eyes.

George hadn't spoken all day. He felt a tightness inside his throat. "Dan?" he croaked, "I know you don't hear me but if you can sense me in any way tug on your left ear." George waited. Dan continued to scratch out what George had no doubt were inanities.

"Okay, I feel a little like somebody telling some guy in a coma I still care but here goes. I don't really know you but I feel attached to you, even though you're not exactly an individual. You're more a type, which makes me some kind of aesthete, I guess, and you the real work of art, not that I buy all your bullshit.

"We had sex. I let you fuck me. That was the hot part, but though it's hard to admit, all the hugging and shit is what I really liked. To be held tight by a person who's had me . . . Well, it's one thing to shake hands and chat awkwardly about art and something else to be fucked then respected.

"I used to think that if lovers got wind of my shit I'd be 'too realistic,' in their words. I kept rolling onto my back, clenching my ass when sucked off so the stink couldn't get out. I had this weird idea that there was something wrong under my looks, not just gory stuff.

"Then some guy ate out my ass and asked for a second date. Since that night I've tried to shrug off each fear in turn. Now I'm dead. It figures no one's around to appreciate or make bad jokes about my 'passing on,' as you'd probably call it.

"I wanted love. Sure, I was attracted to sex-crazed types, their faces so overcome by the need for me it was as though leers were sculpted right into their skulls and their skin was just draped over bone like a piece of cloth. But I was a stupid jerk.

"This part is meant for my father's ears. I've felt more than you thought or I'm able to spit out. My moods were really mysterious, even to me, which makes them not worth the time to you, no matter how long you stared in my 'great eyes' last night.''

George felt faint and teetered slightly. He wished he had a banana, something with sugar to pep him up, but he imagined he couldn't eat, that food would perch in his waist like a caged canary, or drop with a thump to the carpet.

Dan filled the postcard and lay back. George could just make it out. "Dean Fran," it began. He didn't notice his name in the scribbles. It was a simple tale: Empire State Building, good view, dinner at Luchow's, love, Dan. (P.S.) I wish (unintelligible) tonight.

Was George beginning to fade away? He wasn't sure. So much depended on the right light. "Umm, this may be it," he mumbled. He hadn't meant to lower his voice. "Shit," and he started to tremble. "I like you. What can I say? Or not you, but you're all I have.

"I blew it." He blended into the afternoon. Outside the window a car honked. Inside the room a man's watch ticked. Dan stood and scratched his ass. He put the card in his shirt pocket. He had a faraway look in his eyes as he lit his cigarette.

KATHY ACKER

A YOUNG GIRL

A GIRL'S TELLING HERSELF THE FOLLOWING STORY:

On the streets of the city in which I'm still living and don't want to escape, crack and other victims, often in packs, turn those who are other into victims. But the city is the only safety I know. Is familiarity safety? I have had nightmares and I hate them.

The more politically powerful Mayor ___ became, the more the city around him decayed.

When I said that I didn't like his photographs, my friend replied that his most famous picture was the one he had made of his girlfriend totally wrapped up in white bandages. Here only eyes and mouth remained unwrapped and had become black. I looked.

Many neighborhoods, lying next to and unrelated to each other, make up this city. The poorer each neighborhood, the more garbage, like shit, piles up in that neighborhood. The poorer the neighborhood, the less frequently garbage collectors, considered half-worker half-homeless, visit that neighborhood. Cops never visit those who are poor.

In the city's late summer when the concrete had been

123

absorbing heat for months, cold air, coming from lost memories, sat on top of the heat and imprisoned it. Diseases had nowhere to run.

Influenced by the Nazi scientists whom the United States government had rescued at the end of World War II, in the 1960s the CIA had begun drug testing in order to find a chemical that would induce total memory loss in those who had revealed political secrets under coercion and torture. Unfortunately, almost all chemicals that cause full memory loss also stop life. Some years after, a monkey escaped from one of the laboratories in a Third World nation and bit a civilian. The disease that developed into the worst plague known in the twentieth century spread from the Third World, through what Mayor ___ and others considered the lower echelon of humans, Blacks and homosexuals, to New York City, a conglomeration of Third World tribes in a First World country. Or a formerly First World country. The white New York society hated Blacks (Puerto Ricans, Chicanos, Africans, American Blacks, etc. without distinction) and homosexuals.

Mayor ___ was homosexual. He was terrified to give any credence to rumors about the existence of the plague or to take any measures to halt its growth in the early days of its appearance, for he rightfully thought that if he admitted he was homosexual he would lose votes.

Father told me that the mayor hired female prostitutes for the purpose of kicking them down flights of stairs.

Eyes, world-blind, in the fissure of dying: I come,
callous growth in my heart.

The man who wrote these lines was a Jew. Russians, then in 1941 German and Romanian forces, had occupied the town in which he had been born. The latter herded Jews into ghettos.

In 1942, they deported his parents to an internment camp. His father, there, died from typhus; his mother was murdered.

He escaped by traveling to Vienna. Then Paris. When he was forty-nine years old, by jumping into the Seine he killed himself.

Darker night.

HAVING LOST TRACK, THE GIRL PAUSES.

On the platform that he'd raise New York out of economic poverty, Mayor ____ won his first election. He fulfilled this promise by transforming the city's real estate. First he made a pact between the largest bank, the real-estate moguls, and himself or the law. He or the law rezoned the poorer districts, areas formerly populated by small businesses and ethnic groups, so these two kinds had to leave. Then huge warehouse spaces turned into white artists' lofts; then rising rents forced out the few remaining Puerto Rican and Black families. Where they went, no white cared. Simultaneously the bank through white artists' organizations was helping these artists gentrify their spaces. It was well known that Mayor ____ loved art. New York City was on its way to becoming the City of Art, not the City of Refugees and Renegades. As soon as white artistic gentrification was established, the real-estate moguls sold these spaces for fortunes. The white artists had to become more interested in profit than in art to hold on to the spaces they had gentrified and from which they had excluded the poor, not poverty. Never poverty.

Celan said: My flesh is named *night*. Complex as night, if not more complex. Whether or not you touch me, my flesh'll feel desire to such an extent, it'll be named *desire*.

During Mayor ____'s first term, the white middle classes had believed that the mayor was assisting them by means of gentrification and artifying. Now soaring property prices were forcing these classes to become rich or homeless. Vacation or vacate. Finally, though there never is finally, the rich and the homeless were the only groups, not classes, left in the city. In a way, history had proved Marx wrong.

The leftover artists, by necessity rich, nevertheless totally relied on the controllers of money for patronage.

> Desire mirror steep wall. Down.
> —Celan

Steam heats the inhabitants and the city all through the dead winters. A trust fund had been established for the maintenance of the water pipes when they had first been built. In order to keep his early campaign promise, Mayor ____ had used up all the trust fund monies. By the end of his third term, the pipes, Fallopian tubes unfucked, unmaintained, wriggled, broke, burst open, upward, rose up through all the materials above them. Sidewalks and streets, building floors and ceilings, air. Then spewed out, writhing and looking below them like asps about to attack, spat out asbestos over all beneath them. In the city, the snow turns to dog piss in less than a day; since asbestos almost never dies, the mayor had made the asbestos clean-up companies into the most profitable in the city.

Two thirteen-year-olds, female, high on crack and low on johns, began patrolling Twelfth Street between Avenues A and First. Everytime an old woman doddered up the pavement, they broke her fingers and grabbed her purse. Similar incidents commenced happening elsewhere. What were the poor to do where and when all the legitimate businesses were run by whites except have a drug business? Victims, not victimizers, become victimized; the nastier the tricks the poor learned to turn, the more the poor and the social exiles went under.

There were two kinds of men. The first was like Mayor ____. When a young child, he had watched his father abandon his mother. His mother then wanted him to be her husband. Now the mayor wants to be daddy. As soon as he persuades a person he's daddy, he shits on him or her, then deserts the person. Mayor ____ , after all, does not want to be daddy.

The second kind of man is the kind whose father abandons his wife just as the man enters puberty. This wife, unable to accept or recover from loss, tries to render her son unable to leave her. Now the son loves to save people, especially women. As soon as a female accepts his offer, he believes that she's putting a contract out on him and walks away. This man is an artist.

The mayor had overdeveloped his heart; the artist, his mind.

In order to keep continuing with this story, I'm walking into dream.

In just his first term, Mayor ____ had made New York into the City of Art. Though not for the sake of art. Then, the common myth held by artists and others was that artists don't care about anyone or anything, which is why they make great art. Artists must be totally devoted to art.

The artist, who was my father, was considered one of the greatest, sometimes the greatest, of these artists.

Like many great men who compensate in one area for another, he was physically ugly or deviant. Half of his face acted as a distorted mirror for the other. A knifelike slit ran diagonally through one eyebrow, then across the other cheek. Eyebrows and eyes more piercing than colored dominated the face. The rest resembled a middle-stage Jackson Pollack painting.

These were now the first, the golden days of American culture when girls grew up innocent. Even I, and I was born past those days of innocence, believed that a baby is made when a man and a woman, dancing together and slowly in formal attire, rub asses. My father's attitude both toward sex and toward his sexual behavior was typical of artists at that time. Any girl (a woman who wasn't a girl wasn't worth existing) had to be fucked over, because she was out to steal his money or his soul. If the chick managed to fight back successfully, the only possible indication of integrity, she might be worth respecting, though then she would probably be too damaged to fuck. Think of ___ and ___.

Since he was one of the greatest artists, he thought, and any female he had fucked or was fucking—it was all the same thing—must be out to fuck him, then any female who entered his studio must be intending to steal a piece, unless she was rich enough to buy one or had been born almost brainless, which was all too possible. So as soon as Dad woke up to a cunt, he kicked her out of his house.

What had once been a city of renegades, of poor who despised government, had turned into a city of artists. It was believed that an artist must be infinitely hungry and rapacious physically and mentally in order to be great. This artist will spend almost all his sleeping and waking time thinking about his work: political issues will no longer matter; personal relationships will be regarded as aborted forms of prettiness or mannerism—above all, as hindrances to the pursuit of direct knowledge of the truth.

It was believed that for a great artist and only for a great artist, sex is shit compared to pursuit of knowledge of the truth.

The only person and female whom father cared about was me.

I adored father because he adored me. Or: I adored him.

I think that children naturally love their parents and parents feel however they feel about their children.

A child loves, but how can a child obey a parent who has no honor? In this city of artists of rapacity, where rats scurry across planks though even the memories of pirates are dead, there's no honor.

I didn't have to be and I wasn't obedient to my father, but because I adored him so much I did whatever he wanted. My father was coming to the apex of his fame and I began to have my period. He told me that I was old enough to start providing for myself. Father said a person makes himself through work. Even a woman. I couldn't conceive of fighting father, though I knew that I didn't know how to do anything. Anything to make money.

Father became so immersed in painting that he forgot I was alive.

Out of the blue, Mayor ___ who was one of father's patrons, said I could work for him. Not because he had need of anything I could do or because he wanted to have sex with me. Since he was in awe of father because father was an artist, he had to show that he, a politician, controlled my father.

Father, typical artist, despised politicians and flattered anyone who could buy his paintings. Not *despised*. Father wasn't *personally* concerned with the mayor's character, because father was interested only in the pursuit of knowledge. Whereas the mayor was obsessed by power, especially by those he suspected might be more powerful than him. But father was arrogant. The more a patron helped him, the more he hated the son-of-a-bitch. Though father was cold, hatred or irritability could reach fever pitch. Then father became paranoid. Paranoia turned anger even more ice-cold, ocean before a storm. What I'm saying is that father was emotionless unless someone managed to penetrate through and touch him. I am going to tell you about the one time this happened.

Once penetrated, father had to close up.

At this time, between the mayor and father, I didn't exist.

Father said, "For a moment consider that Freud's model of female sexuality, that a woman and her desire is defined by lack of a penis, is true. Then, in a society in which phenomenal relations are as men say they are, women must radically contest reality just in order to exist. According to Freud, a fetish for a woman is one means by which she can deny she's lacking a dick. A fetish is a disavowal."

The era of pirates had yielded to the one of artists and politicians. At the same time women began getting into more than fetishes.

Father was a great artist. The wife he took after my

mother was an artist herself, sculptor and dancer, respected in her own right. After several years she decided she had to leave him, though not because he was continually fucking other women. She knew it would be impossible for her to leave him unless he first decided to leave her.

To accomplish this she fucked another man. Nameless, the pirates of yesteryear. Made certain that father learned about this.

As soon as she had left our loft, he smashed most of her video equipment with a hatchet then threw the rest out a window onto the street. She returned to the loft. He chased her down the building's back stairs, around the block, with the same hatchet.

Though sexuality moved strongly through him, father wasn't interested in sex or in women, but in seeing. Paranoia, which occasionally appeared as sensitivity, enhanced his longing to see.

"An artist isn't and must not be a moralist. Within the realm of art, both the seer and his work occur outside of morality and social judgment."

Father loved to see women in the throes of sexual ecstasy so that he could draw them. "Whereas a man at the highest possibility of his development wants to see, a woman is infinitely sexually avaricious. She'll do anything, moving through physical and mental cons and disguises like a snake through his or her own coils, her tongue flickers, in order to get a man to sexually use her. To let her use him sexually. As they grow older, many European women, being among the most intelligent, learn to control appearances to such an extent that men don't see that women aren't human."

I read a Japanese ghost tale. A man because he was hot married the Dragon King's daughter. They didn't have a single quarrel and never stopped fucking (being rich) until she informed him she was going to have his baby. She said, "You can't watch while I'm having this baby." He refused to do what she had told him to do. When he looked, he saw a snake whom he had believed was his lover whose head had horns growing out of it giving birth to a human baby. The female monster saw him looking at her and fled in shame.

(*Ghosts* equals *pirates*. The graves of sailors.)

("The dead woman fucked him again," Pedro Resaca muttered between his teeth.)

Father said, "Women don't smell human because they smell of cunt."

Father about sight: "If I could, I would replace all sight with all smell."

Due to his understanding of femaleness, father desired me to have nothing to do with sexuality. He felt that he didn't even need to say this.

I felt that he was the Forbidder of all and kept me safe.

Father knew that whenever I left his precincts, sex surrounded me. It was dangerous for me to work, even for the mayor. (Father had forgotten this when he had become totally involved in painting.)

Though Mayor ___ was gay.

But because Mayor ___ was in awe of and looked down on my father and hated himself for this awe, he wanted, to fuck, me.

It was the era or democracy in which the state of art was the art of the state.

My fathers have taught me that if I let a man touch me, he'll touch me red.

Father, as soon as he emerged from painting and remembered, tried to stop me from entering the mayor's mansion. But the more he fought against his patron, the more the patron pulled at me. They hated each other. Mayor ___ commissioned my father, as the most well-respected artist of his time, to make a portrait of New York large enough to cover a wall of Gracie Mansion's main reception room.

Father was a businessman.

(The Dutch pirates invaded, set up their world of shacks, of the outlaw city, of the dens in which the body moved from disease to disease, of dens of iniquity of all sorts of vices or longings for the ways of the low longings for deliriums. Where men cached their hushed pasts, hid their names and realms of names from the authorities. If not born into loneliness, hopefully about to slip into Newfoundland.)

Intended to start painting this by painting a street at night. A black street. But there you could see. The staircases and tenements like hands reaching. No out. A girl who is tipsy is beginning to walk down the street. Two teenage males, partly hidden by a piece of architecture's doorway, watch her. She looks up, sees one of them, shrugs her shoulders. It is the city of anarchy, not of anarchists. One of the boys behind her is reaching for her purse. He's a crack victim and she's not. When she turns around to hit him, his fist smashes into the top of her head. She falls down. The teen-ager is racing across an empty parking lot.

This is the era of artists and of businessmen.

Next to this section is a park. Blankets that are mainly holes sit on the black iron fence that encloses the concrete. The homeless live here. No civilization is a new civilization. A girl walks out of one of the gentrified tenements that surround the park and meets a homeless teenager. She takes him back home and they fuck. For several months, he lives with her. At that time he cooks soup for the other homeless in the park. Then his girlfriend tells him that since she's going to move to another city, he will have to leave within the week and be homeless. He's boiling her cut-off head in a pot of liquid and vegetables so that he can feed the home-less in the park.

Father wasn't satisfied with these, not even sketches, be-cause they weren't the horror of New York. He said, "I can't see anything until I'm it. Since in my normal life I'm too habituated to horror to see it, horror must occur out-side my perceptual habits for me to see it:

"In order for me to paint horror, I have to see the horror in myself."

(Back, for those doomed to silence, unable to recount the fantasy that, though the only life, no one believes. Sensed,

on the doorstep of preternatural senectitude—the sense-
lessness of all adventure.)

Father taught me that the mind of thoughts is a snake in
the whole of the self. It wants control: whenever it or he
feels he can, he begins swelling, winding around himself
until he's eating himself. Therefore, if you allow this mind
or part of the mind control, you can't paint. Father began
painting New York by painting a portrait of the Brooklyn
Bridge. The sounds of boats sailing under is brown like old
menstrual blood sitting on cunt lips. A good number of the
Bedford-Stuyvesant inhabitants, skeletons in the distance,
were walking across the bridge. They were going to join
tribes of homeless and packs of crack victims for the purpose of breaking into the apartments of the rich and the
home owners (same as "the rich"). "Soon, New York City'll
be in flames," father said. "Most of all the populations'll be
smashed; the city'll be shredded."

Father said, "Prophecy is only opinion. If I want to paint
New York, I have to paint horror. In order to paint horror,
I have to see horror. Prophecy might come from sight: that's
not my business as a painter. In order to see horror, I have
to touch or fuck horror."

Father said, "It's necessary to know. For no reason at all.
For art."

I'm innocent. Horror can't take away innocence. If a
murderer murders me, it's not that I am no longer innocent;
it's that I and innocence have died.

Father said, "A painting is simultaneously an object and
a mechanism. Paint, canvas, etc. compose the object. People can buy and sell the object. My purpose for my making
or the object's purpose, if objects can have purposes, is to
make people see. In this case, since I've been commissioned
to do a portrait of New York, see the horror in which
they're living. See the horror which they cause and in which
they reside.

In terms of the process of sight, a painting is a mirror
only if identity is, too."

Father said, "It might suffice, but I don't know for what, for a painting of horror to break down and through its viewers' perceptual habits so that they can see what their minds and hearts refuse to see and what is."

Father began again painting by listing taboos. A taboo is a rule or law whose breakage will cause a society's collapse. Father's two laws or taboos were the untouchability of vision and of me.

Father didn't want anyone to touch me or me to touch anyone.

Father said, "To paint horror, I must violate both vision and my own child."

In those days, father thought that, since a painting was partly an object, a painting was or utilized fiction. Father decided to make the center of his portrait of New York one of me. A crowd of males including him would stand around me. They'd set my cunt on fire.

The men surrounding me'd be either homeless or art patrons.

Father said, "I'm the only man who can take care of you." Perhaps *to take care of* meant *to paint*.

As soon as father returned to painting, he forgot the world, about which he was usually only curious, and me. Except insofar as he made us fictive subjects.

The more my father abandoned me, the more I turned to the mayor. Who didn't want to fuck me but wanted to control father through me. So the mayor acted as if he wanted to fuck me.

His fictive desire made me want to run away, but I had nowhere to run. Not into emptiness.

Father said, "I see through the imagination."

Every day he tramped the streets of New York in search of material or specific desires. On Christmas Day, he penetrated the main cop morgue. No danger here. Corpses can't puke. The cops wanted to return home to their Christmas dinners. No other material or desires here except in the realm of death.

Father walked over to the St. Vincent's emergency ward, where humans were dying rather than dead. A TB victim was sticking his tongue into the mouth of a former lover because he was still in love. Father wondered, was it easier to be dead in a cop morgue or here? No material or desires here except in the realm of death.

Father said, "In order to see, I have to touch or be what I see. For this reason, seers are sailors. When seers become artists, they become pirates. This is about identity."

Father finally began painting his portrait of the city when, one night, between waking and sleeping, he saw my mother. She was sitting upright on the top of his thighs. He looked up at her. Then she lifted her cunt over his cock and lay down on him. She moved herself up and down.

Father, "Are you telling me to come? Come where? Come to hell?"

When father woke up, he drew pictures of my mother in orgasm. These formed the frame of his portrayal of New York.

I see through the imagination.

There's a point at which when I start to know a man well. This isn't true of women. I wonder whether there's something in him that's evil. Something that's pure and can't be touched. This quality of evil may be related to the quality of artistry, for an artist has the same characteristics.

The time when father embarked on the second stage of his painting wasn't the dead of winter. But it was winter and there was more death around than usual. The era of art and business, or capitalism in its finality, is the era of anarchy. No one had the same language; the homeless couldn't communicate with the crack dealers. I began strolling through dying and dead bodies as if they were garbage.

The more the artists became like businessmen, the more common it was for artists to have assistants who made their art. ("Realized their ideas.") Father took an assistant.

Father said, "It's necessary to see (to know, to be) something in order to paint it. I've been commissioned to paint horror. Is horror torture? Can I paint horror by painting torture (or various forms of torture, such as homelessness and crack dealing)?''

So to see torture, father strung his assistant up by his ankles. The assistant dangled in ropes from the ceiling of father's art studio while father's python played with his balls.

Father looked and looked at his assistant, whose face was red, and saw only his own curiosity.

He tightened the assistant's binds. When father realized that he could keep on tightening them because of rapidly increasing curiosity, he desisted.

Father said to his assistant. ''You're in pain so you know you're in pain. Whereas I'm not in pain so I perceive neither pain nor happiness. How'm I going to see the pain and horror that I'm making you feel?''

Father decided that the answer to his question was more violence.

One day while I was masturbating though I didn't yet know what I was doing, I heard screams. I saw the assistant, now right-side-up, bound as tightly as possible in chains, an unknown snake around his neck and about to bite. The assistant, not in pain, was totally scared. Daddy, so entranced in his vision he had stopped drawing. When daddy grabbed the snake's head between bite and about-to-bite in mid-air, I knew that he was incapable of hurting anyone.

And I loved him even more.

Father was growing more irritable and noncommunicative because he couldn't find the next step in his painting. Skulls and owls, death and life, inhabited one corner of his studio. Turned away from humans to animals. He would stare at the owls for days, at their curved beaks and claws. It was as if he were staring at impenetrability. At the limits.

A sailor on the ocean.

(Pirates knew that animals, kin to them, were their natural enemies. As if civil war. Even if you hack animals to ribbons, pirates understood, if your sword hashes their flesh and rips their insides apart, in no time they recover their animal image and life. Not even if you thwack off an animal's head with one blow can you make, pirates said, the demons disappear, since animals not only possess the fabulous magic ability to know what others, including humans, feel and therefore think, but also are immortal and as all-powerful as the gods of their forebears.)

In a piece of literature, in accordance with her will and desire, a man takes off a woman's clothes. To make her more naked, he places a headdress of owl feathers, gray and black, over all of her head but her eyes and mouth. Trails down her back. Then he leads her out into public.

Father said, "My problem's that I'm not listening to myself, my intuition. I must see horror. I said that to see must be to touch or become what is seen. But like most Americans, I keep pretending that horror is taking place outside America's shores."

Father said to me, "I love only to paint and you. To paint horror, I must violate both. In the center of my portrait, I'll paint the most horrible act possible being done to a fictive version of you. A fictive version of me will be part of the crowd around you, watcher and perpetrator. Vision, both in reference to the painter and to the viewer, will occur only for the purpose of murder."

What father didn't say but knew, and he wanted to escape this, was that in order to paint a young girl's torture, he had to see it.

Like thoughts or a snake, coils tightened; father became more unable to paint.

The deepest impotence of all made father neglect, then avoid me. I had been used to what seemed to me egomania when he had entered into painting. This was something new. My hurt grew beyond my understanding. Into an appearance of irrationality named *loneliness*. I didn't like it when bad things grew in me.

I knew that my boss didn't want me because he was gay and wanted me in order to touch my father. The more he

showed he wanted, the more I had to show and did show
that I didn't want him. The more he began to want to hurt
me.

(In their darkest hours, pirates rumbled love songs:

When the flesh shrivels,
you're dying.
When the flesh is shriveled,
you're dead.
When the flesh is red,
love occurs.
If I'm lying
when I say "I love you,"
the winds will kill my words.
What disillusion:
the winds are killing these words.)

Someone with the stupid name of Iyemon, who's come
down in this world, is forced by evil circumstances and an
evil world to support his innocent wife and even more innocent child by constructing umbrellas in an umbrella factory. His brain deteriorates. He can't help it, but he resents
his wife and child who are forcing him to do mindless man-
ual labor.

Next door to him lives a beautiful girl whose family has
real money. To Iyemon she's everything that his wife isn't.
And as soon as he fucks her, she can't live without him.

The beautiful girl and her family convince Iyemon to poison his wife. But Iyemon poisons his wife badly. Only her
face is mutilated and one of her eyes drops out red.

As is usual with women who are dependent on men, Iyemon's wife doesn't have any friends. Finally, her hair-
dresser, to whom she's turned for friendship, reveals the
truth to her: he shows her her face in a mirror. Hairdressers
are very fond of women. The wife, who's been thinking
she's going to see a new hairdo, a new person, looks at
herself and screams. Oh. For some reason, she is a cross

between the Phantom of the Opera and Miss America. Even though one of her eyes is no longer seeing because it's dropped out.

She realizes that it's her husband, a man, who's done this to her. Made her into Miss America.

"I understand what's going on in this world. I'll cut off his dick and mince it into red pieces. I'll give it . . . them . . . to the bums to eat so they won't go hungry."

The wife's become so angry that she's forgotten everything else. That she's one of the most mutilated people in the world.

When love dies, there's nothing and this world is only horror.

Perhaps love has not died. Perhaps there's never been human love.

Perhaps all that human beings have ever meant by *love* is *control*. Iyemon believes above all that he is a man who doesn't hurt other human beings. So when he learns that his business partner knows about the poisoning, he murders the partner, whose name is Jesus.

Then Iyemon took Jesus's and his wife's bodies (his wife had finally died from being poisoned) and nailed them to the opposite sides of a door. The door was discarded in the garbage of the East River.

Finally Iyemon believed he had mended his ways and was ready for marriage. He loved the rich girl, Beauty, and she loved him and this was the only happiness in life. Under the law and religion, they mutually pledged themselves to each other, and as he was lifting up her veil to seal her, he saw that he was really pledging himself to his mutilated wife. He saw an eyeball dangling red from an eye. She hates me, he thought. I don't hate women. I'm just the opposite. I guess I'll again have to explain to her why she's acting the way she is. I always get involved with these neurotic Jewish women. Instead of kissing her, he put his hands around her neck and strangled her. Then he saw he had murdered his bride instead of a dead woman. So he ran out of the hotel.

Just as he was running away, Beauty's grandfather tried

to stop him. Iyemon thought that the old man was Jesus and killed him.

Iyemon started seeing his first dead wife's visage everywhere just like some women keep seeing the face of the man they love. Love's obsession. He especially saw his dead wife's face with the red eyeball hanging from a red thread of mucus—just as if human bodies in this world don't rot when they're dead—in street lamps. When the lamps were bright, late at night, sometimes the rotten but not rotting face was on fire. At that time, holes emerged in its flesh. Simultaneously, water pipes burst openings through the streets' concrete. Through these holes. Through holes in the flesh, the faces of the dead stare at the living. Iyemon's mother said, "He murdered tons of people and, for that he can never atone." Then the beautiful mother stuck two fingers into her mouth and, instead of vomiting, stretched her mouth, as if it were rubber, out so far there was only emptiness.

The dead're screaming. "Through human guilt, we can see."

Iyemon screeches. But there's no help in this world except from the self, and all of us die.

What is it to see?

"Now I can see," said the young girl. Iyemon screeched and screeched. He ran into the river in which he had dropped the door. In the narrow streets that ran along this river, cats were eating dead fish. The cats were dying. Iyemon decided to go fishing. He threw a string into the liquid for something. His patience was rewarded. He pulled his-first-wife-and-his-business-partner-nailed-to-the-door out of the river.

If we forget history, public and private, we're lost.

In order to escape all his actions or the consequences of his actions, which were the same, Iyemon ran to the tip of Manhattan Island, where no humans could live. Here was the other side of nature, which the island's inhabitants think is nature.

A rat was eating a cockroach.

Iyemon decided this was his home. Iyemon decided that he had finally escaped from human beings and all their ignorance and horror. Since there were to be no more humans, there would be neither love nor murder.

There was only part of an apartment building.

Perhaps there is an escape from horror through love, but there is no love.

As soon as Iyemon thought, I'm safe, his first wife's brother killed him.

Finally Father informed the mayor that in order to paint what he had been commissioned to paint, he had to paint an innocent girl.

Mayor ____ said, "Girls come cheap."

Father said, "Not for my purposes."

When Mayor ____ asked father what his purpose might be, father replied that he wanted a crowd of men to set fire to a young girl. Including the mayor. That is, he wanted to see a crowd of men set fire to a young girl. Seeing isn't the same act as doing.

Mayor ____ asked, "Why don't you visit one of our prisons? Or walk into one of those slum apartments Puerto Ricans inhabit?"

(In the era in which men searched for and lived according to absolutes and women didn't exist, only their sexual organs, the pirates were renegades. When businessmen and artists came into power, in accordance with the necessities of late capitalism, men's desires for absolutes stopped. Became nostalgia and romance. The history of the century can be seen as defined by the struggle between a model of or desire for an absolute reality and a model or recognition of reality as indeterminate.)

Father said, "No. Normal life in this city isn't horrible enough, for my purposes, because every New Yorker is so habituated to what's taking place in the streets, in the jails, in the burnt-out areas, that he or she no longer recognizes horror as horror."

Mayor ___ asked, "Why're you so concerned with horror?"

Father answered that he hated violence. He was both a liberal and a humanist, even though today both these concepts were treated with disdain. Because he was as he was, he saw that life in New York is violent and that violence is unacceptable. Father said, "Political violence, above all, isn't rational. When I portray violence, and this concerns how I portray violence, I want it to be clear as hell that violence is not understandable."

Father continued, "I'll give you an example of that which sits outside our capacity to understand. About a year ago, I saw a large apartment building flaming. The cars around the building exploding. In the imagination, there were charred human bodies inside the walls. Since I was living half a block away, I should have been scared. Instead I felt unlimited gratitude for being able to see so tremendous a sight."

Mayor ___ asked, "Does horror come from Nature?"

Father said, "The point is that when I saw these flames and thought that people were dying, I felt joy. Not horror. The horror has to do with me. In order to paint horror as horror actually is or a portrait of New York, I need to show myself doing what's most horrible for me to do."

The mayor said, "Shit."

Father said, "I have to paint myself killing my own daughter."

The mayor said, "More horrible things're taking place in this city."

Father said, "The point is that if, as if I were writing a magazine article for a targeted audience, I painted what I thought was horrible to other people, I would be putting a distance, ironical, between myself and horror and then the horror in and of my painting wouldn't be so horrible. This is why I paint for myself, not for other people. To paint horror, I have to eradicate all distance between horror and me: I have to see/show my own horror, that I'm horrible."

The mayor said, "Do what you have to do. I want the painting."

Father reiterated, "To paint my daughter's murder, I have to see it. Since painting's partly fictional, I only need to see a young girl being murdered in order to see my daughter being murdered." Father asked, "Could you have a young girl killed? In the manner I've described?"

(The pirates knew, if not all of them consciously, that the civilizations and cultures that they were invading economically depended on the enslavement of other civilizations and cultures. Pirates took prisoners, didn't make slaves.)

Mayor ___ decided that the safest procedure would be to take a dead girl out of one of the city morgues. The girl or the dead person would be set on fire in a part of the city where there were no dead buildings. Almost no buildings. For the mayor wanted this painting, but he also had to preserve real-estate values.

(On dreams and actions in pirates: Their rotten souls burn in their bowels. They only go for pleasure. For them alone, you see, naked bodies dance. Unseizable, soft, ethereal, shadowy: the gush of cunts in action. Running free. With a thousand silken fingers, the hands caress the pirates' cocks, maddened by sharp fingernails, red clouds, hurt then cradle, in the darkness of the holds. Sing lullabies mixed with passions' irrational moans, sing of the nipples' erect buds.)

Father said, "Also I need to see a crowd of men standing around the girl. While she burns up, they do nothing to stop her from burning."
Mayor ___ said, "The fucking homeless're everywhere." The girl or the dead person would be sitting in an oversized black limo so that the homeless couldn't touch her. The politician added, "Men're easy to get."
Father said, "If men are easy to get, why's a good man so hard to find?"

STORYTELLING METHOD: THE ACT OF BODYBUILDING PRESUPPOSES
THE ACT OF MOVING TOWARD THE BODY OR THAT WHICH IS SO
MATERIAL THAT IT BECOMES IMMATERIAL. THE SPIRIT OF PIRATES.

The history of New York City.

The more my father turned to, into, his painting, away
from me, the more I wondered whether he was evil. I
wasn't dumb. By *dumb,* I mean *ignorant.* I knew that
though my father thought he was a cowboy, his strength
came only from his desire to see. It was this same power,
resembling and perhaps kin to will, that made him turn so
away from human morality that he no longer knew what
that was. I was his sole link to ordinary emotion; in his
painting he was finally choosing to turn away from me.
That which exalted my father was destroying him.

Sexual desire was a simple hunger and easily satisfied.

Unlike father, Mayor —— wanted to be powerful for no
reason other than power and, like father, thought he was.
As is the case with most politicians, he confused appearance
with reality, money with reality. This confusion was hol-
lowing him.

I hadn't yet realized that no one can ever know another
person.

Then I decided that I wasn't going to do anything or say
anything unless I meant it. I hated the city during day and
loved it most when night was deepest. When, since humans
no longer appeared as they thought they should because
this lack of light allowed anonymity, all who were still living played.

They put blindfolds around my eyes and wrapped what
felt like bandages, only thicker, around the rest of me.

Now every neighborhood was black.

As previously discussed, a section of the city about which
no one cared had been chosen. No one cared what hap-

pened. Cops never visit disaster and we're all cops. Their future disaster.

Most of the section was a parking lot. At the peripheries, apartment and canine parts lay silent. The color of the lead air varied from gray to a gray that resembled black and overlay whatever constituted ground as if the ground was an ocean if an ocean could rot.

The section had been written off before it had been born, as such sections're born.

There weren't many buildings anyway. In this section of rats and dead fishermen. Three inches above the wet, winds crawled on knees that no longer existed like the whores they were imitating. Pirating.

No one lived here, for the poor live nowhere.

There were condoms, needles, small fires.

Do humans rot in the same ways animals rot?

(The pirates loved women who were sexual and dangerous. We live by the images of those we decide are heroes and gods. As the empire, whatever empire, had decayed, the manner of life irrevocably became exile. The prostitutes drove mad the pirates caught, like insects in webs, in their own thwarted ambitions and longings for somewhere else. In the time of pirates, the prostitutes radiated with the knowing patrimony of priestesses whose religions are culturally valued. The pirates worshipped the whores in abandoned submission.)

They put me in a car. I didn't know why this was being done to me. Bound up, I could feel the plastic under my thighs. I didn't know where I was being taken, but since I was bound, I wasn't scared.

On the New York City streets, children play with used needles. Therefore, it's the dead who determine how the living act. Mother had taught me to avoid allowing a man to touch me correctly because, as soon as one man would begin to touch me correctly, I would begin to need.

Now I was being taken somewhere and I didn't know if it was against my will.

Father had said, "I see when imagination joins material."

METHOD: A MUSCLE'S BUILT WHEN AND ONLY WHEN ITS EXISTING FORM IS SLOWLY AND RADICALLY DESTROYED. IT CAN BE BROKEN DOWN BY SLOWLY FORCING IT TO ACCOMPLISH MORE THAN IT'S ABLE. THEN, IF AND ONLY IF THE MUSCLE IS PROPERLY FED WITH NUTRIENTS AND SLEEP, IT'LL GROW BACK MORE BEAUTIFUL THAN BEFORE.

The blindfold was taken off my eyes. At first, I saw grayness or I was hardly able to see. Then I started seeing light.

Differences in qualities of light became forms. I didn't see emptiness; I saw desertion. I saw no neon lights. Then I saw, through the car window, black wire fencing.

Here was the beginning of the world.

The quality of its light defines New York City as the beginning of the world.

I didn't know if Father knew this.

In my heart and outside, the light was turning pale gray. I sat still bound by thick bandages to the inside sides of the car. The only parts of me available for use were eyes and, partially, head.

Heard, "Going to set on fire."

On each side of me, forms. On each side of me, men who looked like the homeless who warm their hands over the fires in garbage cans.

Lit up Mayor ___'s face.

When seven years old, as had been told to do, on the laps of father's patrons and asked them to buy his art.

A match fell, in an arc, through the beginning of the morning. Couldn't see around it. The flame disappeared.

Face appeared in, though it was probably against, the car window on my left. Face like silly putty ridged. Must be homeless. I didn't want the face. Asked me for a match. No mouth. Went away.

As saw a second flame, heard, "A young slut who became

diseased from doing that which was natural to her and unnatural to everyone else and who died from her disease is sitting in that limo.'' Mayor's voice, ''I tied and bound the dead body for your appreciation.'' Was this to my father? ''Throw the next match into the car.''

Father (?) said, ''Want to see this.''

''If the car doesn't go up, throw gas over its cushions and try again.''

''So there'll be enough light for me to draw.''

Another voice. ''Rip a hole in her. Her mouth. The three of us in her at once. Rip. Rip. Rip.''

Voice. ''But then since our dicks'd be touching, we'd be fags.''

Mayor ____ . ''Now throw that match into the limo.''

After hearing these voices, I asked myself what it could be that made me want to live.

Something physical. Something to do with the physical.

Somehow I knew that my father was looking, but still didn't know who I was.

Thought, things must happen for a reason. I can't be sitting in this car solely for the stupid pleasure of stupid old men.

Mayor ____ said to my father, ''If you're going to draw this, you'll need to see every detail of her face and body. Before and as she's burning up. Walk up to that limo right now.''

Walked up to the limo. My father didn't see anything.

Though gagged I said, ''Set me free.''

When Mayor ____ lit another match, my father saw me. A bum set fire to a pile of rubbish and dead dogs.

In the light, I saw my father looking at me. Father seeing every detail of my face as if he owned it, me, without wanting to possess it, me. Has every victim chosen victimization? Then I knew that I had, also, put myself in this limo for my father and that he was looking at me.

That which is beautiful is muscular, not diseased.

I could no longer run away. When my father recognized me, he didn't try to free me.

TOWARD A LITERATURE OF THE BODY.

The homeless gathered to watch the only spectacle in their part of town. At this time. One member stuck his head through the hole in the car where the window was almost down. He asked me whether, when I grow up, there'll be men whom I want to marry.

I couldn't answer.

The beggar asked, "Maybe you like women better?" Bums're sentimental. A flame's igniting of the cushion on which I was sitting stopped the sentiment.

I was scared. I cried and cried and cried and cried.

A small part of the fire ate the bandage on my right side. One of my arms and mouth were freed. I used the hand to gesture to the men around me. "My father's responsible for this."

"Yeah," a bum said as if at a football rally.

I said, "I'm not a criminal. I only look bad now. I'm good and I love my father."

Mayor ＿＿ cut me off. "This girl's a hardened criminal and we're taking her back to where she belongs."

A bag lady asked, "What dirty words did your father use to turn you into a hardened criminal?"

"No," I protested. "Love doesn't work that way." The flames were beginning to rise.

"Did he ask you to do things that are sexually unacceptable?"

I said "Yes" so that the homeless threw themselves like rats upon Mayor ＿＿ and my father. I had managed to free myself from the remaining bandages. The smoke obscured my exit.

Exit means *rose*.

During the following days, a public controversy ensued. One side wanted to give my father the death sentence for what he had done. The other side argued that, despite his and Mayor ＿＿'s actions, his painting of New York City whose centerpiece was a portrait of his daughter in flames was one of the masterpieces of art in the twentieth century, that century in which totalitarianism vied with humanism. Mayor _____ continued to hold the second view.

My father killed himself.

(Piracy seemed like an adventure dreamed in a night of passion, an illusion lasting exactly the time it took for a blind man to rub his only eye, an impossible sexual desire crumbling like a pillar of sand, blowing like winds. Legal punishments ranging from a simple fine to more fearsome ones—torture, loss of property and of personal liberty— gradually succeeded in quenching even the pirates' illicit ghosts.)

ESSEX HEMPHILL

HEAVY BREATHING

. . . and the Negro every day lower, more cowardly,
more sterile, less profound, more spent beyond
himself, more separate from himself, more cunning
with himself, less straight to himself,

I accept, I accept it all . . .

—AIMÉ CÉSAIRE
Return to my Native Land

At the end of heavy breathing,
 very little of my focus intentional,
 I cross against the light of Mecca.
 I recall few instances of piety
 and strict obedience.
 Nationalism disillusioned me.
 My reflections can be traced
 to protest slogans
 and enchanted graffiti.
 My sentiments—whimsical—
 the dreams of a young, yearning bride.
 Yes, I possess a mouth such as hers:
 red, petulant, brutally pouting;
 or at times I'm insatiable;
 the vampire in the garden, demented
 by the blood of a succulent cock.
 I prowl in scant sheaths of latex.
 I harbor no shame.
 I solicit no pity.
 I celebrate my natural tendencies,

photosynthesis, erotic customs.
I allow myself to dream
of roses
    though I know
    the bloody war continues.

I am only sure of this:
    I continue to awaken
    in a rumpled black suit.
    Pockets bulging with tools
    and ancestral fossils.
    A crusty wool suit
    with salt on its collar.
    I continue to awaken
    shell-shocked, wondering
    where I come from
    beyond mother's womb,
    father's sperm.
    My past may be lost
    beyond the Carolinas
    North and South.
    I may not recognize
    the authenticity
    of my Negritude;
    so slowly I awaken.

Science continues
dismantling chromosomes.
Tampering with genetic codes.
I am sure of this
as I witness Washington
change its eye color
from brown to blue;
what kind of mutants are we now?
Why is some destruction so beautiful?

Do you think I could walk pleasantly
and well-suited toward annihilation?

with a scrotal sack full
of primordial loneliness
swinging between my legs
like solid bells?

I am eager to burn
this threadbare masculinity,
this perpetual black suit
I have outgrown.

At the end of heavy breathing,
at the beginning of grief and terror,
on the X2, the bus I call a slave ship.
The majority of its riders—Black.
Pressed to journey to northeast,
into voodoo ghettos
festering on the knuckles
of the "Negro Dream."
The X2 is a risky ride.
A cargo of block boys, urban pirates,
the Colt 45 and gold-neck-chain crew
are all part of this voyage,
like me, rooted to something here.

The women usually sit
at the front.
The unfortunate ones
who must ride in the back
with the fellas
often endure foul remarks;
the fellas are quick to call them
out of name, as if all females
between eight and eighty
are simply pussies with legs.

The timid men, scattered among
the boat crew and crack boys;
the frightened men

pretend invisibility
or fake fraternity
with a wink or nod.
Or they look the other way.
They have a sister on another bus,
a mother on some other train
enduring this same treatment.

There is never any protest.
No peer restraint. No control.
No one hollered STOP!
for Mrs. Fuller,
a Black mother murdered
in an alley near home.
Her rectum viciously raped
with a pipe. Repeatedly
sodomized before a crowd
that did not holler STOP!
Some of those watching knew her.
Knew her children.
Knew she was a member of the block.
Every participant was Black.
Every witness was Black.
Some were female
and Black.

There was no white man nearby shouting
"BLACK MAN, SHOVE IT IN HER ASS!
TAKE SOME CRACK! SHOVE IT IN HER ASS,
AND THE REST OF YOU WATCH!"

At the end of heavy breathing
the funerals of my brothers
force me to wear
this scratchy black suit.
I should be naked,
seeding their graves.
I go to the place

where the good feelin' awaits me
self-destruction in my hand,
kneeling over a fucking toilet,
splattering my insides
in a stinking, shit-stained bowl.
I reduced loneliness to cheap green rum,
spicy chicken, glittering vomit.
I go to the place
where danger awaits me,
cake-walking
a precarious curb
on a corner
where the absence of doo wop
is frightening.
The evidence of war
and extinction surround me.
I wanted to stay warm
at the bar,
play to the mischief,
the danger beneath a mustache.
The drag queen's perfume
lingers in my sweater
long after she dances
out of the low-rent light,
the cheap shots and catcalls
that demean bravery.

And though the room
is a little cold and shabby,
the music grating,
the drinks a little weak,
we are here
witnessing the popular one
in every boy's town,
a diva by design.
Giving us silicone titties
and dramatic lip synch.
We're crotch to ass,

shoulder to shoulder,
buddy to buddy,
squeezed in sleaze.
We want her to work us.
We throw money
at her feet.
We want her
to work us,
let us see
the naked ass of truth.
We whistle for it,
applaud, shout vulgarities.
We dance like beasts
near the edge of light,
choking drinks.
Clutching money.

And there I was,
  flying high
  without every leaving the ground
three rums firing me up.
The floor swirling.
Music thumping at my temple.
  In the morning
  I'll be all right.
  I know I'm hooked on the boy
  who makes slaves out of men.

I'm an oversexed
well-hung
Black Queen
influenced
by phrases like
"the repetition
of beauty."

And you want me to sing
"We Shall Overcome"?

Do you daddy daddy
do you want me to coo
for your approval?
Do you want me
to squeeze my lips together
and suck you in?
Will I be a "brother" then?

I'm an oversexed
well-hung
Black Queen
influenced
by phrases like
"The love that dares
to speak its name."

And you want me to sing
"We Shall Overcome"?
Do you daddy daddy
do you want me to coo
for your approval?
Do you want me
to squeeze my lips together
and suck you in?
Will I be "visible" then?

I'm an oversexed
well-hung
Black Queen
influenced
by phrases like
"Silence equals death."

Dearly Beloved,
    I am looking at the inevitable
    deterioration of my flesh
    as time takes what it wants
    of my pleasures,

as I move in and out of love
like an exile.
Spoon-fed on hypocrisy,
I throw up gasoline
and rubber bullets,
an environmental reflex.
Shackled to shimmy and sham,
I jam the freeway
with my vertigo and delusions.
I return to the beginning,
to the opening of time and wounds.
I dance in the searchlight
of a police cruiser.
I know I don't live here anymore
but I remain in this body
to witness.

I have been in the bathroom
weeping as silently as I could.
I don't want to alarm
the other young men.
It wasn't always this way.
I used to grin.
I used to dance.
The streets weren't always
slick with blood,
sick with drugs.
I keep telling myself
pain will evaporate,
but my only life
appears to be
one long laceration.
I continue having
altercations with reality.
When I fuck
the salt tastes sweet.

At the end of heavy breathing
    for the price of the ticket
    we pay dearly. Don't we darling?
    Searching for evidence
    of things unseen.
    I am looking for
    Giovanni's room
    in this bathhouse.
    I know he's here.

    I cruise a black maze,
    my white sail blowing full.
    I wind my way through corridors
    lined with doors closed
    or slightly ajar,
    or thrown open to darkness,
    seductive light, the future.
    Some rooms are empty,
    their previous occupant
    soon-to-be-wiped-away,
    then another tenant will arrive
    with towels and sheets.
    The last corridor
    at the back of this cathouse
    is lined with lockers.
    We rent time here
    so we can fuck each other.
    Everyone hasn't gone to the moon.
    Some of us are still here,
    breathing heavy, earthbound
    creatures of desire,
    navigating the deadly
    sexual turbulence.

Occasionally I long
    for a dead man
    I never slept with.
    I saw you one night

in a dark room
caught in the bounce of light
from the corridor.
You were intent on your buggery,
pushing your swollen cock
into the depths of a squirming man
bent over to the floor,
blood rushing to both your heads.

I quietly watched
stroking myself in shadow.
I wanted to give you
better sex,
but you rejected my offer
choosing blond,
milk-toned creatures
over my dusky allure.

You cast my eyes aside like peasants
because they lack a hint of blue.
I wasn't the only Black man wanting you.
We were all denied your touch.
You grunted gruffly if we came near.
But you were one of us
even in the dark
you despised in us.

Occasionally I long
to fuck a dead man
I never slept with.
I pump up my temperature
imagining his touch
as I stroke my wish bone,
wanting him to be alive,
wanting my fallen seed
to produce him full grown
and breathing heavy,
the moment it spills

to my stomach;
wanting him to be here,
to be alive again,
intent upon his sweet buggery,
undisturbed by the motion of time,
even if my eyes do
lack a trace of blue.

At the end of heavy breathing
the fire quickly diminishes.
Proof dries on my stomach.
I open my eyes, regret
I returned without my companion,
who moments ago held my nipple
bitten between his teeth,
as I thrashed about
on the mercy of his hand
whimpering in tongues.

At the end of heavy breathing
does it come to this?
Filtering language of necessity?
Stripping it of honesty?
Burning it with fissures
that have nothing to do with God?
The absolute evidence of place.
A common roof, discarded
rubbers, umbrellas,
the scratchy disc of memory.
The fatal glass slipper.
The sublimations
that make our erections falter.

At the end of heavy breathing
who will be responsible
for the destruction
of human love?
Who are the heartless

sons of bitches
sucking blood from dreams
as they are born?
Who will have the guts
to come forward
and testify?

We were promised
this would be a nigga fantasy
on the scale of Oz.
Instead we're humiliated,
disenchanted, suspicious.
I ask the scandal-infested leadership
"What is your malfunction?"
tell us how you differ
from other criminals
who use automatic weapons
and butcher knives.

They respond with hand jive,
hoodoo hollering,
excuses to powder the nose,
or they simply disappear
like large sums of money.

And you want me to give you
a mandatory faith
because we are both Black
and descendants of oppression?
What will I get in return?
Hush money from the recreation fund?
A kilo of cocaine?
A boy for my bed
and a bimbo for my arm?
A tax break on my new home
west of the ghetto?

You promised
this would be a nigga fantasy
on the scale of Oz.
Instead, it's "Birth of a Nation,"
and the only difference
is the white men
are played in Blackface.

At the end of heavy breathing
as the pickaninny frenzy escalates,
the home crew is illin
on freak drugs
and afflicted racial pride,
the toll beyond counting,
the shimmering carcasses
all smell the same.
No matter which way
the wind blows
I lose a god
or a friend.

My sadness is too common
to arouse the mercy of angels.
My shame is too easy
to pick up
like boy pussy
from the park
and go.

I'm supposed to honor paranoia,
automatically trust a dream,
a reverend, hocus-pocus
handshakes.
I risk becoming schizoid
shuffling between Black English
and assimilation.

My dreamscape is littered
with the shattered remains
and effigies of my heroes.
I journey across
my field of vision
raiding the tundra
of my imagination,
three African rooftops
are aflame in my hand,
I ride wild and naked
on the back of a winged gazelle.
Compelled by desperation,
I plunder every bit of love
in my possession.
I am looking for an answer
to drugs and corruption.
I enter the diminishing
circumstance of prayer,
the murmurs of believers
rise and fall, exhaled
from a single spotted lung.
Inside a homemade Baptist church
perched on the edge
of the voodoo ghetto,
the congregation sings
to an out-of-tune piano,
while death is rioting,
splashing blood about
like gasoline,
offering pieces of rock
for throw-away dreams.
The lines of takers are long.

Now is the time
to be an undertaker
in the ghetto,
a homemade
Baptist preacher.

Now is not the time
to be a Black mother
in the ghetto,
the father of sons,
the daughters
of any of them.

At the end of heavy breathing
I engage in arguments
with my ancestral memory.
I'm not content
with nationalist propaganda.
I'm not content
loving my Black life
without question.
The answers of Negritude
are not absolute.
The dream of King
is incomplete.
I probe beneath skin surface.
I argue with my nappy hair,
my thick lips so difficult
to assimilate.
Up and down the block we battle,
cussing, kicking, screaming,
threatening to kill
with bare hands.
The sheer velocity
creates a spectacle.
It reaches the shrill
pitch of bloodshed
like domestic violence.

At the end of heavy breathing
the dream deferred
is in a museum
under glass and guard.
It costs five dollars

to see it on display.
We spend the day
viewing artifacts,
breathing heavy
on the glass
to see—
the skeletal remains
of black panthers,
pictures of bushes,
canisters of tears.

NOTES

p. 152 "Do you think I could walk pleasantly and well-suited toward annihilation?" Walt Whitman, *Leaves of Grass,* "To Think of Time, #8"

p. 154 Mrs. Catherine Fuller, "a petite 48-year-old grandmother, was pummeled, kicked and violated with a metal pole as a crowd looked on." This brutal act occurred in an alley near Eighth and H Streets, NE, within walking distance of her home on the evening of October 1, 1985, as she was on her way home from a nearby store. *Washington Post,* January 5, 1986, "Fuller Killers Bred by Mean Streets," page A–1.

p. 154–155 "I go to the place where the good feelin' awaits me, self-destruction in my hand," Marvin Gaye, *What's Going On,* "Flyin' High (In the Friendly Sky)" © 1971, Motown Record Corporation.

"I go to the place where danger awaits me," Marvin Gaye, *What's Going On,* "Flyin' High (In the Friendly Sky)" © 1971, Motown Record Corporation.

p. 156 "Flying high without ever leaving the ground," Marvin Gaye, *What's Going On,* "Flyin' High (In the Friendly Sky)" © 1971, Motown Record Corporation.

"In the morning I'll be alright. I know I'm hooked on the boy who makes slaves out of men." Marvin Gaye, *What's Going On,* "Flyin' High (In the Friendly Sky)" © 1971, Motown Record Corporation.

"The repetition of beauty," from the exhibition "African Islam," presented by the National Museum of African Art, Smithsonian Institution, 11/30/83–4/22/84. "Islamic art everywhere has certain characteristics. Foremost among these is the decoration of surfaces with balanced designs and the endless repetition of identical forms to fill entire surfaces." *African Islam,* © 1983 Smithsonian Institution.

p. 156 "We Shall Overcome," a civil rights anthem, first used in the media by "labor troubador" Joe Glazer, in a 1950 film for the Congress of Industrial Organizations' Textile Workers Union called *Unions at Work.*

p. 157 "The love that dares to speak its name," Oscar Wilde.

"Silence equals death," a slogan of empowerment created by the gay and lesbian movement of the late 1980s.

DOROTHY ALLISON

PRIVATE RITUALS

I WAS ABOUT EIGHT or so when I discovered that my little sister, Reese, was masturbating almost as often as I was. In the middle of the night, I woke up to feel the bed shaking slightly, the big bed where the two of us slept. Instead of sprawling across the bottom of the bed as she usually did with her legs and arms thrown wide, Reese was pulled over to the far edge of the mattress, her body taut and curved away from me. I could hear the sound of her breathing, fast and shallow. I knew immediately what she was doing. I kept still, listening, my own breathing quiet and steady. After a while there was a moment when she held her breath and then the shaking stopped. Very quietly then I slipped my right hand down between my legs and held myself, thinking about what she had been doing. I wanted to do it too, though I couldn't stand the thought that she might hear. But what if she did? What could she say to me after doing it herself? I held my breath, I moved my hand, I almost did not shake the bed at all.

Reese would go back to our bedroom alone every afternoon after we came home from school. When she would come out, I would go in there. Sometimes I even imagined I could smell what she had been doing, but that could not have been so. We were little girls. We smelled like little girls. I pulled my shorts down and made sure of it, carefully washing between my legs with warm soap and water every time I did that thing I knew my little sister was doing too.

One afternoon, I went outside and stood under the bedroom window, listening for the sound of Reese alone in the bedroom. She was quiet, very quiet, but I could hear the rhythm of her breathing as it slowly picked up speed and the soft little grunts she made before it began to slow down again. I liked those grunts. When Reese did it in the middle of the night, she never made any sound at all. But then I was just as careful myself, not letting myself make a sound even when I was safely alone. I wondered if Reese did it differently in the daytime. I wondered if she lay on her back with her legs wide, the way I liked to when I was alone, rather than on her stomach with both hands under her the way she did at night. There was no way I could spy on her to see, no way I could know. But I imagined Reese sometimes while I did it myself, seeing her as she lay across our big bed, rocking only slightly, showing by nothing but her breathing that she was committing a sin.

Reese and I never talked about our private games, our separate hours alone in our room, but then we never let anyone else go in the bedroom when one of us was in there alone.

My stepfather, Daddy Glen, married my mother when I was four and Reese was still running around in rubber pants. He never spanked us that first year, never even raised his voice to yell at us. He touched my mama like she was something fine and fragile, touched us as if we wore the shine of her on our baby skin. But by the time I was five he started beating me, spanking Reese, but beating me, and screaming all the time. He still stared at Mama as if she were something marvelous and strange, and handled Reese carefully, shaking her so that her loose blond hair flew back and forth but never slapping her. Reese looked exactly like mama's child, with mama's eyes, mama's chin, and her sunshine-streaked curls, but she had a sweet-natured passivity that was totally unlike Mama or me. *I* was Mama's firstborn and her favorite—smart, dark, sharp-featured and too often cuddled up close to Mama's side.

"He's jealous of that child," my aunts warned Mama. "A man grown and he's as jealous of that child as if she were a lover."

To spank Reese, Daddy Glen used his hand. On me he used a belt, sometimes lifting me in the air with one knotty fist clamped on my shoulder, pinning me against the wall and beating me as if his life depended on the intensity of my screams. There were shadowy bruises on my thighs and blood spots on the sheets. He announced that I was "arrogant," that I "thought too much of myself," that I was "spoiled" and "talked back" and gave him "hateful looks." I was five. I didn't hate him yet. I hid from him. Daddy Glen would lock me in the bathroom for a while to think before coming in to punish me. He would go on until my screams reached a certain satisfying pitch, or until Mama on the other side of the door began to scream louder than me. In the beginning I think I was too young to matter as much as she did.

When Daddy Glen yelled, Reese would flee. When he shouted my name, I would shudder like a bird, stopped by an arrow in the air. I schooled my face to have no expression. I admitted that I was a bad girl, evil, nasty, willful, stupid, ugly—everything he said, anything he said. Nothing helped. By the time I was seven, I did hate him. I hated him, my sister, my mother, the air that hummed with electricity when he got mad. I was a bowl of hatred, boiling black and thick behind my eyes.

Sometimes I tried not to scream, sometimes I tried not to fight him. It didn't matter at all whether I screamed or fought or held still. There was no heroism in it. There was just being beaten until I was covered with snot and misery. It wasn't until I was almost twelve that I realized Daddy

Glen was pinning me against his thigh and beating me until he came in his trousers. It made it worse. It made everything more horrible. There was no reason in it, no justice. It was an animal thing, just him using me. I fell into shame like a suicide throws herself into a river.

I think I was five when I started masturbating. At least I can vaguely remember doing so. What I clearly remember are the daydreams of fire that accompanied doing it, being tied up and put inside a haystack while someone set fire to the dry, stale straw. I would picture it perfectly while rocking on my hand. The daydream was about struggling to get free while the fire burned hotter and closer. I am not sure that I came when the fire reached me, or if I would come, and then imagine escaping it. But I came. I orgasmed on my hand to the dream of fire.

I'm not sure when I got the science kit. I think it belonged to Daddy Glen's brother's children and I actually only got part of it. But I got the important part, the set of three glass test tubes in their little rack. Cold glass tubes, crystalline and gleaming and dangerous. What might happen if you pushed them inside you? What if they broke?

I pushed one inside myself.

In and out. Gradually it became warm.

I pushed the tube at my asshole and told myself it was going to hurt terribly when I actually shoved it in. When I heard myself say that out loud—"It's going in"—I came so hard I thought I'd broken it. Terrified, I hid all of them and ran outside. It was the first time I hid something, but not the last.

I made up stories for myself, changed some of them a little and told them to Reese and my cousins. I was very popular for those stories though my Aunt Raylene got upset when she heard some of them. If she had heard them all she would have beaten me harder than Daddy Glen. I would tell stories in which boys and girls were gruesomely raped and murdered, in which babies were cooked up in pots of boiling beans, stories about vampires and soldiers and long razor-sharp knives. Witches cut off the heads of both children and grown-ups. Gangs of women rode in on motorcycles and set fire to people's houses. I was very popular as a babysitter, the children were always quiet and well behaved while I whispered my stories, their eyes fixed on my face in such a way they made me feel like one of my own witches casting a spell.

I walked in on Reese one afternoon while she was lying on the bed with a pair of mama's panties pulled over her face. All of her features were outlined under the sheer material but her breath puffed the silk out over her lips. Frantically, she snatched them off and shoved them behind her on the bed. I grabbed up a book I had been reading from the dresser, and pretended I hadn't seen anything.

Reese played out her stories in the woods behind our house. I watched her one afternoon from the top of the tree Mama hung her bird feeder on. Reese hadn't seen me climb up there and didn't know I had a clear view of her as she ran around wearing an old sheet tied to her neck as a cape. It looked like she was fighting off imaginary attackers. Then she dropped to the ground and began rolling around in the grass and wet leaves, shouting, "NO! NO!" The haughty expression on her face was replaced by mock terror, and she threw her head back and forth wildly like the heroine in an adventure movie.

I laughed, hugged myself tightly to the tree and rocked my hips against the trunk. I imagined I was tied to the branches above and below me. Someone had beaten me with dry sticks and put their hands in my clothes. Someone, someone, I imagined. Someone had tied me high up in the tree, gagged me and left me to starve to death while the blackbirds pecked at my ears. I rocked and rocked, pushing my thighs into the rough bark. Below me, Reese pushed her hips into the leaves and made those grunting noises. Someone, someone she imagined, was doing terrible, exciting things to her.

When I was nine, determined to finally have some privacy, I moved myself and all my stuff out into the utility room, setting up Mama's old fold-up bed next to the washing machine. The latch I had put on the door made it possible for me to play the game I had dreamed about for so long. I started tying myself up, using scraps of clothesline and worn belts. I would spread my legs wide and use rope that I had already tied to the bedframe to pin my ankles. I fastened clothesline to the top of the bed and I wrapped the rope around my wrists, pretending I was tied down. The stories I made up while lying like that were so exciting, I felt as if they made me drunk. After a while I would free one hand and slip it down between my legs to play with myself.

It was a sin what I did alone in there. I was a sinner, a bad person. I told myself I would have to stop doing those things, that sooner or later someone might catch me, and then what would happen? Everyone would know. But maybe, secretly, everyone did the same thing, like Reese behind the closed bedroom door. Maybe everyone was committing the same sin, secretly, fearfully. I looked in people's eyes to try and see if something showed. "We have all sinned and fallen short of the glory of God," the preacher intoned. Yes, I thought, probably so.

I don't think Reese ever tied herself up, but I'm not completely sure.

My uncles were big men with wide shoulders, broken teeth and sunken features. They kept dogs trained for hunting and drove old trucks with metal toolboxes bolted to the reinforced wooden sides. They worked in the mills or at the furnace repair business, or sometimes did roofing or construction work, depending on how the industry was going. They did engine work together on the weekends, standing around in the yard sipping whiskey and talking dirty, and kicking at the greasy remains of engines they never finished rebuilding. Their eyes were narrow under sun-bleached eyebrows, and their hands were forever working a blade, or a piece of wood, or oiling some little machine part or other. "You hold a knife like this," they told me. "You work a screwdriver from your shoulder, swing a hammer from your hip, and spread your fingers when you want to hold something safe."

I worshiped my uncles; Uncle Earle, Uncle Lucius, Wade and Butch and Bo. I begged my aunts for their old worn shirts so I could wear them just the way they did, with the front tucked in my shorts and the back tail hanging out. My uncles laughed at me, but affectionately. They raked their callused fingers through my short black hair and played at catching my shirttail as I ran past them, but their hands never hurt me and their pride in me was as bright as the coals on the cigarettes that were always held loosely between their fingers. I followed them around and stole things from them that they didn't really care about—old tools, pieces of chain and broken engine parts. I wanted most of all a knife like the ones they all carried—a buck knife with a brass and stained wood handle or a jackknife decorated with mother-of-pearl. I found a broken jackknife with a shattered handle that I taped back together around the bent steel tang. I carried that knife all the time until my cousin Grey took pity and gave me a better one.

One summer afternoon, I found a broken length of chain from off the tailgate of one of the trucks. I cleaned and polished it and locked it around my hips. Sometimes when I masturbated I would push the links up inside me. I had read in one of Daddy Glen's paperbacks about women who did something like that. I couldn't stop thinking about it. I collected various sizes of chain for it. It took me a long time, however, to learn to run that chain between my labia so that it rubbed from my vagina to my asshole, and the links pulled up tight to press my clit as I moved. But the first time I did it, that chain was sun-warmed and tingly against my little girl's boyish thighs, as shiny as the sweat on my uncle's freckled shoulders, and as exciting as the burning light behind their eyes. Every link on that chain was magic in my hand.

I became ashamed of myself for the things I thought about when I put my hands between my legs, more ashamed for masturbating to the fantasy of being beaten than for being beaten in the first place. I lived in a world of shame. I hid my bruises as if they were evidence of crimes I had committed. I knew I was a sick, disgusting person. I couldn't stop my stepfather from beating me, but *I* was the one who masturbated. *I* did that, and how could I explain to anyone that I hated his beating me, hated being beaten, but still masturbated to the story I told myself about being beaten? I was a child. I could not explain anything.

Sometimes, I imagined people watching while Daddy Glen beat me. I imagined this only when it was not happening. The times when he actually beat me, I screamed and kicked and cried like the baby I was. But sometimes when I was safe and alone, I would imagine him beating me, and then I would imagine the ones who watched. Someone had to watch—some girl I admired who barely knew I existed, some girl from church or down the street, or one of my cousins, or even somebody I had seen on TV. Sometimes a whole group of them would be trapped into having to watch—they couldn't help or get away. They had to watch. In my imagination I was proud and defiant. I'd stare back at Daddy Glen in outrage with my teeth set, making no sound at all, no shameful scream, no begging, no crying. Those who watched admired me and hated him. I imagined it that way and put my hands between my legs. It was scarey to think that way, but it was wonderful too. The girl's face that watched me, loved me. It was as if I were being beaten for her. I was someone wonderful in her eyes.

I lived a completely schizophrenic life. I was just about the best little girl in South Carolina, made straight A's at school, took care of my little sister, cleaned the house so Mama wouldn't have to worry, told lies to the bill collectors that came to the door, and went to Baptist Sunday

School in clean white dresses. But I was a sinner. I knew I was a sinner. I kept switching to different churches every few months, while pretending that I was struggling over whether to take Jesus into my heart. My mama finally caught on to the game I was playing and had me baptized. Church wasn't any fun at all when no one was trying to save your soul, so I quit going after a while.

I stole laxatives out of the medicine chest and swallowed them in large quantities to punish myself. But I couldn't stop telling myself those stories. Instead I promised Jesus I wouldn't put my hands between my legs anymore. I curled my hands up close to my neck. I gritted my teeth and wore thick cotton panties. I even started going to sleep with my arms stretched wide as if tied to the bed frame. In my imagination they were. It was a way not to sin.

Jesus, help me not to sin, I prayed. It was a joke on Jesus and me that I started having orgasms in that position, arms wide out, not touching myself, the movie playing in my head working more efficiently than my fingers ever had.

My favorite of all my uncles was Uncle Earle, known as Black Earle for three counties around. Mama said he was called Black Earle for that black, black hair that fell over his eyes in a great soft curl, but my Aunt Raylene said he was known for his black, black heart. Black Earle Boatwright was a pretty man, pretty and soft-spoken and hardworking. He always had money in his pockets, a job he was just leaving and another one he was about to take up. He always had some tender young girl on his arm—some seventeen-year-old child who watched him like his spine was outlined in pearls and rubies, his teeth with diamonds brighter than the highlights in his shiny black hair. He'd had a wife when he was young, a Catholic wife and three daughters, but she had left him for his running around, and since then he'd made a career of it, taking up with a new young girl every year or so—always young enough to boast about and as madly in love with him as only a young girl could be.

He married them, each of them, in a courthouse wedding over the line into Georgia or North Carolina after getting them to swear they were of legal age. "It's a sin," my aunts declared. "He's never divorced a one." And he didn't. He stayed married to them as if the marriages were more than the law or men could understand, as if that piece of worthless paper had meaning only he and they could put on it.

"Why do you bother?" Mama asked him after he brought the fifth or sixth of his young brides to stay with us for a week.

"Because they want it so bad," he told her where I could hear. "It seems like the least I can do."

I loved my Uncle Earle absolutely, so I decided all those girls were lucky to have had any kind of marriage at all and too stupid to deserve pity anyway. Besides, he always brought them to stay with us sooner or later, and I would find a way to plant myself up against the bedroom door while he honeymooned loudly on the other side.

"That's sex," I told myself. "They're having sex in there." I hugged myself and listened for every girl's gasp, every thud of my uncle's body against the bed. It had to be something good if they both wanted it so bad.

I became very very afraid someone would find out the kind of stories I was making up for myself. Because of the fear, I stopped telling my stories to other people, except for rare and special girlfriends who first had to win my trust by telling me something scarey about themselves. I knew that people would think it strange that there were no boys in my stories, no men. Probably it too was some kind of sin, the kind of sin people locked you away to purge.

My stories became more detailed, more violent and more complicated. The world I was creating in my mind was full of violence and sex. It was dangerous and terrible, the women in it powerful and cruel. Sometimes those women would even bring in men to beat and fuck me. Then again, sometimes I would be captured by evil men, tortured for my bravery and then rescued by beautiful women who wrapped me around with their great strong arms. That world was both complicated and simple, a place of dreams, adventure, sex and ritual. I was thankful that no one knew what hid behind my carefully blank or smiling face.

Once or twice a week, regularly as Sunday School, Daddy Glen beat me with one of the same two or three belts he'd set aside just for me. Oiled, smooth and supple as the gristle under chicken fat, those belts hung behind the door of his closet where I could see them when I helped Mama put away his clothes. I would reach up and touch the leather, feel it warm under my palms. There was no magic in it, no mystery, but those belts smelled of him and made me grit my teeth. Sometimes I would make myself go in that closet and wrap my fingers around those belts as if they were something animal that could be tamed.

I don't remember how old I was when Daddy Glen actually got his cock inside me. I don't remember the fucking but I remember exactly how it felt to stand up afterward, the way I hurt and how angry and afraid I was. I remember going outside and watching Reese ride her bicycle around the house. He was shouting my name but I kept heading off across the open fields behind our house. I lay down in the high grass, but I didn't cry. I started telling myself a long elaborate story, a long, long story. I didn't go into the house until it was dark. Mama was mad at me. She had been calling my name. Daddy Glen took me in the bathroom and beat me. I wrapped my hands in the pipes under the sink and watched the black hairs on his legs below his shorts.

I think it was the first time I didn't scream.

It was only in my secret stories that I was able to defy Daddy Glen. Only there that I had any pride. I loved those fantasies, even though I was sure they were a terrible thing. They had to be; they were self-centered and made me have shuddering orgasms. In the fantasy, I was very special. I was triumphant, important. I was not ashamed.

I learned to push a hairbrush handle inside my vagina to masturbate. I pretended someone else was doing it. I wore a belt fastened very tightly around my waist under my clothes where no one could see. I pretended that someone else had put it there and I couldn't take it off.

I enjoyed my other world so much that I began to live in it, plotting it out like a movie in my head, escaping to it whenever I could no longer stand the real life I did not want to be living at all.

Uncle Earle came to stay with us after a construction accident, hobbling around on a cane. I found excuses to spend time with him and get him to tell me stories. He told Mama that all the girls loved him because he looked like Elvis Presley, only skinny and with muscles. In a way he did, but his face was etched with lines and sunburned a deep red-brown. The truth was he had none of Elvis Presley's baby-faced innocence; he had a devilish look to his face and a body Aunt Carr swore was made for sex. He was a big man with a long, lanky body and wide hands seamed with scars. "Earle looks like trouble coming in on greased skids," my Uncle Bo laughed. All the aunts agreed, their cheeks wrinkling around indulgent smiles while their fingers trailed across Uncle Earle's big shoulders as sweetly and tenderly as the threadlike feet of hummingbirds.

When Uncle Earle talked, I made my eyes wide, so he would think I believed his stories. I laughed at his jokes, even the ones I didn't understand. He would take me riding in his Pontiac with the top down, riding around dirt roads kicking up clouds of dust. He drank whiskey out of a pint bottle and let me sip a little. I would giggle and fall against him, pretending I was dizzier than I really was. I wanted to touch him. I wanted to smell him up close. His voice would get deeper after I fell against him, and he would tell me to sit up straight, that we had to get home. I didn't want to go home. I wanted to feel the muscles in his shoulders. Behind his sideburns and below his ears, the skin of his neck was as soft as if he were a woman. It took a lot of gentle persistence before he would sit still so that I could touch him when I wanted.

He gave me dollar bills for letting him rub against my backside, something I was happy to do. I wanted to turn around and pull his shirt up so I could smell his belly. But he would get nervous if I touched him too much and he got angry the one time I tried to take my pants down so he could see. I felt guilty then, and angry at him. One day when we were out in the country all alone, I pretended to be afraid and ran away from him. I walked around in the heat under the pine trees, imagining a secret installation built under the ground and the mutated, grotesque creatures who lived there. I lay down and looked up blindly into the sunlight. I began to play with myself, rubbing against the pine cones scattered around. A smoky dust came off the dried cones when I rubbed them together, a bitter dust that hung in the slanting sunlight and made me squint. I pushed some of the pine cones down in my pedal pushers before I heard my uncle coming, and quickly sat up.

Uncle Earle didn't say anything. He just sat down beside me and offered me some warm Coke. I could taste the whiskey in it. He told me I was going to be a beautiful woman. I was gonna drive men wild. He rubbed my neck and shoulders and breasts and told me he would never hurt me. Then he got me to roll over and lay down on my belly. His long body came down on top of me, smelling the cigarette smoke and hair grease. My chin was pressed into the pine needles and dirt. His chest was heavy on the back of my neck. I could feel his cock against my ass, steadily rocking against me. Every time he came down the pine cones in my pants ground into me. They were rough and scratchy but felt good to me. I began to rock with him, squirming to push the pine cones around. I got so excited that he must have gotten scared. When he came, he jumped up and ran back toward the car. I ignored him and reached into my pants to shove the pine cones farther down until they were pushing at my labia. I told myself I was going to shove them up inside me, with the dirt and the grass. I came so hard I peed myself.

It took me a long time to get up the nerve to go back to the car. I wanted to tell my uncle that I had been dreaming about him for years, that I had wanted him to do more than what he had done. But I was afraid to say anything. Uncle Earle didn't say anything either. He poured his little bottle of whiskey out the window onto the dry ground. His face looked shadowy and scared, with the shock of his hair hanging limp over his eyes. He never took me out driving again, and his eyes would slide away from me when I watched him across my mama's dinner table. When I came up behind him on the porch and hooked my fingers in his belt, he jerked my hands out roughly and pulled away from me.

"Ain't gonna touch you," he muttered.

I didn't really know if I wanted him to, but I think I did.

Masturbation for me was a mystery, private and terrible, desperate and glorious. Knowing that my sister did it too helped me to believe that I was not alone. Listening to my Uncle Earle with his teenage lovers made me think sex might be worth the price you had to pay for it. Listening to my parents fucking in the night convinced me that it was an inevitable sin. Listening to my aunts' jokes about men and their ways taught me that sex was also a subject of great humor and bitter enjoyment. But still, I believed that what I did was somehow different from anything anyone else had ever done. Maybe it was because Daddy Glen was fucking me. Maybe it was because on some level I could make myself forget that was happening and go on as if life were normal, as if we were just like everyone else.

When I thought about how different I was, it seemed to me that my difference lay in the things I thought that no one else imagined. The things I dreamed of doing with my life, the stories I made up for myself were clearly something I had to keep secret and protect. In my stories, women did things that I knew they were not supposed to do. They carried knives and rode motorcycles and spat in the faces of those that dared to touch them. I played an incredibly complicated game with every book I read, every movie or

TV show I saw; I turned it over in my mind. The heros and active characters became female while the men receded to a vague blur, not really interesting at all. The stories I made up, in which I was captured and tortured to save my girl-friends—the ones I used so successfully to bring myself to orgasm—they were only the smallest piece of what was scarey and dangerous about me.

Finally, I told. One night late while she was babysitting us, I told Cousin Temple that Daddy Glen had "done things" to me. She climbed out of the bed and ran down the hall. When she came back she had a little comic book with cartoon drawings of men lying on top of women, pushing their dicks between the women's legs. "Did he do that?" she asked me. Temple's eyes were pale, pale blue, burning. "No," I whispered. "He does it with me standing up."

Early the next morning my uncles all stomped in the back door, their faces flat, red, and dangerous. Temple had told the whole damn world. My uncles took Daddy Glen away and beat him up, the same way they had when I was six and he had whipped me so badly that Aunt Raylene had seen the marks. Mama moved us out to a motel. But after a few weeks, Daddy Glen came over to the motel and cried in Mama's arms until she forgave him. I understood that we had to go back to live with him. I understood that Mama loved him. We went home on a Sunday afternoon and he had a big basket of take-out chicken waiting for dinner. I went for a long walk and kept making up stories for myself, talking out all the roles as I walked for hours. When I went home, Mama had gone to bed exhausted. Daddy Glen was sitting at the kitchen table, staring out the screen, his hands loose on the oilcloth, cigarettes spilling out of a saucer. His blue-black eyes were mirrors in his pale face. I say myself in his pupils, my own face brown and empty, my own eyes shining like wet glass, reflecting nothing.

I invented a series of new tests and rituals for myself. I put things in my pants and made rules for how long I had to keep them there—pine cones, rocks, a letter opener I stole from the library whose handle I gripped with my buttocks, little ceramic figures from my aunt's dresser. I added details to my fantasy world, pretending I was required to carry messages tucked in locked containers that the enemies would try to steal from me. I experimented with actually pushing things up inside me. My test tubes were long lost. I graduated to screwdriver handles, my mama's potato masher, various vegetables and most of the tools in my stepfather's toolcase.

My uncle had left his cane. It was blond wood with a knobby top about the size of a closed fist. I discovered that if I put it between my legs it was just about a half inch higher than my cunt. I tied a clean washcloth over the head of it and used masking tape and rope to fasten it between my legs. I walked back and forth with it riding high up against my clit, stumbling painfully. I made myself promise that I would walk back and forth across the room ten times before I could stop. Even if I should come, I promised, I would not let myself stop. When I actually did come and could not finish the required laps, I made a vow that I would have to do it all over again, and double the number of times I would have to cross the room. Doubled again and again, no matter how I sweated and limped, riding that cane like a wooden horse on a merry-go-round, I never caught up, never met my vow. Expiation was impossible. Sin was endless.

I was thirteen. Uncle Earle had moved to Florida. I was rummaging through the house, restless, irritable, looking for something new. In my sister's room, I started opening drawers, pulling out boxes, looking through her things. In Reese's bottom drawer there was a box with a cord tied around it in a complicated series of knots. Slowly I picked it apart, keeping the pattern of the knots in mind so I could tie it back together the way it had been. The process took a long time and calmed me down. When I had it completely untied, I sat still for a moment with the box in my lap. I could hear a lawn mower in the distance, a radio, and someone yelling. I opened the box. Silk panties, an old pair of my mama's. I lifted them carefully. Underneath was one of Daddy Glen's handkerchiefs, loosely wrapping a long smooth ivory handle that looked as if it had once been fixed to a mirror. It fit my hand solidly and felt almost soft, so cool and yellowed as if it had absorbed years of sweet oil. I lifted it to my mouth wanting to run my tongue over it, but the smell stopped me. I knew that smell. It was my smell, girl smell, sex smell, heady yeast and piss smell. I breathed deeply and grinned, put that handle in my mouth.

"Little sister." I giggled. "Little sister . . ." I sucked the handle into my mouth, pushed my fingers down in my jeans for a little of the juice from between my legs. Carefully I rubbed it into the ivory before wrapping it back up and tying the knots all over again. "Little sister." I kept laughing, almost singing. "Little sister, just like me!"

It was true then. All of us hid the same thing behind our eyes. I went and got my chain, locked it around my hips, took my uncle's knobby-headed cane and ran out into the thick summer heat. My stepfather was unloading boxes out of Mama's gray Chevy. My Uncle Wade was helping him.

"Come on over here," they yelled at me.

I planted that cane in the damp grass in front of me, and stood rock still, rock steady, memory rolling up like an endless, powerful story. Fire behind my eyes, light and shine, chain in the dark, whiskey taste beneath the Coke, my little sister's face through the back window of the car, Daddy Glen's forearms ridged in muscle, my uncle's eyes narrowed under thick brows—I put my head back and smiled. The chain on my hips moved under my jeans. I was locked away and safe. What I really was could not be touched. What I really wanted was not yet imagined. I looked down at my hands on my uncle's cane, remembering the fear and excitement in his eyes. Somewhere far away a child was screaming, but right then, it was not me.

WANDA COLEMAN

POEMS

why i don't write love poems for you

for Austin

"evahbody wanna do da horizontal bop"

what would i say in them?
that i keep making typos at work becuz i can't stop
thinkin' about you

that i'm coming down with a cold becuz
i've spent too much time sleepin' in the buff
after we've made love

that i'm broke out in a rash because all this sudden
attention from you racks my nerves

what do i say?

i don't write many of 'em
that word has been terribly abused
i don't want to contribute

plus i've been in love so many times with terrible results
i'm beginning to question my judgment

what kind of monster are you?

"beware—anything cums between open legs"
a friend once said

i'm on society's bottom
all things shift down here sooner or later

i know the expertise with which Amerikkka destroys my
    kind
black male & female alike. to seek a mate
outside my people-culture, one of the alternatives to

    abstention & loneliness
    lesbianism
    the church
    asexuality
    intimacy with pets
    opium
    suicide

    or staying wed to my
    present monster

and you. all over me. so fast so total
have you lost your mind? do you know what price will be
extrakkked from you for taking on a black woman
& her three children???

plus you're unemployed

and i don't want the world in my biz-in-ness
lessin' i allow it in
i don't want to be your poem stuff
cuz you's a poet too

love between us seems impossible
but here it is

for now

the black princess has a love jones
for a jewish frog with warts
and don't care

even if

worse come worse

he's some kind of monster in disguise
may eat her up as a midnight snack
or
she contracts warts, becomes covered with them &
all her kisses
can't transform him into a prince

even if

it fails and months from now
she's penning pain messages & making juju
to ward off this possession

of me by you

black madonna

screaming legions/her children chase her down Shame
Street. they stone her lover into flight. they violate all
sanctuaries. there is no place for her to hide. fouled/her
breath is foul, her hole is foul, her soot skin ashed with
filth—pustules and granulating sores. biblically speaking,
she writhes in Manifest Pain/forsaken. plagued. the
screaming legions of her children tear at her breasts and
partake of her flesh. they slit her consciousness that she
may never sleep. she of the Night of Nights. she
conceived without vaginal birth/without woman. unclean.
she—the victim of victims.

father, the crucifixion did not take

what i know of my man

how his head turns when desire enters his mind
how he smells me how my smell arouses
how he absorbs my
breasts legs buttocks how my feet, hands and nails
evoke touching how the color and textures of my skin
agitate how in black lace i stir his saint, white
his beast, red the john, blue the romantic
how his eyes experience and transmit entry imagined
how his ears taste my hot breath and listen acutely
for expressed fantasies how his nose opens how
his too moist mouth broods over my nipples
how his dickhead tears in worship how he sometimes
pauses to savor my anticipation how his
adventuresome tongue explores and excites my rapture
how his blood rushes how our bodies glow together how
friction exacerbates his final exquisite suffusion

baby baby

death 213

this time only one body on the divan

rhythm mortis/soul creep/holed out
this time no limbs askew
(she believes in
tidy endings)

one electric eyeball winks dingy melodrama
overhead—a blues beacon
sweetly radiant heavenward. this time

the silent stereo. a bass monotone pulses up from the
apartment below
penetrates the floor

> woman causes fizzle in suicide attempt
> turns on the gas then empties
> her mind

this time beyond novelty
this time beyond television—this time

no bruises. no sigh/signs of solipsistic violence
mere limp prick resignation and terminal relief
(she loves him she always
    loves him always)
no blood pools. no semen spills
no rape no murder no needle

this time there's no chance of schematic mishap/discovery
by friends (nobody
evah drops by 'ceptin' strays sniffin' pussy)

nuthin'

but cold lifeworn flesh the rugless bare waxed floor
the obscene intrusive electric eyeball

this time
it is painful/slow
laying stares on the ceiling/rampant thoughts
seeking bone-soaking rest and fetal sleep
the simplicity of carbon monoxide
and headlines

> the pathologist will note a last meal of
> bile and Sartre

this time no tears no rush no sting no thrill of expectation
no finger pops no do wops
no so longs and no you-done-me-wrongs

and this time, no savior

MANUEL RAMOS OTERO

THE EXEMPLARY LIFE OF THE SLAVE AND THE MASTER

DO IT TO BE the way I tell you to or don't do it all. spit in my face. dripping dripping the saliva dripping dripping all the way from your lowered eyes to the end of your rough chin spittle hangs like jungle vines. spit while your hand is clenched. spit the way I tell you to or don't spit on me at all. on his eyes so he can't see. he rubs the slimy saliva with his sticky hands. from his throat the spit that crashes down on my face. his fingers displacing space on my face. do it harder or don't do it all. rigid hands like hard pumice redden the deserted surface of the face. the gummy spit on the black hairs of the mustache that covers the mouth and the saliva in his mouth mix together. he contracts his lips. I spit on the photographs glued to your eyes. I break your face from side to side on the pillow. do it the way I tell you to do it. harder, more. the back the ass the face squashed by the hands trampled by the master's stinking feet. and I your slave. If the blinds had been open on that hot noon of the city the smells of carburetors and chimneys would have reached us, there would have been sunlight streaked by the rose-colored blinds and this would not have had any importance.

When he walks. With his jeans worn at his knees on the hips that form two moons on his cheeks and a scorpion on the curve of his dick. But when he walks. The left thigh which is where the above-mentioned dick rests takes a step forward and moves like a pendulum, rubbing the jeans, between the flesh not so tanned by the sun of course but covered by fuzz and the worn-out denim of the jeans. When he walks. His balls with their delirium over the bridge of the thighs move indecisively from side to side but prefer to spill over the right thigh.

and I his slave I've said. piss on my life or don't piss on me. piss on the violet interstice of my solitary cheeks. piss on my veins like channels of all the islands constructed on water. piss on my islands of flesh made purple by the suctioned blow of the mouth. the master pisses on the white stone that I am. golden torrents run whirling down on the ends of the slave's body. piss on me the way that I tell you to or don't piss on me at all. hot. sun of water. hot sun of water am I. liquid sunflowers. burning petals of wet light. the master urinates. his sleeping hose unwinds. he shoots jets of solitude. I used to fuck with Chopin or I wouldn't fuck at all. fuck like Chopin or don't fuck me at all. From the bed only the record player can be seen but the record (the "Military Polonaise," Opus 40, No. 1) can't be seen and since the closed blinds don't allow the other to be seen (the edge of the island, the docks, the jail where the *Rhymes and Legends* of Gustavo Adolfo Becquer are read, the indigo blue policemen fucking in the back alleys and the number-one macho with his forty inches of torture) and I can't even see myself reading my novel.

He smells like a sweaty dick at night. He smells like an asshole observed but not touched. He leans against the perpendicularly perfect edge of a building. But when he leans. It must be because the left leg angles and the foot (I didn't mention it before, sin of omission, but he's wearing white tennis sneakers worn down from so much walking around here hoping that his slave walks by, that he looks at the dirty and torn canvas sneakers and that he is enthralled with the stench of his feet). He smells of death. The street where he is. Christopher Street. Or. The alley of the chapel where the master mortifies himself. His thing is dead but if it wasn't.

put your whole fist inside me or don't put it in at all. finger by finger. first put in your big finger. he feels the carnivorous walls. wild orchids hanging on the walls. put your whole fist inside me. that's what I said. but he didn't hear me because he put in the thumb knife edge threat of murder illuminated by the moon. put your whole fist inside me. the index finger slid in like a candle and it bent the way rainbows do. finger by finger he exited. the master smeared his hand with saliva. hydra of green spit. he enters. but he doesn't exit. saliva lubricant. put your fist in me. he was up to the first knuckles. he was forcing the joints. we were shouting almost always. we were shouting because we were fucking. we were shouting because we weren't fucking. putting in his fist. whole. anus poppy in live flesh. I live the flesh of my flourishing asshole. the fingers poking the spilled pool of the magical mucous membrane. put your whole fist inside me. the palm of your hand. the lines on your hand. long life. fortune. the wandering fist of the gypsies. the hungry shufflings of fate. the master read the slave's fortune when he put his hand in. he opens his hand. he was up to the wrist and the entire fist. the whole fist. the. fist. the. If not, we wouldn't have come up against nothingness, the ceiling fan would have stopped, the images would have sputtered out and for what purpose would we have smelled life? for that very reason.

The bed moved. It moved from side to side. From side to side on top of the bed. Under the sheets it moved. Under the sheets of cum it moved. It stopped on him as if there were a snake under the sheets. It stopped on him. Like a watch.

spurt by spurt the master is coming on his slave. spurt. by. spurt. in his mouth form white pools of marble honey. come in my mouth or don't come at all. he shoots his cum over my sleeping tongue. I cry for the master's cum. spurt by spurt the cum. bubbles of boiled cum from a billy goat. milking the master. a flood of cream up to my edges. it rolls. it moves like a crab in the throat. spurt by spurt it comes down. swallowing it. the tongue awakens. my tongue moves over his skin. moves head to foot. head. to. foot. the neck and the tendons in the neck. the shoulders and the muscles of the shoulders. arms that embrace and the tongue on that embrace. on the chest. entwined in the down of the master's body. my tongue inside. agitating the soft skin. the knees. behind. the downy buns. the master's heel. the ankles. and finally the fingers in my mouth. suck on me the way I tell you to or don't suck on me at all. suck on my body face up. suck on my body face down. suck on my damp asshole. swampy. plunge your pointed tongue into the abyss that I am. I am the master's slave. I am the slave's master. The paintbrushes of our dicks are painting us a round prison cell. enters. and. exits. the tongue. sucking on my anxieties about the nothing that I am. If the telephone hadn't rung, I had to put down the novel (long distance), over there the snake under the sheets and between them both the rim of the asshole of the bottle that permits the slave to protect the dream or the master to dream of his slave (it seems as if he has died), but he wasn't listening to the voice on the telephone (they found the body in the sugarcane field where they burned Correa Cotto), the master didn't even awaken with the noise (how many pools of cum did they find inside him?) (they shot the pistol in his deepest throat), I closed the novel and the master opened his eyes (later they broke a Coke bottle in his asshole), the master's hand on his sweaty dick had to move I suppose (later they cut off his dick with a barber's razor and shoved it in his mouth so that he could continue sucking in the afterlife), the odorous leather belt for punishment the whip with metal points the immobile ropes the knife sharpened on stone flesh and the Smith Wesson .32, he had to jerk off hanging from the bars—because I wasn't sitting on him but his cream reached as far as the telephone after having inundated the room and the rose-colored Venetian blinds, the record of the "Military Polonaise" and the record player, the ceiling fan and the police siren, the uniforms of indigo blue, the wooden clubs, the open eyes of the cadaver, the novel *(Exemplary Life of the Slave and the Master)* and nothingness, besides.

TRANSLATED BY GREGORY KOLOVAKOS

LYNNE TILLMAN

DIARY OF A MASOCHIST

REMEMBER WHEN YOU PISSED on me in San Francisco? You waited at the bottom of the stairs; it was dark. I came down the stairs and you crouched there, leaped on me, hit me, tried to stick it in me. C. was upstairs. You pissed on me, I turned over and tried to absorb the piss. C. had been scared you'd destroy her work, ruin her films. Don't worry, I said defending you, he wouldn't do that.

In Phoenix you said I was Kissinger because I couldn't explain a line in H.'s story. "I was eight when I had my first affair." You told me you tried to put your hand on your aunt's cunt when you were five. I didn't call you Tricky Dick for that. Kept me up all night long in a Phoenix motel room, calling me Nixon, all night long, TV on, your eyes holes in your head. I made phone calls my invisible thread for sanity.

Back at the beginning—but there's no way to compare beginnings and middles and ends—in Amsterdam you put your cock in my hand and said my cock is yours. You had been my friend for three years. You held me all the way to NYC, and our first night fucking, worried that my sister

201

would hear us. I thought that was strange, but already I was gone and thought if you were concerned, probably you were just more sensitive.

In Buffalo you got the flu. Your hands turned red, you cried and wanted to go back to Holland. I nursed you; in the morning you told me my breath stank—I was eating less and less.

I dream two men are watching us as we lay in bed. I go up to them (they are very tall, I am barefoot) and demand that they stop. I tell you my dream and you say they were in the room and you saw them too.

You warn me against S. in Pittsburgh. I dream about your wife and how I'll be isolated again in Amsterdam. I run the bath in the dream and it overflows. I swim in its pool to turn off the faucets and my mother is angry with me for making love with "a married man."

We are not making love. That's what you decreed in West Lafayette, Indiana. There we are at Purdue University, showing films to cheerleaders, and in the Purdue Guest House, you tell me you don't want to make love with me because it deteriorates our relationship. We show the films, eat Chinese food, you can't understand why I'm upset.

I sleep alone but every night you get into bed with me, then leave again. In the morning you beckon me to you and kiss me. The phone rings. You say I'm glad because we were being drawn in again. I want to go, you can do the trip alone I say. You say you'd blame me and so would everyone else. Next day you'd act ok, the day after, it's murder again.

We get to Minneapolis. A Hyatt Hotel. I write in my diary that I can't resist my desire for your tongue on my cunt. As I undress in the hotel, thinking about you and sex, I look out the window and notice a man on the sidewalk, beating off, watching me.

We change hotels. You say you've been keeping yourself from me frantically. You don't want to come, don't know what to do with the feeling. You want me to come—you start me, you stop me. You piss on the floor in your sleep.

I tell you in the morning and say I'm not angry. Your wife would've been, you say.

You wake me in the middle of the night and stand at the foot of the bed and say, I feel I am eating myself up.

You are eating me and biting me so hard my skin turns blue and red. You bite me on the cunt and I ask you to stop. You say it hurts you more than it does me. I look at my shoulders after one of our sessions and think, the stain of you lasts so long.

The bus ride to Omaha with Chicago Blacks. One calls himself a professional fucker and puts his hand on my thigh. We change buses in Omaha, get a bus all to ourselves. I'm ready to fuck you in the toilet, going Greyhound. You say your wife would be shocked. We don't.

Get to Cheyenne. I buy boys' cowboy boots. We play pool and some man promises me a silver dollar. A whore tells me there are two ladies rooms, a nice one and a nasty one. She asks Which do you want? We both laugh, we're in the shit together.

You say you don't like my body, but you like making love with me because I'm more skilled, more exciting than your wife. I dream a man who is crippled tries to lure me to his floor #9, and I want to get out at #4. Somehow I'm forced to glide past him.

In Boulder we meet B., the filmmaker. You tell him he's afraid to die. B. says he made his wife choose making art or marrying him. B. kisses me on the forehead. Feels like the seal of approval and the kiss of death. I dream four babies are placed in a plastic box as a work of art.

In Boulder we come and fight. Our host hates me, thinks I persecute you, until the last night when he sees. He apologizes to me and I defend you. I understand you, I say to our host.

On our way to San Francisco. Fifteen hours to Salt Lake City, where we register as man and wife. You tell me again never to have any expectations, any needs. We're in the Palace Motel.

On to Reno. I read "but also all journeys have secret destinations of which the traveler is unaware." You write a letter to your wife. I ask why you're so much clearer now about the situation with your wife. You say because you are with me now. You say you're not turned on by me.

San Francisco. C.'s house. I dream about prostitutes and in the dream you say it's better to be a prostitute and not married. C. and I are not married. You hate C. and try to turn me against her. You tell me she's in love with me and can't love me. C. tries to put up with you. You go mad; she screams at you but you're too gone and I'm scared, everything's collapsing. We see W.'s films and you tell him one side of the screen is brighter than the other. It's such a crazy thing to say, I wonder if you're right. This is the night you pissed on me. In the morning you tell me you knew what you were doing. C. tries to help me and says you're going crazy. I can't admit it to myself. She takes me to the bus and we go to Portland.

We make love in Portland. Over Chinese food you talk about your wife, your kids. We are interviewed about film for a radio program. You tell me you were C.'s victim. The next morning I tell you how my father hurt me and you say you'll never betray me.

There's money just for one of us to do the show in NYC, to fly there and back, and besides, you're scared to death of flying. The morning I'm to go, I awaken in your arms and we begin to make love. Your cock was hard on my ass. You enter me from the back, the front, then pull out. Let's have some tea instead, you say. I cry and you accuse me of trying to make you feel guilty.

I do the show like a champ. Two days in NYC alone. Am down 15 pounds and I can't sleep or stop talking. I show G. and S. 8mm films of our trip. The hotels, the bath water, you lying asleep in bed, views out windows to streets, an American flag, endless miles of America from a bus window, C., desert, mountains, bathrooms, lamps, snow, room after room.

Your wife phones me from Holland. I fly to Vancouver; you meet me and do not look at me. I ask you to return to your wife. I try to ignore you. We argue in front of our host again. Our host asks us to stop. We stop and you ask me what I want to drink. Surprise me, I suggest, smiling. You say you don't think you can.

There is a party. Everyone seems so normal. I cower and when I dance see you watching me. You say only your wife can dance well. You say I should seduce my partner. You watch everything. We leave the party and in a French restaurant become friends again, get high together, go back to the party and fall asleep in the midst of it. Your cock is again hard at my back and I don't move. I feel nothing. You ask if I'm comfortable and I lie, Yes—and you? You say it's none of my business.

The Dutch are supposed to be good at business. You put my hand on your hard cock and thank me for the birthday present I gave you, a fish, a jade fish. It is the end of March. We're tourists in Vancouver and taken places. Sadomasochism feels out of place in this young dusty town, only seventy-five years old. Drunk Indians fall out saloon doors into our path as we walk at night. Our hostess is pregnant.

I write to J., who should have been on this trip—"each day a dream flies out the window." You read the card and question me three times. I refuse to explain. I know you will take your revenge when I'm weaker.

On the bus again, going to Los Angeles, where I've never wanted to go, you start the day by asking me why are you more hysterical? You're afraid I'm cracking up because I use my hands and gesture more. I ask that you leave me alone. You imitate my movements.

Medford, Oregon, another fight. This time you say I'm claiming you by writing in my diary. The letters I once wrote you are fraying in your pocket as we eat dinner and you insist I stop writing. I keep notes of our film shows. You tell me you don't need notes, that you'll remember. After dinner I vomit; an enormous shrimp salad, the portions are so big in America. A friendly waitress with a ribbon in her hair served us drinks while we fought.

Before we board the bus to L.A., you say, Let's be friends.

You throw your arm around me and I think about Amsterdam, before all of this, and can't believe that fucking can breed such bad results.

C. meets me at the San Francisco station on our rest stop. I am still defending you. C. is still my friend. F. comes with her to say goodbye. This time, as I board the bus for L.A., I feel I am voluntarily committing myself to a concentration camp.

The first night in L.A. at the Hotel Cecil, a death camp for the poor who live in the strip outside the wealthy. We get a room with a bath and no stopper. A room with numbers marked in black ink along the edge of the door frame. Cigarette holes in the carpet and a TV chained to the ceiling. Here you try to fuck me again and can't. It hurts you. You say we don't fit. I never know if you mean physically or not and you won't tell me. We fall asleep watching TV: a live wedding, a prayer drama with Raymond Burr and a policeman telling us about the latest criminals.

The next day we are picked up and taken away to the hills, to E.'s house, to art, to lizards in the backyard. I feel privileged, just out of the death camp, then adjust quickly. The Governor lives down the road from E.'s house and two secret service men are always there. We sleep together in her house; I always try to sleep alone, you always follow me. Sunday night your cock is all bloody. You refuse to see a doctor. I phone B. and S. in Amsterdam and see blood on the phone booth wall. An uncircumcised cock sometimes has that problem which is nameless in our litany. I have no one to get information from and am shy about asking W., a Dutchman in L.A., to explain why your cock is bloody. I taste blood in my mouth.

More arguments with filmmakers about film. The East Coast vs. the West Coast. We play chess, you make me play. I write long letters that I can't send; you send yours to your wife. I wonder what E. thinks, we're up all night. I try to stop you from biting me on the cunt. Neither of us wants to have orgasms now; and even with a bloody cock, you still try to fuck me. You tell me over and over how much you love me. You tell me you hate me because I lack passion. You tell me my pain hurts you more.

Finally we leave L.A. and are heading toward Texas to stay with my other sister, the one I haven't seen in years. I am nearly able to consider leaving you in Phoenix, the morning after you called me Nixon and Kissinger. Instead I try to exact promises of good behavior. The motel we're in is on Van Buren Drive. I take a Valium and sleep on the floor. You put your hand on my cunt and I push it away. You tell me you love me, I'm a fascist and you hate me.

Get to El Paso, midway to my sister's place; we stay at the Hotel McCoy. I fall asleep but you keep waking me during the night. The next day, passing Fort Stockton, a notice at a gas station reads Dean and the Fat Boys—Dance Tonight. I write it down to enjoy later.

My sister and her boyfriend meet us at the bus station. They've come from a party and are in a good mood. We have a beer with them and are taken to her home. You and I sleep together again.

Back with a family, my niece and nephew, my sister, a cat and a dog. I sleep in my niece's room. You get the guest room with the TV, so that you can smoke and drink all night. The third night you drink a quart of vodka and tell my sister you're not attracted to me. You tell her she's your type. My sister walks out. Your wife and her sisters had the same lovers, at the same time. I talk to you some more, then give up. Wake my sister and cry. She thinks I'm crazy and you're drunk and mean.

I sleepwalk through the next day. You ask me if I want to talk about last night and I say no. I mean it. I have no choice. I have nothing to say. Later that night you talk to me about your wife, the film co-op. I listen and say things, then go to sleep in my niece's room. I avoid you.

The dog gets hit by a car. I see her go under the wheels. It's a disaster the whole family can share. The dog survives.

I don't want to leave my sister's house. Back on the bus with you, I know I don't stand a chance. Fifty-six hours to NYC. We're almost broke. Just one motel more. We stop in

LYNNE TILLMAN

Atlanta. Pizza in the Underground. I push you away two times when you get into my bed drunk. The third time I let you enter me. The last time.

We get to NYC and stay at N.'s. I sleep near the door, on the floor, You get the couch. We have dinner at my sister's, where we began our trip, and you pick a fight with us about Joan Little's defense. You talk about it for two days. N. gets upset watching us. One morning I phone KLM and make a reservation for you that night. You agree to go and we buy gifts for your family. I phone your wife and let her know you're coming. N. takes us to the airport and after you're out of sight, I start laughing with her. Louder and louder. Can't cry. Now that you're out of my life, there's a weird hole as big as the La Brea Tarpits we saw together. I feel like one of those animals stuck there.

Days pass and I fly to Florida to see my parents. There's a message waiting from you: it says you've arrived safely. I get a bad sunburn and my parents buy me clothes. I fly back to NYC with my mother's cousin who says my mother was always too much in love with my father. I have to go back to Holland and I'm scared to death. I imagine you apologizing to me and things going back to normal. I see a therapist who says I don't have to let you know when I'm arriving.

I land in Amsterdam and J. meets me. The first time I see you we meet with M. You're cruel and M. is shocked. He says he thought you'd never treat me like that. You phone me and call me Toots, say you don't understand what's wrong.

The last time I set eyes on you we do some film business together. I'm trying to get out clean. You drive me to S. and B.'s and tell me you love me and that I don't understand. I look at you and ring my friends' doorbell and go inside.

One year later, I'm in NYC and you write me that you nearly killed yourself in a car crash and now you're even more beautiful. I don't believe you.

TERENCE SELLERS

IS THERE LIFE
AFTER SADOMASOCHISM?

THE LATE AFTERNOON SUNLIGHT cast its frail rays over the dusty furniture. Two aging jades stirred vaguely amidst the velvet—Byron, the brilliant author whose infamous subject matter had rendered him notorious and adored, and Amanda, the St. Theresa of Bernini come back as sculptress. Both were Ecstatics, of the Ecstatic School of Thought— that fin-de-siècle tendency to seek the extreme in all things—but most particularly, extremes of Beauty.

Refugees they were, from the darkly glittering byways of lower Manhattan. Their seclusion now in the deep styx of New Mexico had enraged some, and relieved many . . . but no matter what the herd lowed, the desert was there to console them.

If Ruskin's gentle analysis of the desert lands being most conducive to the production of religious art were true, it might be said that these two were in serious difficulty. What art of religious power could come from two hearts blackened by pain? From two minds still crawling through the dry streambeds of despair? We shall see. . . .

Desert and labyrinth—labyrinth and desert. The labyrinth—Manhattan.

Their plunder of the *demi-monde new-yorkais Sadomasochiste*[1] circa 1970–1988 had left them both prostrate—romantically. Romantically prostrate? But this is no affection. To have seen, to know to ground zero—how much horror humanity is capable of, how much pain and cruelty exists within mankind, beneath the whitened veneer of normality—who could look at that and remain the same?

Once you have seen inside the body like that . . . seen the poor frail bravery of the living animal, naked, helpless and exposed . . . once you have been inside the body like that, and felt your strength ebbing, and seen the flesh melting, and known how easy it is to die . . . once you have known your own violence, and stopped yourself just inches from crushing, seen the writhing pleasure of the thing before it self-destructs, and known how easy it is to kill . . . you know there is no safe place inside the body . . . cozy and well packed in the happy flesh as you think. Those who choose to look at this do not return from hell unscathed. Cocktails came early in the afternoon, and the birds all twittered on cue.

There was something of the great *Apatheia,* those ultimate philosophers, about Byron in particular. Was that the tearful glaze of nostalgia, or were they only drunk?

"What next?" he sighed. "Why don't we drive the car off Devil's Throne?" she suggested again. "I've told you— he won't let us die yet." "But is there life—after Sadomasochism?" "I've told you. No," he affirmed, and refilled his glass. "How are we then to nourish our bright lives?" she quoted. "No longer with the 'baser prey' . . . but how can I sublimate another day?"

There in their private waiting room to hell they watched the clock go around again. These once proud encyclopedists of desire now listened as the instruments of pleasure ran down, coughing and shuffling off in old carpet slippers. Their pulses beat faintly on the growing void around them. Byron counted over his dead lovers, as Amanda muttered, "Nostalgie de la Boue-Boue."[2] Perhaps a new sensibility would emerge; perhaps not. Sex was still the only thing that concerned them, and as artists they were bound to keep their powers free from any bondage. Libido as life, the lotus of creation, must flow, and no matter where, must break through all restraints of deadly convention.

Exhaustion was upon them . . . and now there was a fatality, a severe physical horror attached to the act of sex. The blood was toxic, the semen was toxic, the body of the lover was toxic. Behind all desire lurked disfigurement; behind the wretched flesh stood the doctors, and sex came again into the hands of the authorities, who had, perhaps, in their own laboratories, by design or accident, spawned the parasite growth—the virus.

Sex was more of a crime than ever; sex was now an act of murder. Was there no choice but dignified abstinence? Crabbily they assumed celibacy . . . and as in Victoria's time, one hundred years ago, it must be that to tremble on the edge of consummation must become more thrilling than consummation.

Exhaling a thin stream of blue, she mused, "I have often wondered why, in the city, there is such a strength to all our so-called illicit sexualities. Out here in the deep styx folks are not so *out*." "In the city, you can be 'filthy and anonymous,'" he quoted, "We're not anonymous here. Anonymity is necessary for hot sex. With total strangers, you can be the hungry body. Raw and Unashamed. Oh the baths . . . the bars . . . I'll never say that time was not beautiful. You could do anything, you could be anything, with anyone. The imagination cannot bring to me the wonder, the strange miracle, nor the pleasure I could gather from one handsome and improper stranger." A tear glimmered in the white of his eye—or was he only drunk.

He went on, coaxing himself to the vision, "It was fantastic. No one knew you . . . bodies in the darkness . . . pleasure a swift-flowing, nourishing constant ecstacy no coming generation will even conceive. I can't stand it!" he

shrieked. "It's over—those days will never come again!"
" 'The Art of our Necessities is strange, and can make vile
things precious.' All our precious instruments . . . the Vile
. . . the Mysterious . . . the Cruel . . . the Holy . . . all required for our creation. So the pleasure is over now. There
are other excitements." "Such as?" "The exaltations of
deprivation." "Horrendous. Spare me. *My* experiment is
over." "Maybe."

"So here we are, exiled in the provinces, where we can't
do any more damage." "Either to ourselves or to others."
"It was either that, or being locked in a cell." "Or strapped
to a hospital bed, subject to their surgical probes." "Feebly
raving under the morphine drip."

"Perhaps we shall evolve, if we stay away from Manhattan. Perhaps we can become . . . less decadent." He
laughed. "As though it's only a *style*? Haven't you been
wearing black since you were twelve? And your five adolescent suicide attempts, demonstrating an early belief in
the uselessness of life? Your polymorphous perversity,
which renders you incapable of marriage, stability, or perhaps even love? Not to mention your extensive research
into every aspect of psychopathy and perversity. All your
morbid predelictions . . . no, darling, you are *marked*. You
are Decadence. But still, you're only a product of our times.
In your forties in the year 2000, I see you as blossoming,
the black flower of the Christian millennium, horribly conscious of every sin that has ever been committed, yet somehow above it all, somehow unscathed. You're healthy, you
see," he said flatly, and with contempt. "You will survive.
But I will not."

She did not protest. The cigarette smoke drifted through
the dense air of the room, caught aslant in the rays of the
setting sun that brought all the dust to life. "We are the
Decadent Ones. We are the Vultures, who shall rid this desert of the dead." He stood and gazed out at the barren landscape. "But how is it . . . that we have ourselves become
talismans of death?"

They stared into the litter of cocktail glasses. "Tomorrow

we should quit drinking,'' said one, and then the other replied, ''What for? Life is meaningless, but so what? It's a little rosy now, isn't it?''

A bit farther down the royal road to nothingness Byron asked her, ''How do you live, without sex?'' ''I don't. . . . I mean, I do have sex.'' ''You do not. Admit it—you hate sex.'' ''No—I hate only those I have to have it with—all the dull groveling . . . the stenches . . .'' ''You are too fixated upon your ideal. Your desire for aesthetic perfection now approaches anaesthetic perfection. Just use their bodies for sex.'' ''Oh, I have.'' She covered her eyes. ''Crying again?'' He looked at her closely. ''Really, don't the old lies die hard.'' ''It's the Christian sickness, still inside me, still craving that *sublime sacrifice,* of the self to something greater than the self.'' ''That in time proves itself to be a snorting hog.'' He concluded her rapture.

''You wouldn't be thinking of . . . falling in love would you?'' He shuddered delicately. She said nothing. ''If you ever fall in love again, I'll have to kill you.'' ''Do you think I could survive . . . another one of those . . . submissions?'' ''You're lying. You're planning to find the True Love.'' ''No. I would come out more dead than alive. To kill me would be redundant.'' ''Enter the Paradox—'All men kill the things they love,' themselves first.'' ''They kill the things they love, along with the things that they hate, and are indifferent to.''

''I wish . . . I could just go. Tomorrow.'' ''Not yet. I haven't got everything down yet.'' ''You must let me see it soon.'' ''No. It's too dangerous. You know what they say happens . . . when you meet your Double.'' ''You die. So show it to me.'' ''No—I haven't got it all down yet.''

The dark paralysis of melancholy settled upon their prone, half-conscious forms. ''We must reopen the schools of Initiation . . . we must revive the ancient mysteries.'' He lay and focused himself intently upon her. Whenever he began to record her, in his fashion, by consciously deciding to write down everything, she became, through some telepathic faculty, an actress. And as she improvised, she waxed

brilliant, and so original that Byron sometimes had a difficult time recalling her erratic and exquisite creations.

"Sex and the worship of god will once again become one
and the same thing." "Meanwhile, you live in a culture
where Tantra is porno." "You don't think the herd is capable of the refinement?" "I think all that must come from
a time more pure, more innocent, before we had so many
variations, so many insane permutations of sex, imbedded
in the collective unconscious. There are so many murderers
in this country. For these people, murder is a form of sex.
And more than ninety percent of these insane murderers
had someone twist, or kill their sexuality at an early age,
usually through some form of Christian hygienic training.
'Sex is dirty . . . wait until you're married . . . be a heterosexual . . . get married . . . spawn . . . what's wrong with
you?' They murder their sex, and their sex does not die. It
merely becomes the same thing as murder." "Is it true—
that they will actually *come* into the pools of blood?" "You
see—you're fascinated. How can we imagine a more innocent time, with the weight of their guilt in our consciousness? Oh pure, more innocent time! It does not exist . . .
except in the minds of the exhausted High Decadence. The
pastoral ideal! A literary product of the last days of Rome."
"The 1960s . . . back to Nature . . ." "Impossible! We do
nature harm by living within her, for we have become so
unnatural we taint her air, we foul her body. We are better
off locked in our cubicles in the air than trampling gleefully
over her face, thinking how holy we're making ourselves.
All we leave behind us is filth and chaos."

"Guess who else died?" "Barry." "No. Not yet. Carol."
"Oh, God!" "Her parents don't want her buried in the fam-
ily plot." "They're afraid their corpses will get infected?"
"I imagine. The priest backed them up." "Hypocrite dirt!
They love the disease. They have destroyed our experiment.
With their science, they have killed our new science. They
will do everything they can to blot out the knowledge we
have unearthed in our *pure indulgence.* We have eaten the

whole apple, worm and all, and it just isn't right that we should live. Thus their pleasure in watching us killed off."

"Sex will harden again into conventional forms. Sex may at last achieve the Christian ideal, and be permitted only in laboratories, at specified times, under direct supervision, for the purposes of procreation only. Good luck with your cult of ecstasy . . . you'll be branded Satanist and hounded to the latest in gallows." "And the last germ of intellect is stamped out." "Probably not." "It's never been easy—always too much persecution." "Live doomed, die hoping." "Doomed—doomed and doomy. O doomy gloomy one!" "Our lives are over."

She agreed, yawned, and partook of an esoteric herbal medicine. "Higher mind?" she inquired, "Yes, please," and he inhaled. Half an hour later, Amanda broke the trance, "But you *are* ridiculous! Our lives are over. What about your imagination? Your huge, ungainly brain that takes you traveling into whatever mind you wish?" "I'm tired of it. All I want to do now is get married to the perfect young boy, settle down in front of the TV set, and drift off downstream in some backwater town." "Be careful, dear, you're waving a loaded gun around. I will have to report you to the Aesthetic Police,[3] on charges of Entropy." "I *want* to be a philistine! I'm tired of Ecstatics. I'm too *ancient* to rebel. To be visionary now is too painful." "Corrupt. I didn't think it was possible that you could become more corrupt." "Corrupt—but not hungry." "Not hungry?" "Not hungry," he repeated with a strain in his voice.

"What if I never wrote again?" he asked her. She cried out in response, and gazing seriously at him, began to weep. She knew at that moment that he was one of the dead. "You must have sex . . . immediately. It's been too long." "I *know* the only way out is through sex. I'm going to start looking. I never have much appreciated sublimation . . . and this may be *the last boy*. . . ." "I wish you luck. Out here in the deep styx they hear 'Manhattan' and flee before the mutant. What viruses might you harbor—in your aura,

man—not to mention what's lurking in your blue and degenerate blood." "I confess. I am a black fiend . . . from
one of the most pungent cesspools of modern syphilization.
I'm a homosexual from Manhattan." "Evil—dark—diseased. Punished by God." "And now ruined. Ruined! I'll
never fuck again. Thank you, God, I've learned my lesson."
"Between the two hells—New York and this radioactive
desert—what's an out-of-work libertine got to look forward
to?"

Amanda shrieked and went pale. "I see it! The prophecy
has come true—it's really happening. THE MAJORITY IS RULING!
Oh God, it's true it's true, the barbarian culture is dominant!" Byron yawned. "I wish they *were* barbarian. Beasts
are fine. It's these modern things—desexed, Lysoled, rub-
berized and *mated*. They rule, now. Breeders! Feeding the
machine, and breeding the feed. . . ."

He took a slow turn around the attic room, not lighting
the lamps as the sun set. "It was the Comte St.-Germain, in
1787, who revived an oracle of Nostradamus, that was
meant to be read every hundred years." He rustled through
the books piled high on the low table, withdrew the small
green volume of Nostradamus, and read:

Whilst princes and kings are captive in prison
Songs, chants and refrains of the slavish mob
Shall in the future be received as divine oracle
By headless idiots deprived of judgment

"St.-Germain warned the royal family to flee from the
mad greed of the rising herd. But the royals were themselves too piglike to budge from their gilded pigsties."
"Louis Seize was a slug." "Glutted. Thus ended one of the
most advanced civilizations we have yet evolved." Byron
and Amanda saw again the white outstretched necks of their
ancestors, upon the dirty chopping block on the Place de
Greve. Felt that swift cut of the blade, severing head from
body, but not spirit from mind. For at least five minutes
their sarcasm failed them.

"You see, we have no choice. We cannot die. We must live, as there are fewer and fewer of us left. I've got to get healthy!" Amanda yawned. "In a more naïve and hopeful time I might have encouraged you. I might have thought there was some intrinsic good in continuing to live. Now I doubt it. Do I care, at all, if the human race is saved from destruction? All our puny arts, all vision, magic, sciences and systems—has any of it really been able to stop the general stupor that is even now coming over the eyes of the huge, ever huger and homogenous masses? And Marie Antoinette thought *she* had it bad. . . ." " 'The man of genius may be insane, but all the sane are idiots.' " "All right." She sighed. "Though I'm feeling a bit too *frail* to pursue my insanity at this very moment."

"What about the acid—is it still fresh?" It had been in the refrigerator for three years.[4] "Only one way to find out."

Forty minutes later it was indeed evident that it had been very fresh. "Eee-whoosh!" sang Amanda. Byron's eye was caught by the passing figure of a young man, going along the lane up the hill behind the house. Twilight lent a melancholy glory to his passage, but Byron could not bear to lose the sight of him. "Passing strange—curioser and curioser—I do feel the need to explore the unknown." And he was gone, in pursuit again of the Golden Ideal, this time manifesting as young, virile and nineteen, who, when he realized he was in the sights of the most notorious of the local derelict aristocracy, began to stroll a little faster.

When he returned, he announced, "Forget Art as Religion. We shall worship boys. These Nature religions . . . your goddesses and what-not—never mind—even you girls will have to worship The Boys." "Please, dear, don't tell me what to do. I will worship no one, not even myself, I cannot live for pleasure, as you can. The point of pleasure is no longer the climax, specifically sexual, but to expand the awareness of the senses outside the body, to treat them as nerves, arraying themselves throughout the entire universe . . . rendering one capable of experiencing exquisite physical pleasure constantly, and from every tiny detail of existence—from sound, color, the scents of the air, the tone of the voice. So we may once again become conscious of Beauty—everywhere . . ." He shuddered. "Who could bear . . . so such . . . feeling?"

Now they emerged from their attic and went out walking into the night. A green half-moon flickered through a thick cloud cover. A few stray, articulate snowflakes fell. They walked up the road to the old country church, whose stained-glass windows had long ago been sold. Plywood boards were nailed in their place, painted over squarely NO TRESPASSING. But the graffiti flowered, with giant cocks, the peace sign, FUCK BUSH, and the inevitable 666 done up in gold and silver. PAGAN ANGELS . . . METAL NYMPH . . . DEATH 101, and VALMONT 1990—BEYOND MY CONTROL." Shotgun barrels stuck out from crooked cut-out slits in the boards. Hippie scavengers had moved on the place, completing the desecration with joy. And from the interior of the church came the sound of the speed freaks drumming . . . drumming on the garbage cans, drumming on their thighbones, beating out their freaky tattoo for the millennium's crazy tailspin. Apocalyptic, man . . . "What *are* they up to tonight? You know they'll keep that up for hours." "Most likely . . . religiously practicing their Satanism . . . having sex all day, and saying their prayers . . ." "Kali, Kali, Dance to Death . . ." "They'll go as they come . . . and come as they go."

The snow flew thicker and began to cover the two entranced figures as they gazed at the renegade church. Suddenly past them flashed the blond figure of the boy, dressed in a sort of silver bunting. Byron gasped. "It's him again, look—he's going in!" And the boy disappeared through a broken pane in the church's basement window. "The basement!" she wondered, as he followed the boy. "Future generations will weep, to hear how he had to have sex in basements." "The catacombs," he reminded her. "But now it's the pagans, hiding from the Christians." "If only they would just throw us to the lions. Instead they bleed us slowly, with fear, with their inhumane morality." "We can reverse it," he assured her. "Construction begins tomorrow on the new Coliseum. We should have finished the job two thousand years ago. We'll stock it with Beasts . . . and laughing Scarlet Women in the velvet-lined boxes." "The Apocalypse is long overdue." "I insist on the pagan rites! I insist on every one of my Perversions! What ever I come upon, I make holy!"

Byron crept up to the broken window and peered into blackness. "He may be . . . the last boy . . ." The sound of someone's excited breathing caught his ear. He swung his legs over the ledge and let himself fall. There was no basement so dark he couldn't find his way around in it. ". . . the last boy . . ."

Midnight sounded in the old bell tower; shadows again spread their dark array. It was the end of the century. Our jades' rather typical *ennui de fin-de-siècle* is but one aspect of the grimmer unease we all shall face in the year 2000. *C'est la fin du millenium*—and worse—as Hell will spring to life on earth, and with some doing, Paradise too . . . and little in between, and certainly, *nothing beyond*. No after-life, only afterhell,[5] as hell follows hell after hell after hell . . . and into the fiery arms of a billion hungry ids shall we watch the old moralities stumble, skid and fall. But so shall we Ecstatic Ones yet remain to sing . . . to sing, and sing on, of the perishing.

NOTES

1. We insist that the word Sadomasochism shall always be capitalized. Aside from the obvious, that the S of Sade shall never be equal to, but always greater than the m of Masoch (though this is no reflection upon the exquisite works of author Leopold von Sacher-Masoch), we must vindicate the honor of the great Marquis Donatien Alphonse François de Sade, 1740–1814. The modern-day Sade family is waging a private war with the Academie Français to have the word "sadist" struck from the dictionary. They feel that the implications of violence and perversity now inherent in the name have cast an unconscionable

slur upon their family honor. We consider this a grave insult to the Marquis. His descendants' inability to appreciate his distinguished achievements is a stain upon the family history, yet another example of modern literary impoverishment. We shall thus carry on the inimitable example of the great Marquis of pre-Revolutionary days, and forever torment these plebeian aristocrats with the religious use of the capital S, that it may be kept ever in the minds of men the name of the genius behind the conception *Sadism* the great author, playwright, natural scientists, rationalist Dionysian, orgiast and humanitarian, the Marquis Donatien de Sade. Throughout three-quarters of his life he suffered from the cruel effects of a *lettre de cachet,* by means of which his relatives kept him locked in prison without trial. It is the least we can do to avenge him, to persecute his persecutors— the hypocrite snobs—his family.

2. This horrendous pun partakes of the French expression *nostalgie de la boue,* used to indicate a longing to return to a more archaic and perhaps purer lifetime, and the American expression "boo-boo," meaning an error. The Ecstatic School is no great believer in mankind ever having been a species somehow more "elevated," or less bestial, than we are now.

3. The Aesthetic Police are a psychic body of regulators charged with punishing those who are bound, by their superior talents, to promulgating the Ethics of Beauty, and who fail to maintain those high standards. Instituted by the Society of Charles in 1972.

4. Acid, or LSD, D-lysergic acid diethylamide tartrate Delysid, was a substance in active use for ecstatic derangement of the senses during the 1960s. It was accidentally developed by the chemists of the CIA as a weapon, to be placed in water supplies to confuse the enemy. It was used successfully by psychotherapists throughout the 1950s in breaking through psychic blocks in psychotic patients. It was made an illegal drug and banned from use in 1970. It was still being manufactured illicitly and taken to induce transcendental states during a "psychedelic renaissance" of the 1980s.

5. *Afterhell* (1990) is the title of a painting by the poet René Ricard.

JANE DELYNN

|||||||||||||||||||||||||||||||||||||||||||||||||||||||||||||||||||||||||||||||||||||

BUTCH

SHE WAS SO UGLY I found her attractive, though of course I didn't want anybody to see me with her. When I left the bar I made her walk several feet behind me, like Chinese women used to do. I told her it was because I didn't want anybody to see me with a woman, but really it was just her—with her crewcut what would people think? This was long before punk had made the androgynous look respectable. Even inside my building I made her walk a flight behind me up the stairs. I was poor then, and lived in a walk-up on the Bowery. And yet I was not unhappy, for I lived entirely for love. Much of the city did then, though it never will again.

I put on a record, took out two beers, turned down the lights, and sat next to her on the couch. I felt relaxed, as I always do with someone less attractive than me, since then it's up to them to initiate sex. I would never have walked over to anybody who looked like her at the bar. And yet as I stared at her pale, soft skin, her short, spiky hair, my pants got wet: amazing. A wave of total peace washed over me and I shut my eyes. The ball game was not in my park.

Whatever happened, happened. I didn't choose it and it was not my fault.

She began to tell me about her life. She had grown up in some small upstate town, the kind of dreary town one might look back at with pleasure but would yearn to escape from at the time. But even in retrospect there was no pleasure for her, because her father had caught her humping her girlfriend on a sleepover date when she was sixteen, and beat her up. A year later he caught them again and threw her out of the house. The girlfriend left her to marry some guy, so she moved to New York, where there were other people like her. It was during one of the lulls in the East Village, and she quickly found a share in a four-room walk-up between First and A. The normal thing for someone like her would have been to become a waitress, but she wasn't attractive enough (though in a few years her short-cropped hair and male suit jackets would be all the rage), so she took this job her roommate found her in a T-shirt factory. They were lovers, though Diane was fat, unattractive, a real cunt. All day long they hammered stuff on T-shirts—shiny little round things that made patterns. It was lower-class, blue-collar, real boring, back in those days before the Sony Walkman. That is, it was boring to Laura to live it, but not for me to listen to it. Everyone I knew was a struggling writer, painter, or some other arty type, so hearing her was refreshing, the way it would have been to spend a day in an African village—or Passaic, New Jersey.

She was supposed to be at work by eight in the morning, but she was a night person and often was late. She'd pick up a coffee and bagel and bring it into the factory. Nobody cared, everybody was in their own world. She had gotten to be friends with some of them, but Diane was jealous of anything that moved. Lately they hadn't been getting on so well; that was why she was with me now, though if Diane found out she would kill her. If Diane had walked into Bonnie and Clyde's and seen us talking, she would have beaten Laura up—and maybe me too. But luckily she hung out at Gianni's, where the serious bulldykes went—the ones who were into cross-dressing. At least that's what they used to call it, before the style seeped into the upper classes and got renamed the "androgynous" look. Most of the time Diane was on the wagon, but when she got drunk she went absolutely crazy. She would push Laura up against the wall, and throw words like "slut," "bitch," "cocksucking cunt" at her. Then she would slap her. Laura was thin, pale, soft, with tiny, birdlike bones, and I could see the pleasure one could get in terrorizing her. Once Diane punched Laura in the face and Laura had a black eye and didn't go to work for almost a week. She made up some story but everyone knew all about it anyway; they always did. Laura would tell Diane that Diane didn't love her, that Diane just wanted to control somebody. But whenever Laura threatened to move out, Diane would threaten to commit suicide, and Laura would end up staying.

"Why did you sleep with her in the first place if she's so horrible?" I asked lazily. But I knew the answer: it was similar to the reason why I was with her tonight, though somebody tall and blond and beautiful was probably lying sleepless now because of me.

"Oh, she's not so bad," said Laura.

The record was over. I thought about getting up and turning it over, but I didn't, then the silence became interesting. I was spacey from marijuana, and I realized how tired I was of being even a little bit in charge. Of anything. It began to seem more disruptive of the mood to put on music than let the silence be—though bits of songs played in my head like a movie track. I realized how rarely it was I was with another person without some kind of music in the background. I wondered if Laura was playing something in her head too. I cleared my throat to speak, but I stopped. The silence grew more and more awkward, but then this very awkwardness should compel her to do something.

As I waited I began imagining Laura and Diane together in bed: a fat bulldyke and a water-pale wisp. The relationship was mysterious, incomprehensible, but what relationship wasn't? The tall blond woman who waited for me—

my "official" girlfriend—who was she and what did it mean when she said she loved me? What could it possibly mean when I told her I loved her? What relationship did the person I thought I was have with the one sitting here on the couch, my pants wet at the idea of having sex with someone I kept telling myself disgusted me. Was it that I secretly liked her, and was embarrassed by my attraction, or was it the disgust itself I liked? Did Laura put up with the fear and beatings because she liked Diane, or was it the fear and beatings that she liked?

"What are you thinking?" she asked.

"Oh, nothing." I waited awhile. "Actually, I was thinking about Diane. Whether she'll punch you out when you go home."

"Does it turn you on to think about that?"

"Maybe."

Her hand slipped inside my blouse and touched my nipples. They were erect. Her hands were cold. I heard myself breathing fast, and the utter shamelessness of this—the person I was breathing fast for—only made me breathe even faster. Had I ever been more turned on? And yet, she was scarcely doing anything—barely circling the tips of my nipple with her finger. Why couldn't she put her mouth there? My body strained toward her as in a bad porno movie. She shoved her hand inside my closed jeans, though because of the tightness of the jeans she couldn't get very far, maybe a little south of my belly button. I twisted to meet her fingers, to move my pubic hairs a little more toward her. I yearned for her to undo my belt, unsnap the snap, push down the zipper, slide her pale white fingers inside my underpants, spread my legs, drive me crazy with her icy touch. But no, she continued this lazy circling of her finger. Gradually the yearning turned to anger, that she was dawdling, torturing me by this slow tease. And yet, oddly, the angrier I got, the more my respect for her grew.

Finally she put her mouth on my nipple, undid my belt, unzipped my jeans, and shoved her hand inside my pants. Even then, she didn't slide her fingers straight in, but kept tweaking my pubic hairs, somehow managing to avoid both my clitoris and vagina. The bottom of my body bucked in a way that was at least partly nonvolitional. Her arm pressed down on my pubic bone and I felt like I couldn't move (though of course I could).

"God, you're wet," she said.

At last she pushed her fingers inside my vagina and crawled on top of me, so that the weight of her body was on the arm that was inside me. Whereas before she had been gentle, now she became incredibly rough, jerking her arm back and forth very quickly. I was so wet it didn't hurt. "I bet I could get my whole hand inside," she said, as if in a question.

"Okay," I whispered. At that moment there was nothing I wouldn't have let her do (though of course there was).

She cupped her fingers, trying to get her hand inside. It was as if I hadn't felt her before, as if my skin had been numb to individual sensations, that I'd been this wet tunnel down which something smooth had been shoved. But now I could differentiate her various fingers. "Three," then "four," she counted out loud. She had to struggle to get this last one in, and so did I. "Am I hurting you?" she asked.

"That's okay."

"If I'm hurting you I'll stop." She started to withdraw her hand. My body sucked after it.

"It feels good," I had to whisper.

"Oh." Was I imagining the triumph in her voice? In any case, she spread me wide, as if she were about to give me a D&C, then I felt her knuckles. She was trying to bend her hand into a fist.

This really hurt, in a way that was hard to tell whether it was pleasurable or not. The tips of my nipples were no longer erect, and the wetness seemed, not a response to some unfulfilled yearning, but a reflex no more interesting than the turning on of a faucet. And yet I was pushing my legs apart as far as possible so she could get her fist inside my vagina. Peaceful, I guess you'd best describe it, almost as if I could fall asleep. I moaned when she put her teeth around my nipple. "You're very sweet," she told me.

I have always felt this to be true, though very few people have recognized it as such. With my nipple still in her mouth she pushed my jeans down so they encircled my ankles. I was sweating and messy. She was much cooler than I, almost clinical as she proceeded, which not only aroused me but made me like her better. Somehow things were more in balance than earlier in the evening. I wished she had brought a camera with her so we could have taken pictures of me masturbating to the sight of her naked body—and ever after I could torture myself as to what she had done with them.

Abruptly she pulled out her hand, then I heard her stand up. I kept my eyes shut, wondering what she was doing, if she were going to search up some strange toy in her pocketbook. I heard her walk away, then behind my lids I saw, or perhaps felt, the warmer glow which I pretended was sun, but which was really a distant light in my apartment. I heard the toilet flush, but not the sound of the sink.

She came back. Her hands made me shiver. I opened my eyes. "Did you wash your hands?" I asked.

"What do you think?"

They were cold, so I decided to assume she had. I lay there, the jeans still around my legs, in the same position I had been in before, as if I were tied up and couldn't move. This passivity both embarrassed me and turned me on. She took my right hand with her left and gently brought it up above my head. She held it down with her arm as she lowered her head onto my breasts and bit my right nipple.

"Ow," I moaned. But I didn't push her away. In fact, the lower part of my body gyrated toward her. She took my other hand and placed it above my head. She held both my arms down with one of hers as she crawled on top of me until her knees held down my arms. She pulled my belt through the loops on my jeans, and wrapped it around my hands. Then she took the end and wrapped it around the leg of my couch.

Both the leather and buckle cut into my wrists. The belt wasn't very long and I had to lean partway off the couch. "That hurts," I said.

"But you don't mind," she said. Silence. "Do you?"

"Not exactly."

"I didn't think so." She stared at me rather impersonally, then slapped me lightly on the face.

"Ow," I said. But it didn't really hurt.

"Come on," she said. She ran her fingers very lightly down my stomach, then all of a sudden slapped me again.

This time it did hurt, but I didn't say anything. "How does that feel?" she asked.

"Okay," I said.

" 'Okay?' Is that all? We'll have to do something about that." She slapped me again, even harder.

"Ow." This time I wasn't so sure I liked it. It was no longer part of my fantasy. I wasn't sure what was coming next. For the first time I really pulled at my hands to see if I could get free.

"Roll over," she said.

"What?"

"Roll over." With the belt around my hands it was hard to do this. I had to move even nearer the couch leg and kind of slip my head around under my arms. Gently she ran the tips of her fingers over my ass. It rose slightly in the air, waiting for her. Whether the goosebumps were from her touch or the cold, I didn't know. I kept worrying I would fart. She stroked down the crack to my vagina, where she soaked up some goop with her finger. She used this to lubricate my asshole.

"One sec," she said. She got up, went over to her jacket to get something out, came back. With my eyes shut I waited for her finger, or maybe even a tongue (this being long before the Plague), but I felt something hard and unfleshy-feeling press against me. "You ever use this?" she asked.

By turning my head as much as I could, I could see the

black leather around her groin and the pink latex in the shape of a penis sticking out from it.

"Not this way," I said. "Won't it hurt?"

"That's up to you." She spread apart my cheeks and moved forward over my ass, then began to press the dildo into me.

"That hurts," I said.

"Just relax." She ran her fingers over my ass, and I felt the goosebumps again. I realized I was holding my muscles tensed, and told myself to let go. As I exhaled she pushed it in further.

"Ow!"

"I told you. *Relax.*" She moved a hand back inside my vagina, and in spite of the pain the wet began to flow, as if there were two separate bodies inside my one head. The other hand continued to help ease the tip of the dildo far enough into my body so that it wouldn't fall out. When I had relaxed enough to open myself to the pain, she put the hand that had been holding the dildo inside my mouth. The hand smelled like wet rubber, and I liked it. She moved her fingers in and out of my mouth in a kind of lulling rhythm; I drooled on them as if it were a cock I was sucking. Then she began to move her fingers along my gums and the muscles under my tongue, even into my nose, then back into my mouth. It was strangely erotic, though I did begin to worry about germs. With all this distraction I did not have much mental space to concentrate on the area of diffuse pain around my asshole where she was still pushing in the dildo. When on occasion I thought of it I moaned, but the pain, although intense, was made bearable by the thought of my strange submission.

Not just bearable—*pleasurable*—at the thought that all my holes were filled, my body possessed, not by just anyone, but by this being who disgusted me. Had it been someone I cared about it might have been different, but since I did not know her, and there was nothing I could do about it, I might as well relax and enjoy it. No doubt I would have been happy enough with her on a desert island, where I could let her make love to me all day and no one would ever know. And yet, with world enough and time, perhaps I would not have wanted to let her do it, or she herself might not have wanted to do it. For is it not often true that when you want someone to make love to you all day, they don't want to, so you have to make love to them in order to get them to want to make love to you—so the person who wants sex the least generally gets more of it?

Then, beyond the pain and mental pleasures, came a powerful sensation of peace. I realized all my life I'd wanted something in there. The hand that had pushed in the dildo now cupped my right breast, as if a boat had capsized and she was hanging onto me. I was tired and I wanted to go to sleep. The sweat on my body was drying up. I hadn't had an orgasm, and I knew I wouldn't get one. "I'm cold," I said.

She kissed the back of my neck, which made me shiver further. Then she took her hands off my breast and out of my vagina and began to push herself up off my back. The dildo pulled out a little, which hurt, though not as much as when she had put it in. "Ow," I said. But what I really felt was sadness. I had gotten used to it in there.

"Shh." She fiddled with something, then abruptly stood up. The peaceful sensation was still inside my body, but less so. When I turned my head I saw that the dildo no longer was attached to the black leather belt. She untied the end of my belt from the couch leg and carried me perhaps fifteen feet over to my bed. "Be careful," I said. She was small and I was scared she'd drop me.

She placed me down on the bed, my ass still in the air with the dildo sticking out of it. The pants belt was still looped around my hands. She took a blanket and placed it over me. It pressed down on the dildo a little, which felt good.

Then she crawled on top of me, turned my head to the side, and kissed me. Her lips were incredibly soft, and in spite of my fatigue I felt sexual stirrings again. "What can I do for you?" I asked. In spite of my disgust, I wanted to bury my head in her, in order to fall asleep.

"Nothing."

"You sure?"

She kissed me again, then stood up and began to walk away. Again I shut my eyes. I wondered what other trick she was going to come back with: blindfold, handcuffs, tit clamps.

"Goodbye," she said.

"What?" I opened my eyes. She was standing by the bed, buttoning up her jacket.

"I got to split. You know. Diane."

Tears rushed to my eyes. Whether it was because I didn't want her to go, or because I didn't want that peaceful sensation that had spread from my asshole to the rest of my body to leave, I couldn't be sure. I began to imagine my loneliness after she'd gone. "I give the best head in the world," I said. "Haven't you heard?"

"So *that's* who they were talking about in the bar." She was so deadpan that for a moment I got paranoid. I never expected anybody I was with to have the slightest sense of humor.

"I really do," I said.

"Some other time."

She moved toward me, and I waited for her to remove the dildo. Instead, she pushed it in further.

"Ow."

"That's in pretty good now, isn't it?" She patted it.

"Yes."

"I'm going to leave you like this."

"No. It *hurts*." But the more it hurt, the more I liked it. And her, standing calmly by in her jacket, indifferently pushing the pink latex into me.

"You really don't mind, do you?" Silence. "Do you?"

"I guess not," I admitted.

"I knew you wouldn't." She gave a last shove, then bent

down to kiss me briefly on the mouth. Then she moved to the door.

I knew it could be dangerous to be left like this, my arms still tied by my belt, but I loved the idea of being able to tell my friends about it in retrospect.

"Will you come back to get it?" I asked.

"Maybe. You never know." She opened the door, then left. The words "I love you" played through my mind, but I knew it wasn't true. But I felt as sad as if they were true. For a while I lay there, then I maneuvered the belt off my hands, pulled out the dildo, and went into the bathroom to brush my teeth and wash my face. Even when I was back in bed, listening to the country music station play songs from a region I wished I had been able to escape from, rather than move toward, as I was doing now, the sadness stayed with me. It was the same sadness that was always there, and it occurred to me I must like it. Why else did I keep going to the bars, if not to find it?

DODIE BELLAMY

DEAR DENNIS

October 10, 1989

Dear Dennis:

KK said Dion and I were two giant screens with different movies playing on each of us.

I certainly never planned him—Dion jutted into my life like Carrie's arm jutted from the grave—and the catalyst was M.S., one of those popular girls who wait in the wings ready to destroy Carrie's life or mine—Dennis, you've never met M.S., but note how her initials mean ManuScript, a woman who's her own scandalous invention. When KK and I entered the raised auditorium the first thing we noticed was She a queen bee perched in the back surrounded by her drones: as soon as M.S. spied us She quipped, "Here comes Kevin Harker and Mina Killian—**the married people.**" *She might as well be calling us plotless.* What was I supposed to do, dump a bucket of blood on my head? I, Mina Harker, the Famous and Feared, my trail of weeping jugulars spanning two continents, two centuries—can you imagine *me,*

Dennis, the joke of a popular coed! Fangs jutting out of my gums like stalactites: before her powerful alchemical hauteur how could I help myself? When Dion came along, trouble on a silver platter, I had no alternative but to bite . . .

How dare She insinuate our marriage is boring—who does She think She's dealing with here—her parents—Mr. and Mrs. ManuScript? And then there's Dion acting as if KK and I were recruiting him for our Anne Rice lifestyle . . . I can see some scholar in the 21st century huddled over our papers in the San Diego archives totally perplexed he takes off his spectacles stares blankly at the shelves of dusty books—suddenly he's transposed to another plane less solid than his own he sees his future in a flash the pages of his award-winning biography fan out before him the book that probes the untold story of San Francisco's greatest authors Mina Harker and KK. Just as suddenly back at the library table he picks up his pen . . . like a space shuttle it slowly arches forward touches down on a yellow legal pad he begins: *The Enigmatic Duo*: Chapter 1. Dennis, I WANT TO SET THE RECORD STRAIGHT **RIGHT NOW**! As a lover the *mot juste* for KK is not "kinky" but "graceful"—you've seen the swanlike flick of his chin as he smokes a cigarette *hands like water flowing over and into every crevice* when I admire this grace he shrugs his freckled shoulders and sighs, "Yes, they used to call me the Baryshnikov of love." So why am I creating a character as white bread as Dion when right at home I have Mr. Exotic? BECAUSE THERE IS AN INVERSE RELATIONSHIP OF FOREST TO TREES! Repetition blurs details in a haze of privacy *anything even Patty Hearst locked in a closet begins to seem normal after a while* on the California Street cable car a worker like myself who rides it to the Embarcadero every weekday would never ooh and aah the way those horrible tourists do—if I hear one more time "Look, that's where they film *Hotel!*" there's going to be a polyester mess across the tracks—I just want to exist on the wooden bench my quiet interiority mingling with the fresh morning air sometimes I even stick my face in your book

I'm just a bunch of blue tubes inside a skin wrapper it takes a stranger or an accident to bring the panoramic view back in focus.

Dion confides he's planning to break up with his girl-friend—we're both still in bed though on opposite ends of the city *the phone stretching from ear to ear* he casually asks, "How long have you and KK been married? . . . That long, huh?" Suddenly his voice goes husky: "You and I should get together and have a little snack on the side." Like the subatomic meson a flurry of desire passes through me. It leaves a faint flash on a photographic plate for a few millionths of a second only to vanish out of material exis-tence. "Dion, I think that would be *disastrous*." A snack— not dinner or even Sunday brunch—something in-between the fat girl's nemesis greasy food products they advertise on TV a nibble that can happen any old time. . . . Dennis, do you remember El Toro the burrito place I took you to before your reading at Intersection? One night when Dion and I were squatting on those wicker stools he picked up his churro and started mimicking fellatio on it—the more I slapped his arm and squealed, "Stop it!," the deeper Dion would plunge the tubular pastry down his throat.

For three years our relationship was casual, innocent even . . . then Dion dreamt there was a plane crash—digging through the rubble he uncovered my unconscious body dug it out and carried me across the mesa I was but a limp shell draped in his arms my torn skimpy gown draped across my trembling breasts: only a dream but in the nuclear region of desire a quantum event *out of nothing a primordial some-thing* Dion began to touch me, tentative pats almost grazes on my arm or waist—was he testing me or trying to bring me back to life? *I warned him there are things on heaven and Earth that mortals shouldn't mess around with but he didn't listen grabbed my kneecap instead of the stick shift* once at the end of a joke he laid his head on my shoulder offering his sweating cranium as the punch line. Though his trapezius looked a little tough his weight against me felt comfortable a big adoring beast—he said he'd always found

235

me sexy that I'd look great in Ray Bans on the back of a
motorcycle *thick engine between my thighs* he had another
dream where we made love and all the tensions between us
dissolved. . . .

*She was aroused and whether she would now behave
right or not—perhaps this hung in the balance for her.*

Dion sat across from me in a café his irises against his
baby-blue T-shirt beaming bluer than nature . . . on the
smoke-stained walls hung an amateur artist's first show the
colors were gaudy and the figurative elements unintention-
ally stiff . . . I fiddled with my bendable straw . . . folding
it back and forth was weirdly erotic . . . the accordion curve
locked as I let go, clasped my hands together on the white
formica table between us. Without missing a beat in the
conversation "When I was a boxer I knew better than to
slam anybody down on the mat . . ." Dion leaned forward
covering my hands so softly his palms were the wings of a
giant insect in a caveman tableau then he puled back
clamped his coffee cup in a grip that could crush it *his
warmth clinging to my fingers infecting me with prehis-
tory.*

SOMEBODY MIGHT GET IN TROUBLE.

We romped across San Francisco, a couple of large frisky
dogs squirming and wrestling until his car shook up and
down like a boat . . . we pretended we were in a Wim Wen-
ders film driving cross-country our itinerary convoluted as
our brains our only destination Pleasure USA . . . we sat on
the concrete ledge at the top of Twin Peaks watching the
changing light—a warm San Francisco sunset *weather rare
as diamonds* from the Bay Bridge to the Golden Gate the
city spread out before us glittering and gorgeous . . . Dion
in his mussed hair and jeans *out-of-bounds, unknown, un-
civilized pockets* baby-blue T-shirt boasting forearms dim-
pled from pumping iron *a body within inches of my fingers
its heat rippling through the evening air* arching his shoulders Dion commands, "Scratch my back" *up here a million
miles away there's no reason not to baby-blue air gels into
a wall of muscle I rub my hand over it* . . . "To the left

236

. . . *now up a bit* . . . **harder**'' . . . blue cotton slides around his torso like bed sheets how can I stand it this craving to wrap my legs around his waist to swallow this savory morsel of junk food whole this corpus delectable that's ten years younger than Dodie.

Dion kept lamenting ''if only''—as if my marriage were a terminal disease. For days I had in fact been under the weather with stomach flu—but by the time we drove home the pallor in my cheeks bloomed to a blush my mouth swelled crimson I felt new as dew TOTALLY REVIVED *Dion my transfusion my 20th-century succulence.* Still, I told him he was crazy if he thought I knew what I wanted.

My parents and me in our brand new '59 Fairlane . . . we're at the drive-in sitting through *another* Western why don't we ever go see anything interesting like Jerry Lewis— in the front seat my father pees in his popcorn container then dumps the gunk out on the gravel *the dark isn't really dark but flickering* I slouch in the back the warm hiss of urine drowning out the passions of the big screen—ever since then I have sensed something obscene in a man behind the wheel *a car is more than motion . . . it can be a bed or a coffin or a room, any room* . . . the second night Dion backed into a spot on Twin Peaks I knew better than to wax cozy in my bucket seat—this time it wasn't the scenic vista but an elongated parking lot, our ''view'' concrete and a few shrubs. Fog formed a blowsy curtain across the windows. I said, ''You're afraid I'm going to take these sex games of yours seriously and what would you do then?'' He smiled as he leaned over and stuck his tongue in my mouth *it was thick with saliva like a dog's* imagine my feigned surprise! Our relationship hadn't even progressed to the point of those dreadful little hugs that people expect you to give them upon departure—stiff and mechanical with a light pat on the back optional graze of smiling cheeks occasionally the slightest peck of a kiss into the vicinity of (but not on) the lips—an embrace like a chastity belt you can never relax into. Someday I swear I'm going to latch onto one of these vacant fondlers and grind my groin into theirs. Imagine the look on Dodie's deeply pinkening face—her mouth an "O" straight out of Sylvia Plath as I proclaim to her, as the space alien with the bird face proclaimed to his shrieking hostage, "Horror is a luxury the desperate cannot afford."

Dion didn't need my memories to make him obscene he was born obscene an animal that humps whatever comes into focus.

I was wearing a slinky silk blouse that really lived up to its adjective . . . Dion's hands frantically roamed up and down my spine as if the knobs were Morse Code he couldn't quite make out, the dots and dashes garbled by enemy static—suddenly in the middle of a deep-throated kiss he stopped, sat back . . . panted . . . stared straight ahead and murmured, "I've been wanting this for three years and it's every bit as good as I imagined." Dennis, I try to maintain some semblance of control but how could I resist a man who made me feel like Jesus Christ on the cross, my ego destined to soar to heaven? And just a few minutes ago we had our first kiss! I kept putting it off . . . that ultimate steamy moment when dreams materialize . . . when corpus eclipses the specific *this really is going to happen clothes will be peeled away ripe flesh revealed body parts played like the greatest hits I dice my carrots to on K-FOG's Psychedelic Supper.* I didn't want to become faceless as the boys in your novels (how could a contour as vague as "cute" stand for anything less than the human condition?)—in that leap across the unfathomable distance between two bodies a formula is set in motion—you can fill in the numbers . . . brackets . . . x's and y's with calculated abandon—kinky or vanilla you always end up on the other side of the equal sign with the same big Z for Zero.

Pushing his Ray Bans up the bridge of his nose Dion declared, "You can't get me in trouble because I *am* trouble."

Dennis, if only I had the tiny passions of a human like the boys in *Closer* endlessly fucking and being fucked acting out a ritual they've memorized but barely comprehend . . . one Saturday afternoon my longing was so huge I felt like

H.D. trapped in Emily Dickinson's body I wanted to screw my brains out . . . so I put on jogging shoes and ran crosstown to North Beach *I made my way by odor and feel and uninhibited touch panting down California then Polk over the hill on Pacific then through Chinatown the streets lined with amber ducks hanging from their feet as if a cartoon butcher had caught them mid-fall* I couldn't shake off these jabs of arousal that had attached themselves to my groin like gnomes that cling to the wings of aircraft fiendishly tinkering with engines making the plane take a nosedive in the most far-fetched places, the Dead Sea, the Bermuda Triangle, Dion's arms.

All those sailboats clinking in the foreground . . . Dion and I are parked in the Marina as far from streetlights as we can get—luckily its a cold night and our breath clouds the windshield a stranger standing right outside wouldn't see us—we might as well be ghosts or ideas *is this really happening?* I roll down my window to let the boats in . . . *an atonal Japanese interlude* . . . Dion leans across me one hand squeezing my thigh the other rolling up the glass wall *the inside is us and forget the rest* he's trying to move things along to the Big Picture while I savor the details: here in the dark I miss the fine lines beneath Dion's eyes running like rivers to his ears: fissures in such a young face *something is coming apart* . . . I'm having my period but Dion doesn't care he hasn't cleaned up from his day job—hauling around carcasses for eight hours his sweat is mingled with cattle ooze blood is caked beneath his nails he pushes his tongue down my throat as he pushes a finger up my vagina *all those discarded unsanitary world bits all that refrigerated death* he whispers, "I'd like to stick my biggest finger in there" *he's pointing in my direction* all I'm wearing is a cotton-knit camisole which might as well be nothing— with every passing headlight I stiffen: cops? Dennis, how can I pass up the chance to fuck in a Camaro—it's so perfectly high school! But like high school it's damned near impossible . . . after numerous failed contortions I turn sideways and sit on top of that glove compartment or what-

ever you call that box thing between the bucket seats—
Dion plunges into me his right hand clinging to the headrest
for balance his left arm around my waist suspending me in
a hot-blooded void *there's nothing solid for me to lean
against or grab onto I can't adjust myself try to ignore the
nagging cramp in my calf* . . . head and shoulder bobbing
around in open space a line of poetry sticks in my mind
reasserting itself like a mantra with each thrust: Sylvia Plath:
something else hauls me through air I imagine Dion imagining himself at work diving into one of those gleaming
pink slabs his cock smearing white to fuchsia à la Francis
Bacon *something else hauls me through air* . . .

The sex part worked because he used all the right adjec-
tives.

Afterward I try to cuddle but Dion clings to his side of
the car like a barnacle—I've heard of passion spent but once
this guy shoots his load he's bankrupt—I guess I'm spoiled
but I want him to curl around me like a shell. Instead he
tells me about a TV show where one cell removed from a
specimen's body could feel the effects of its home cells miles
away. Waving a bloodstained finger back and forth Dion
concludes: that's why people know each other so well after
they make love . . . they leave specks of microscopic sen-
tience behind. I snap back, "Don't start telling me that now
you can read my soul." His cum in my cunt *sticky radar*
while I'm washing the dishes will his emotions zap through
me will I drop a plate—from now on when I'm happy will
Dion smile to himself will he saunter to the bathroom
whenever my bladder's too full?

In build and character Dion was wolfman rather than the
aristocratic Dracula of my young dreams—I've always pre-
ferred men with long bodies and soft asses—like KK or
yourself. Rubbing against Dion's acres of muscles his red-
wood thighs I felt like Jayne Mansfield in a leopard skin
jumpsuit. He was pushing thirty and leading a sedentary life
I had to taste him quickly before he went stale all of him:
unshaven jaw broken nose scars chipped yellowing teeth
skin you would never mistake for candy armpits reeking

of musk and meanness. His views on poetry were tedious and naïve he thought Chopin was a great composer decorated his apartment in a style that I could only call "boys dorm" cooked jambalaya with a prepackaged seasoning mix—none of this mattered as he lay down on my back his arms looming on either side *pterodactyl wingspan* his colossal heart pounding through the flesh barrier filling my rib cage *I am hollow a drum resounding with alien pulsations.*

If I don't calm down Dodie's threatening an exorcism what does she expect from me the pineal gland is a snake that pokes through my forehead making me eat psychiatrists' brains.

The room was subtly lit like a case full of perishable objects . . . Dion's arm a dead weight across my naked waist I deliver my line: "We're not having a relationship," I avow, "We're having an affair!" *understated yet driven* **Mina Harker in her greatest role ever—Mildred Pierce.** The last time we lay on this futon KK walked in on us— well almost—Dion and I were entwined *oblivious to that ambiguous inch between facial expression and soul* when I heard a suspicious jingling and scratching OH MY GOD HIS KEY IN THE LOCK I hurled myself against the door and threw the bolt: "Just a minute!" Hopping around the floor on one foot Dion looked like a pagan performing some ritual **Oh Great Pants God—Please Cover—My Bare Ass!** *I was trying to lead a life so trashy I'd be personally responsible for San Francisco's landfill crisis*—KK seemed embarrassed and amused as if watching an X-rated episode of *I Love Lucy* . . . later when the three of us sat in the living room discussing the weather that cat jumped on Dion's lap . . . with a sly smile KK remarked, "I see she's got a new boyfriend." *Oh, Ricky!* Dion is still freaked out by the Cat Comment: "I could understand if the guy wanted to beat me up but this talk about the cat . . . you guys are so decadent!" His boyish features tighten in such a grimace I expect his irises to spin around like blue pinwheels. "I've never cheated on a girlfriend, never had sex with a married

woman, never had sex with the wife of a good friend . . .''
I recognize his expression: a younger version of my own
face in a movie theater—I was so stoned on hash I couldn't
tell if my body was moving or still—and I was watching
Satyricon. In Dion's eyes I'm more wicked than anything
in Fellini's film—*wicked as Salome, but not any old Salome—the only man who can do me justice is Beardsley
. . . or maybe Oscar Wilde.*

Dion's intensity was ultimately inaccessible to me. I hated
him for that. I still do.

Dennis, I've been caught before . . . playing doctor with
Beth. When I was nine I had to go once a week to the
Hammond Clinic for a shot of penicillin. The nurse always
let me pick which side of my butt I wanted it on. Beth lay
on her stomach on my twin bed, her pants pulled down—
I didn't have a needle but I did find a pencil and was pre-
paring to jab the chosen cheek of Beth's ass when my
mother walked into the room. Instantly she turned from
housewife to Fury, wresting the pencil from my little fist
and yelling, ''Don't you *ever* do that again! Beth pull your
pants up.'' I was confused why my medical endeavor so
upset her, but she hadn't been exactly understanding either
the previous summer when my night lamp caught on fire
from the pajama top I'd thrown over it to attempt dim lighting—I'll never forget her shock when she found me in the
90-degree weather lying on my back on the floor beneath
the smoking lamp wearing mittens, earmuffs, and my father's motorcycle goggles stuffed with cotton balls. It had
taken all day to set up this sensory deprivation experiment
based on my reading of *Science Digest* and she ruined it
with one shriek: ''What the hell are you doing!'' I shoved
the goggles under the bed. ''Nothing,'' I said, ''I ain't doing
nothing.'' This rage over Beth's shot went beyond her re-
curring fear that her daughter was insane—I felt hurt MOM I
WAS JUST PLAYING! but looking back with the jaded eyes of
an adult I see how my girlish exploration of Beth's ass isn't
all that different from some of the sex kinks KK and I occasionally treat ourselves to—to this day, I'm sure if my

mother walked in on us, she'd bellow, "Don't you *ever* do that again!"

When I told him the above story, KK replied, "Because you didn't have a hypodermic needle you used a pencil . . . ummm . . . sublimation . . . no wonder you became a writer." He's full of theory. Fifty percent of female serial murderers, he tells me, spell their first name with an "i" at the end. Dodie or Cindy is okay, but watch out for the treacherous Patti Judi Suzi Cheri or Mimi. Pushing his Korean barbecue around on its styrofoam plate KK adds, "Take my friend Theresa—all of a sudden she switched from signing herself "T-E-R-R-Y" to "T-E-R-R-I"—and she was a grown woman! I knew from then on that she spelled TROUBLE."

With Dion, his girlfriend Tiki, and KK all jostling for elbow room I felt crowded out of my own bed. I'd bitch, "If all you can think about is your girlfriend why don't you go home and fuck her instead of me." That was the extent of my understanding *having been an Other since the day I was born, being the other woman was small potatoes to me* . . . Dion in his muddy backyard yelling through the cellular phone, "Well, maybe I'm just too young and inexperienced to have sex with someone as demanding as you!" His rage made everything very abstract, not just the ideas but the objects *souls hovered in the dark air under the moon* eventually he looked up and through his kitchen window he focused on Tiki taking in *everything*—a forbidden history and its confused future—his misbehaving cock. "Oh shit," he said. "Can I hang up now?"

Real Life was sneaking up on him threatening to commit mutiny on the ship of his story it took some fancy navigating to switch tenses from the dangerous "I did" to the purely literary time frame of "If I were to . . ."

I like a lover with lips that talk as well as kiss. Hours of Dion's arousal (observable tactile elongated) pale before his offhand remark: "Last night you looked so good I got a hard-on just crossing the street with you." We were on our way to a Cambodian restaurant . . . I ordered green curry, traded him a shrimp for a cashew having no idea I was in the midst of a sexual situation beyond my own vague urge to get the business of public eating over with. Predator that I am I have an instinctual need to keep moving—at work I take as many trips to the bathroom as possible—rinsing my hands in the antiseptic white sink I gaze at my reflection on the wall—framed in a simple rectangle it moves like a painting . . . I try to imagine what he finds attractive in the creature before me: tattered grave clothes spattered with mildew and mud fluorescent skin of a undead chapped lips oozing blood *no temperature whatsoever like a piece of paper* . . . who else could he be seeing? . . . blond hair . . . green eyes . . . a woman who crumbles with his touch into pure sensation? A rush of fear swells through my chest: "You made me hard crossing the street" his testimonial superimposed onto my perceived image like matter and antimatter an impossible contradiction that's bound to explode *the world is an unwelcome drug* the mirror glares in the afternoon sun I've tapped into the essence of horror: the crack in one's perceptual framework *who am I to believe: the government scientists with their cover-ups and whitewashes or the slimy thing thumping down my hallway whenever I turn my head I catch a glint of fangs or extraterrestrial metal.*

His cock curled back on itself, a finger beckoning.

The funky sheets have been supplanted by freshly laundered cotton—a team of forensic experts wouldn't find any traces of hair skin blood NO INCRIMINATING MOLECULAR FLAKES. Dennis, how did it feel to sleep four nights on this futon where half of the X-rated action took place? Were your dreams shot through with flashes of heat and confusion the way a psychic clenching the dead boy's shirt glimpses his killer's face? Were your nights restless as mine—waking then waking then waking again, lips parched cheek pressed against a vanishing chest—Dion's—I can't hold the dream just its afterimage no limbs no head a wide-angled close-up of his disconnected torso: a panorama of beige skin so smooth it looks oiled or polished with unnatural highlights like airbrushed metal: whenever I move my eyes the frame fills with rippling muscle, strata upon strata of muscle a Grand Canyon of tortured flesh stretching above the sun-drenched horizon—the camera backs up to reveal long skinny stick legs and arms poking out at awkward angles, a huge upturned screaming mouth by Salvador Dali.

DENNIS, ARMAGEDDON—NOT GOD—WILL COME IN THE FORM OF A KISS.

A perfect Saturday night: pizza and a slasher video: *everything edifying ennobling morally elevating collapses in a series of gradual dissolves punctuated on the sound track with electronic rumbles mimicking thunder or heavy traffic—the elemental breaks through:* the serial murderer's M.O. is true to the true-crime literature KK's such a fan of: *Fatal Vision, Fatal Dosage, Blood and Money, Bad Blood, Poisoned Blood, Bitter Blood* . . . during the credits KK gets that faraway look that I know so well—blue eyes boring through the flittering screen to the delicate web of intelligence that holds the world together, he absently picks up his Tab takes a swig and sets it back down beside the 50s panther lamp. "Do you know the three things all sociopaths have in common?" A shake of my slouched head from the other end of the couch. "Well, as children they all wet the bed, tortured small animals, and lit fires. Mina, if you ever meet anybody who did *all* those three things they are NOT NORMAL—STAY AWAY!" A few days later when Dion started talking about vengeance in the 7th grade how could I help but latch on to KK's ever-so-interesting trivia. We were driving down Haight Street and I couldn't wait for him to finish his story about the girl who framed him—to get even he filled a balloon with urine, climbed on top of a roof . . . she was drenched and screaming when I "innocently" asked, "Did you used to wet the bed?" "Didn't everybody?" STRIKE ONE "Did you light fires?" "Yeah, I lit Kleenex boxes and put them on the dining room table." STRIKE TWO "But you never tortured small animals?" "Yeah, I hung snakes from a fence—upside down—so they'd bake in the sun." STRIKE THREE—LET ME OUT "I'd rub them with suntan lotion it kept them alive longer, it kept their skins soft." TO HAVE YOUR METAPHOR LEAP OFF THE PAGE AND LAND BESIDE YOU IN THE DRIVER'S SEAT RAISING AN AX—ON HAIGHT STREET NO LESS! I thought I was going out for a cup of coffee and here I was living the second reel of *Frenzy the 13th, Part II* . . . my mind reversed itself rooting out all the "quirky" anecdotes Dion had entertained me with the past few months: how he stuffed dog shit in his enemy's mailbox . . . slammed his co-worker enemy down on concrete— "lucky nothing broke" *no spinal snap no leaking cerebral mush* . . . he trashed his neighbor enemy's house . . . poured sugar in his roommate enemy's gas tank . . . slammed his fist through his landlord enemy's window and smeared the blood over his face like war paint as he raced home . . . the list of Dion's enemies swelled irrationally, out of control like anything exposed to radiation in the 50s—would he stop making dates and just break into my apartment whenever he wanted to see me, make me his moll like Stephanie Zimbalist—poor Stephanie—complacently observed by millions of Movie of the Week viewers, an uptight lawyer who falls head over heels for her imprisoned client—with his X-ray blue eyes who could blame her—she hides a gun in the court bathroom and they drive off together in a baby-blue van pretending she's his hostage—end of romance, beginning of hell. She winds up in a cheap hotel her hair dyed cheap blond, her middle-class life dissolving in a puddle at her feet, broke, desperate, not even liking her beer-guzzling con very much. I began searching for a reason to storm away from Dion, shouting that "it" was over.

I wanted his heart on a silver platter I wanted to have some kind of effect on him—but his cock curled back on itself like a question mark—I should have guessed I'd never know what he wanted.

Did you hear about Audre Lorde? Her house was swept away by Hurricane Hugo! These writers—tragedy is always befalling one or another of them. Like my friend B.—he went to the dentist for a root canal and six months later was wheeled out of the hospital, a plastic valve in his heart: college student turned high-tech hybrid: on last Saturday's

Outer Limits one minute the scientists are flying into the eye of a hurricane a puff of smoke and they're trapped in an Alien observation chamber—it's clear we're dealing with an advanced culture when the short one touches a wall and marvels "it's made out of some kind of plastic!" Imagine how amazing they'd find B.! Malpractice scar bisecting his chest from neck to navel B. sat in the row behind me at your reading . . . I could hear his heart clicking like the crocodile that swallowed Captain Hook's watch . . . then B. stood up and left. NO wonder he couldn't see you pointing beyond the mutilated boys in *Closer. Your finger so holy it should be snaking across the ceiling of the Sistine Chapel instead of tapping away at a typewriter.* It's NO accident that I Mina Harker am a vampire rather than a serial murderer: Dodie's never going to run into me in a dark alley or mall parking lot: about me the neighbors the former classmates the co-workers will never say, "She seemed so normal kind of quiet volunteered to man the barbecue NO one would have suspected anything she did her job kept to herself." *Beside a nightstand* Fatal Vision *might be titillating but I don't want a maniac messing up* my *bed . . . to take a student into your body only to realize that on either end of his cock there is TERROR* . . . KK says the sociopath always knows who suspects him and goes after her first . . . I'm tired of walking around in the middle of *The Bad Seed* wavering between tenderness and fear toward Dion my demented little darling (overgrown and sans pigtails though still very Patty McCormack) he seems so sickeningly sweet but inside his tightly packed cells hides a gene that spells M-U-R-D-E-R: KK my crime buff neighbor is the only one who can read the clues, the dead bodies that litter our neighborhood like candy wrappers. I want to move to *Woodstock* Nation where shaggy-headed promoters call their financial disaster a huge success because success is about Something Money Can't Buy: Meaning—and the meaning of Woodstock is: being afraid to walk down the street at night isn't living. The aerial camera tracks over an amorphous mass of stoned hippies . . . there are NO streets in Woodstock I feel so safe want to follow the guy from Ten Years After squinting and frenetically pouting "I'm Going Home"—I want to live back then, and before—to the era of the fake fur coat I wore in college an ancient *faux,* one of the very first—it wasn't the fuzzy gray stripes I paid $2 for, but the satin label in the lining its brand name embroidered in red script: "Mutation" with a heart instead of a dot over the "i": a label I could flash before my friends, casually cooing like a drag queen, "How do you like my Mutation?" I want this coat to fly me to a streetless world where consequences are unheard of: pre-Hiroshima pre-pyramids pre-overdose pre-Patty McCormack pre-fig leaf pre-toxic overload *can you dig it the New York State Freeway is closed man* a world where people pick up each other's garbage and it's inconceivable a civilization could sink beneath a heap of non-biodegradable artifacts *where plastics are awesome and it's diamonds that mean forever.*

Dennis, we both know there's more to being normal than not having hallucinations.

All you wanted was a place to crash for a few days as you trekked through your reading tour but Fate inserts you into *my* story—you are the innocent who stumbles onto the scene of a murder only to find himself chief suspect *his fingerprints all over the gun a white-haired woman across the road sees him running away when the squad car siren comes blaring up the street.* After your radio interview you sit alone in my living room—writing—it's very quiet and from time to time you stare out the bay windows . . . in the distance you see a giant crane and towering beyond, Twin Peaks . . . Dion and I appear beside you a couple of iridescent ghosts half on the floor half on the couch unzipping each other's pants in slow motion . . . you lean closer to examine the last decadent flowering of Dion's flat stomach *his navel protrudes his gut so full of funk it's ramming against the umbilicus ready to erupt* a lover's carcass never can top a spectral seduction—I Mina Harker never should have materialized for Dion I should never have slept with one of my own characters *what is a body in sex anyway but a handful of moans and undulations, a highway of secretions* I should have stayed behind the scenes like you pushing around commas—then I wouldn't have to worry about Dion's warnings MINA I'M A **VERY** PRIVATE PERSON! imagine the growl when he peruses these intimate confessions of mine—what if he trashes my apartment pisses on me what if my teeth turn up in Daly City my wallet in Sacramento? *Her body was shredded like paper the insides pushed through some holes in her shirt blue and greasy and jumbled.* Dennis, you let your fingerprints all over me—the whole world knows you've got no alibi—as I read *Closer* I found myself losing my sophisticated cool *poor Youth poor disfigured Desire!* I couldn't concentrate on your pyramid structure, make sense of your images, appreciate your *qu'est-ce que c'est*—the more I read the more retro I became *the Moors Murderers started to sound like just plain folk* horror swelled my moments both waking and sleeping *I had to turn on my night lamp just to get up the nerve to go to the bathroom* but I didn't know whose horror I was feeling—that of your deadened characters or my own.

I got my belt off, stripped naked, and threw myself onto a mattress that someone had left in one corner years back. "Hurt me," I yelled in a hoarse voice. "Fuck me up and I'll never forget you." "Leave a mark," I whispered. "Leave marks wherever you want. Make it memorable or whatever."

How ludicrous to presume our sex demons or even our partners will allow us to maintain any composure—they'll fight you prick and claw until your sassy aspirations expire in smoke until you forget who you are until you're nothing a question mark with legs pumping inanely like a full-frame porn shot of two anonymous pink asses connected by a piston of cock—it is only through the context of the film and some subliminal knowledge of anatomy that we recognize both as male—in the dark we become these asses or Chuckie the Killer Doll, blurred between animate and inanimate our mechanical moving body parts possessed by

Santeria we each are Ella the monkey who loves too much, murdering our quadriplegic desires we are all insane twin gynecologists devising jagged instruments to gouge out alien genitalia—GIVE THE BIG THINGS IN LIFE A BREAK—sex shouldn't be shouted over a scotch and soda but whispered with a scarfed head—I don't want to be tasteless as those dead who come back, not to haunt us, but to boast of death, as if they had any say in the matter as if the living should be awed by their wind without substance *flimsy blue in the foreground pale and swirling a muffled woooo woooo.*

One of the attributes of sociopaths is phosphorescence . . . matchlike, quick, they make connections that flash brilliantly in the dark, drawing the unsuspecting into this warped reality they create. Typically they invent wild tortuous pasts to gain sympathy from women *their fantasies gather strength over their heads, insidious halos black as dried blood, glittering with the thunder of snapping bones* . . . KK doesn't believe men from the neighborhood bar gave Dion quarters to go buy ice cream so they could be alone with his mother. *Dion was knee-deep in a lime-green fog populated by see-through ghosts skimpy as the Kleenexes that scorched the dining room table*—but I swallowed his fable hook line and sinker, felt pity for burly little Dion standing outside his mother's bedroom window licking his Rocky Road to the rhythm of creaking springs. With such a gastronomic beginning no wonder he performed sex acts on a Mexican pastry. KK scoffed, "That's not anybody's childhood—that's the plot of *Marnie!*" Against the screen of my mind shadowy figures arise . . . blond girl . . . scantily clad mother . . . a strange threatening man, a sailor maybe . . . the three of them having an emotional scene near a stairway. . . . KK continued, "That's why she became a kleptomaniac and stole the money from Sean Connery's safe. And look at Tippi—she spells her name with an "i" at the end!" A few days later on *Santa Barbara* Dr. Scott Clark confesses to Heather that every Tuesday his mother would give him a quarter to get a soda after school. And what was she doing all those afternoons alone in the

house? You guessed it—turning tricks to pay for his Christmas presents. When Scott found out he threw those tainted
toys down the cellar stairs. I know how it feels, Scott. **I
know how it feels to find out.** Damn that Dion! I'm Mina
Harker Queen of the Undead—no man will ever reduce me
to a gullible woman! I'm turning State's Evidence, Public
Enemy Number One in Dion's screwy cosmology. *I broke
into his private parts trashed his secrets word-processed his
cock slammed my fist through his persona smearing the
details all over the page.* The way I've sucked the lifeblood
out of his story who cares if it's true or merely a dream
spiraling into the darkness, a piece of cheap dinnerware
covered with jewels.

NOT A SOUL! Dion tossed me around the bed like a rag doll,
pleading PLEASE DON'T TELL—favor escalated to warning DON'T
TELL escalated to vow PROMISE YOU WON'T—TELL—which in
practical terms meant I only blabbed to C.R. and A., and
with A. I didn't mention his name. How could Dion demand such a sacrifice of me—it's my nature to sprout erotic
tentacles I'm an artiste *secrets rattle around in my cunt like
bones* those four days you stayed in my apartment I was in
agony . . . hoping you wouldn't notice the bedlam vibes
. . . trying to pull off composed and low-key when I was
dying to burst out, "Dennis, you wouldn't believe what's
been happening!" *I can't reveal any details his forehead
his nose his eyes his lips were all quite distinctive in a way
that I found attractive.* Maybe it *is* true the body's full of
memory *last night's quarrel is buried in my left shoulder
a lifetime of love and anger lies hidden in this galaxy of
cells* but I don't have a Rolfer at my fingertips to unlock the
sensation of **all that smoothness Dion crouching over
me on all fours his chest gliding the length of my back**
by the next morning his touch is already dissolving just beyond the reach of my synapses like a ghost—it's imperative
I translate this mute soup of physical undulations hissing
atomic whirls into a syntax the mind can comprehend **all
that smoothness Dion crouching over me on all fours
his chest gliding the length of my back** *the delicate*

chiaroscuro of aging bodies and young gestures it's impossible for me to roll over his arched physique is a giant mouth I feel completely swallowed in him I say, "I'm completely swallowed by you."

Love,

Mina

Mina

This piece is from a collection of letters written in the persona of Mina Harker, the heroine of Bram Stoker's Dracula. *This letter is written to the novelist Dennis Cooper, on the occasion of the publication of his latest book,* Closer.

ROBERT GLÜCK

WORKLOAD

I'VE STARTED JERKING OFF to porn; I'm allowing into my sex life some hopelessness, capitulating to loneliness, glamorizing and eroticizing it. There are three horny clerks, "American youth," regular guys—white jockey shorts, white socks, white cocks, essential jock. Larry is a baseball cap, a wiry frame, a "Good morning, Mrs. Cleever" smirk; J.T. is a blue Oxford shirt, sneakers, brown hair, brown eyes; Sean is jeans and a blond reserve. I guess it's naïve to ask these simple images to contain my loneliness; I guess only these images are empty enough to contain my loneliness. The future will take this contradiction for granted.

In one photo Larry fucks J.T., the two observed by Sean, whose tilted gaze is a peephole in a pillow book. I can't help liking J.T. for his ripe body, juicy really, fucked between tan lines between cheeks between marrow bones on his hands and knees, his body not even very manicured, but floral, generous as a peony. How flattering to all of us, his body and pleasure. I think of medieval versions of naked men and women, pink sacks with arms and legs and the appendages, insulting to the species, closer to the truth.

The still represents motion (the legend at the top reads Slam It In), but conveys a stronger impression of immobility. I meditate on J.T.'s rosy ass, immobile receptor. If J.T.'s ass is supposed to be passive, Larry's rigid cock hardly embodies a principle of action—its motion is internal, like a TV antenna, stationary but receiving signals. Slam It In Harder may be one of those signals; a bat slams a load of jism into the bleachers—an outsized description of an activity that more truly resembles, in its mechanical optimism, a cuckoo striking twelve.

Sean is an observer in this picture; he's blond and cool. Later he gets into the act. Sean lies woodenly on his back while J.T., still on his hands and knees, still getting fucked by Larry, gives him a blow job. I have to stop and consider this. I am committed to J.T.'s excitement. Does penetration at both ends really work for J.T. and me, are we saturated with providence or is this blow job a distraction, a visual flourish? My asshole is either much farther away from my head than the distance of J.T.'s beautiful torso, or it is my center, the capital city, that radiates meaning onto the empire.

It's J.T.'s excitement and I need to borrow as much of it as I can. I need to witness his excitement and I need to be him, the one whose excitement is witnessed. His image provides access to both sides of the sexual proposition. The lack of that circuitry is masturbation's drawback; jacking off resolves physical tension but it exacerbates the imagination's need to witness and be witnessed. The only recourse is to trick myself into believing my body is an object by dramatizing masturbation, with mirrors, with contraptions say, to provide the effect of a keyhole or proscenium arch, a window, so to speak, a photo, in other words. My mind goes ahead talking to itself in this vein, so to speak, but runs out of material before the essay impulse has expired, in other words, so it keeps the same tone and measure almost mechanically until that wears out...........................
....

I begin again: I need to borrow the excitement I feel J.T.

feels. The entrance to this excitement is not only through J.T.'s body, general in beauty, but through the specifics which give the scene its particularity, its effect of the real. So "It was in the little town of X in the year of 18—" lives again in the band of underwear elastic, the white sock and inside-out denim that dangled from J.T.'s left leg, documenting this stud's eagerness; still, they could be, must be, props. The slight indentation made by Larry's hand where it rests on the skin of J.T.'s rump is more exciting. There's a patch of shine on J.T.'s inner thigh, catching the light just at the shadow made by Larry's cock. I realize it's lubricant, grease from Larry's cock; that's as arousing as J.T.'s disheveled brown eyes, as the goofy off-center expression he wears while being fucked or blown. The grease shine is still inside the controlled daydream the photos moniter; it plays a chance role and therefore conveys more authority. In these accidents I most exist, most take part, like the marks that suddenly become apparent on J.T.'s ass—bruises shaped something like a hand. There's no spanking in this photo session. A discoloration of the skin or of the magazine? The magazine is in so-so condition; it was used when I bought it, giving the images a patina, the reader another depth to fall into. But the other photos have this same discoloration so I say okay, it's on J.T.'s ass.

What does J.T. think when he sees his ass? Does he ground diffused global sensations in the image: slam it in harder? I bet he doesn't. He sees his ass and mentally nods in recognition as though a secret has been divulged; it's what he would imagine in the first place, yet different, like hearing his voice on a tape recording. A reality based on glamour and distance impresses him, he's excited by the photo and this is erotic for me; he wants to be alone with it to scrutinize and love as he loves something nameless inside himself. He studies the headless figure: I should have sucked my stomach in on that one (he should have but I'm glad he didn't). His ass impresses him with its generic quality, lacking the stamp of character it appears rather abstract, or mute—but *full*—not only full of cock but full of life.

What does J.T. think when he sees the bruises? Does he know how they got there? Birthmarks? His big red asshole declares such nakedness that the rest of him seems dressed and composed, his cock regular, normal as a necktie. He feels moved by the image even though it's contained, orchestrated. He's all for technique and also for the unmasking of technique. He imagines writing this letter: Dear Abby, I am a man but I want to be so extremely excited that my body goes rigid and milk spurts out of my nipples." Now the sex seems ordinary, pulled along like a dull crime show by the thump thump of its background music. He tries to sort out the limbs—that's Larry's hand. He looks for signs of extremity that document loss of control.

I'm assuming J.T. sees this image on June 2, 1987—I bet this magazine is old. I look for a date: it's under a photo of J.T. and Larry. Larry wears a blue baseball cap; Larry's lips purse as J.T., lowering the red nylon trunks, sucks the tip of Larry's hard cock: MCM, that's 1900, and then L, fifty, then XXX, thirty, so that's eighty, 1980, and then V. 1985. These orgasms were in 1985, my orgasm is a time traveler, an allegory, everything either didn't happen or it's in the past.

1985—J.T. had better watch out—he'd better be careful. That obviously wasn't the first time J.T. took a stiff one. Is he contracting the virus right in that picture? It looks like Sean and perhaps Larry come on J.T.'s chest a little later, I hope so. J.T. could have AIDS right now, I could be jerking off to the image of a man contracting AIDS—in fact, he might be dead. By now my daydream of the image is outside the controlled daydream of its presentation. J.T. looks at his picture, at the marks on his ass. A plane blocks the sun for an instant or his heart skips—some physical shift divides then from now, timelessness from time. Now he knows what the fevers mean, the fatigue—he knows even before he drops the photo and finds the cancer on his skin. Other photos appear, collections of grainy faces on the obituary page. The intimate snapshot public for a second— the best likeness smiling above two dates.

Then what can I do but take part in J.T.'s dismay as I took part in his pleasure, borrow a share of his pain in order to feel the grief that accumulates in my own life. Like myself, J.T. is too guileless to hide his unhappiness; maybe he doesn't understand the implications, his nature being fluid spilling over rather than drying up. Even with the evidence before his eyes and in his body, he can't imagine a wasting disease. He dwells on the impossible accumulation: Ken left us recently—passed on to glory—Mark fought bravely—Ty succumbed—never afraid to die—fondly remembered—John died peacefully—deeply missed—

I pass through the curtain of a dusty web, the spider's skeleton jumps and trembles like a dry leaf.

Meanwhile J.T. visits me after this article is published—things like that happen. My pain does not diminish; it continues as its own story read at the same time as other stories. If they all take the shape of J.T. getting fucked, then let the doctrine be mystical, that there is more content in the world than form. A knock at the door—Hi, he says, it's me. I don't recognize him in clothes. He tells me. I'm amazed, I'm awed. I am back in my daydream, controlled and unlimited. My second thought is a threatened one— have I got in deeper— Then I'm overjoyed to see J.T. in the bloom of health, though I'm too polite—especially after all my speculation—to ask about it directly. We take a quick look at each other in the moment that quickly changes; we go upstairs; we enter a physical willingness; we don't use rubbers—the imagination is a reprobate; the bruises are gone, but he wants new ones. His mouth tastes like spearmint gum.

KATE BORNSTEIN

TRANSSEXUAL LESBIAN PLAYWRIGHT TELLS ALL!

MY ANCESTORS WERE PERFORMERS in life. The earliest shamanic rituals involved women and men exchanging genders. Old, old rituals. Top-notch performances. Life and death stuff. Cross-cultural. Rising way way way above being a man or a woman. That's how my ancestors would fly. That's how my ancestors would talk with the goddesses and the gods. Old rituals. I'd been a performer of one sort or another for over twenty-five years, and now I'm writing plays as well as performing in them. See, I had never seen my story on stage and I was looking. I used to go up to writers I knew. I used to wish you'd write my story. And I'm only just now realizing that you couldn't possibly. I write from the point of view of an S&M transsexual lesbian, ex-cult member, femme top and sometimes bottom shaman. And I wondered why no one was writing my story? I'm writing from the point of view of used-to-be-a-man, three husbands, father, first mate on an oceangoing yacht, minister, high-powered IBM sales type, Pierre Cardin three-piece-suiter, bar mitz-vahed circumcised yuppie from the east coast. Not too many women write from that point of view. I write from the point of view of a used-to-be-politically-correct, wanna-be butch, dyke phone sex hostess, smooth-talking, telemarketing, love slave, art slut, pagan tarot reader, maybe soon a grandmother, crystal palming, incense burning, not-man, not always a woman, fast becoming a Marxist. And not too many men write from that point of view. My ancestors didn't write much. I guess they didn't need to. Y'know, people try to write about transsexuals and it's amusing it's infuriating it's patronizing and it's why I'm writing about transsexuals now. I wrote one play in college twenty-one years ago. And one play last year. Both of them I pulled from my chest until they pulsed bleeding on the stage. Saint Kate of the bleeding heart. The first play was young love gone bad. Spun out my soul as just so much cotton candy romanticism god it felt great. The second play was a harder birth. *Hidden: A Gender* is my transsexual voice the voice I speak with, cry with, bellow with, moan with and laugh with don't forget laugh with. I always hid that voice away. I always used your voice spoke your words sang your hit parade. Until I heard them whisper, my ancestors. And I whispered and you heard me and I said hey you weren't meant to hear that and you said tell us more. And that was the second play, the harder birth. The one I had to write. I write when nothing else will bring me peace, when I burn, when I find myself asking and answering the same questions over and over. I write when I've begun to lose my sense of humor and it becomes a matter of my life and my death to get that sense of humor back and watch you laugh. I write in bottom space. I open up to you, I cut myself I show you my fantasies I get a kick out of that—oh, yeah. I perform in top space. I cover myself with my character and take you where you never dreamed you could go. Yes. My ancestors did this. My instrument is not my pen or my typewriter, not my cast of characters, not my body on stage. No, my instrument is my audience and oh how I love to play you. And to what end? I've come to see gender as a divisive social construct, and the gendered body as a somewhat dubious accomplishment. I write about this because I am a gender outlaw and my issues are gender issues. The way I see it now, the lesbian and gay community is as much oppressed for gender transgressions as for sexual distinction. We have more in common, you and I, than most people are willing to admit. See, I'm told I must be a man or a woman. One or the other. Oh, it's OK to be a transsexual, say some—just don't talk about it. Don't question your gender any more, just be a woman now—you went to so much trouble—just be satisfied. I am not so satisfied. My ancestors were not satisfied. I write from the point of view of a gender outlaw because I don't want to hear: You're not welcome in this bar/You're not welcome at this party/You're not welcome in my home. And I say I don't know why separatists won't let me in—I'm *probably* the only lesbian to have successfully castrated a man and gone on to laugh about it on stage, in print and on national television. (Geraldo, are you reading this?) My ancestors were not shunned. They were celebrated. Look, I know you try to fill in the blanks in my life. I write to let you know who I am so that you *can* fill in the blanks. (Mom, are you reading this?) I work in theater because I really enjoy working *with* people, and theater is not an alone art. And current theatrical forms reflect a rigidly bipolar gender system. They aren't fluid enough for what I want to say, and I feel that form and content in theater as in life should be complimentary, not adversarial, so I work on my own gender fluidity and sometimes it works and sometimes it doesn't. And I work on the fluidity of my theatrical style—and sometimes it works and sometimes it doesn't. My life and my theater—my form and my content—sort of do as I say and do as I do. Like my ancestors.

MICHAEL LASSELL

DREAMS IN BONDAGE

My dreams are slung in hammocks
like refugees
waiting embarkation,
like sailors in the nude
rocking in their fetal sleep and far from shore,
like novices in slings
waiting for the long loose hands of strange love
to untie their nipples,
waiting for the bee-stung petals of tulips
heavy with honey
to unlock their thighs,
for the cave dwellers' tongues
to plump the earthy caverns and
lick the echoes off
undiscovered streams and screams.

My dreams are hung on hooks
like hams in palace kitchens
waiting for the hungry mouths of
foreign boys to pull the gristle

from their bones with gleaming teeth and
suck the sugar from the
marrow of their dormancy.

My dreams are guyed
like slain deer on birth poles
waiting for the hunter's knife
to slice their bellies and
release their steaming innards from
girdles of hide and muscle,
are trammeled up
like poached pheasant forgotten in their wires
and rising in the sun like bladders filling with blood.

My dreams are pods of spores
swelling in anticipation of
spring's lust to burst apart and
spread seed on fecund ground;
are ripe fruit
dangling in the face of autumn
like the testicles of choirboys before the slack jaws of
unrepentant clerics;
are blisters on the brink of leaking,
bruises engorged with violets,
elder sons encumbered by conformity
who ache for prodigal younger brothers.

My dreams are Renaissance paintings
of the Flagellation of Christ
that hide a sadomasochistic secret
in the tortured flesh of
triangular composition.

My dreams are icicles
impatient for thaw in midwinter,
a complex civilization clinging to the
mountainside of extinction by a
lewd tattoo,

a city groaning at the gates with
fevered populations,
tumescent labia of
a bitch in heat,
a lynched man
strung up at night and
swaying in the stained breeze,
his eyeballs straining from their sockets
like animals raging against tethers.

My dreams are the bound feet
of a Chinese concubine
who sings at night:
Oh come, you barbarous invaders
from outside the wall
and batter these stones with onslaughts of log rams
and fiery boulders,
pierce the breasts of the warriors with
arrows and spears,
impale the custom of my incarceration,
unlash the wounded feet that are my dreams
and let me limp
along your country roads
sowing dream seeds
sweetened by tears.

COOKIE MUELLER

|||||||||||||||||||||||||||||||||||||||||||||||||||||||||||||||||||||||||||||||||||||||||||||||

THE ONE PERCENT

DODGE LEE HAD A secret life. It was the kind of unimaginable, unacceptable, and grisly secret life that would horrify most friends and casual acquaintances. In fact this secret life was something that horrified ninety-nine percent of the population of the world.

For Dodge, who owned and lived the secret, it was something else. It wasn't so peculiar or terrible. He was comfortable with the secret and he knew that one percent understood.

Dodge's secret was his thirst. He was a golden showers guy, a man into water sports, a pee hag. During the day he was like everyone else, he ate eggs and toast and drank coffee for breakfast, and at dinnertime he drank mineral water or wine at the table, but late at night in damp pee bars he drank urine. On these nights his secret life came to full flower like a rare night-blooming jasmine under a swollen summer moon. It was wrong, he thought, to relish pee the way he did, but it was his secret which he proudly carried after midnight among the one percent who had seen a lot and hadn't blushed in fifteen years. There he was, sassy in the dark, the Dodger with a mug of gold.

Dodge truly loved urine, it wasn't just that it was fashionable in the bars he frequented, he really loved it. For him it was fluid of gods, a liquid elixir for bliss, and he couldn't get enough of it, couldn't get his fill, it was so dear. Sometimes he felt his heart would burst with love for pee.

This obsessional love he callously blamed on his mother, the battle-ax. She had messed him up. It was all her fault he turned out the way he did, he thought, even though most times he was not in the least unhappy with his little quirk.

His mother, Hilda Lee, had been a slob, a boozer. It was fortunate she was dead, otherwise Dodge would have had to kill her. He almost strangled her a couple of times out of sheer pissed-offedness. If she hadn't fallen drunk in an asphalt pit one night, after the bars closed, right on a busy city street, he would surely be on death row for her murder.

Dodge told the story of her death to fellow water sports people and his psychiatrist, Dr. Bernstein. He said she had probably moaned all night, and no one heard her. He said the next day when people were going to work they saw her down there covered in litter: empty beer bottles and Coke cans, potato chip bags, and candy wrappers. She was in the right place, he said, dead she was a shell, a wrapper, an empty bag, the contents were gone, the container to be discarded.

"Good thing she's gone." Dodge would shrug his shoulders. "Nasty broad was a witch. I'm this way because of her."

One has to wonder what a mother could have done to make a child so interested in urine. Does a mother wear a tasteful rubber dress and strap a toddler to a toilet seat in a bathroom that is warm and soothing and smells great? Or maybe the mother is just an innocent oddball, a weirdo, a knucklehead with a twisted take on reality that makes strange things seem perfectly normal. Certainly Hilda Lee was from white trash hillbilly stock, but so was half of the population of the United States. Being a hillbilly wasn't necessarily a factor that contributed to anyone's perversion.

"She never had an ounce of class," Dodge would tell his psychiatrist, "and if you didn't believe it all you had to do was look at her head. She always had her hair set in pink foam rollers and black crisscross bobbie pins. I never saw what her hair looked like without these things in it. I used to wonder when was that big party she was getting her hair ready for."

True there was always something mysterious about Hilda, aside from the pink foam rollers that is, something to really blame her for. Once when Dodge was little he found in her possession a book of witchcraft with one cryptic passage underlined. It said something about witches stealing the penises of God-fearing men to collect them in boxes where they would writhe like worms. After reading this he immediately knew his mother had a ton of penises in her black pocketbook. There she kept all the family's dicks . . . his father's, brothers', the cousins'. Oddly enough he still had his own penis, thank God for that.

"So I looked in the pocketbook one night," Dodge explained to the quiet Dr. Bernstein, "but there were no penises there. Nothing except a wad of money, a hairbrush, lipstick, a pint of bourbon and a roll of toilet paper . . . toilet paper because she was too cheap and low-down to buy those mini-packages of Kleenex."

Dodge told the psychiatrist that he had to accept the fact that his mother hadn't really robbed anyone of his dick, not literally or physically anyway, but she had emasculated all of them just the same. She had robbed their power, and hid it from them.

"No wonder they all despised her," he added.

So Dodge blamed his mother for everything and that belief exonerated him. It wasn't him, it was her, he was a blameless victim of particulars. What he couldn't see was that she had been a victim too, just like him.

His psychiatrist listened silently for a number of long tearful years to Dodge's ranting about his poor mother and then one day, finally, after these years of being mute, years of literally not saying one thing, the doctor had something to say. Dr. Bernstein, the faithful, patient, rich, psychiatrist, told it this way: "Dodge, look, here it is. You say when your mother was carrying you she drank a lot of beer. Beer is a diuretic and everyone knows how the baby in pregnancy presses on the bladder so that the mother has to urinate more frequently. Anyway you say when she started to go into labor she was sitting at a bar stool drinking beer. By the time she got to the hospital and you started to come down the birth canal her bladder was bursting. She must have urinated on your head the minute you were born."

Dodge's mouth fell open. This doctor could not possibly be serious, could he? Was this textbook psychiatry? Was there any validity to his wacky opinion? Probably not, this doctor was just an asshole, a moron grasping at straws. He almost lost his appetite for pee right there and then. He called Dr. Bernstein an idiot and stormed out. He never went back. Later, with a more benevolent insight, Dodge considered that maybe Bernstein intended him to lose his appetite for pee by telling him this. Well, it hadn't worked.

So Dodge decided to stop trying to analyze his obsession and just enjoy it. He let the past go, it was too dark, he gave up thinking about the future, it was too obscure. He concentrated only on the present, and this he found clear. He found bliss in this. Finally he decided to come out of the closet and openly admit to the world his love of pee. He shared his secret with everyone, thus he lost a lot of old friends, but made some new ones.

He found to his surprise that the majority of pee lovers weren't sleazy at all—in fact, they were much like him, they held down respectable jobs, had loving families and were generally wholesome types. He had always had a prejudice against and felt superior to the people he used to call the "piss reptiles," the people who he believed were the worthless, soulless types, the kind that hung around in sex and pee bars waiting for urine to flow and not seeing the beauty of it. He also used to feel superior to the people he called the "wee-wee hobbyists," those people who were weekend urine enthusiasts. He wasn't at all those types, he wasn't a sleazo and he wasn't a mere weekender, he was a first-class guy and pee was his life.

After he eliminated his prejudicial judgments by opening his mind and the closet door, he became a happier person. New Year's Eve 1978 he even made a resolution to stop blaming his mother for everything.

So Dodge went along peacefully and normally enough, going to his job as a design consultant for a major international architectual firm and at night frequenting the bars. He was a polite man, and not too wild. He wasn't the type that would sit naked in the back-room piss tub accepting just anyone's fluids and he certainly had never waited in shadows at toilet bowls. He always went home at a reasonable hour, usually three A.M. He had a few long-term flings with leather men or guys that wore yellow handkerchiefs in the left-hand-side back pocket of their jeans. He had good and loyal friends, male and female. One winter he even attempted to settle down with a busty Irish fag hag who had admired his collection of blown-glass vases.

Everything was fine until one spring night when he heard about this disease called GRID and how it wafted through the air at gay discos. At first only handfuls of people were concerned about it, but after all kinds of people started coming down with it, and the name was changed from GRID to AIDS, and it was discovered that it was a virus contracted through body fluids, naturally Dodge got really scared. He worried constantly. It ate him up. Finally he got a test and unfortunately the results were positive for the virus. A few months later he got angry magenta-colored lesions on his thighs and went to the hospital to die. What else was there to do?

He was so confused. How could the beautiful golden fluid, the pure honest liquid, have been so bad, so evil, so unsafe? To him it had not only been an obsession but his sanity. Everything meant nothing now. Suddenly there were no footholds on reality for Dodge. He saw all the important things of his life become like the leaves on a tree after the summer. Those plump, green leaves turned brown, became shrunken and flimsy, and fell in October. By December the leaves were no longer existent, they had just disintegrated and totally disappeared.

He was ready to die as soon as possible. No one blamed him.

Feeble, despairing, and brokenhearted he decided to get prepared so he could meet death with everything in order. Along with drawing up his will, planning a big furniture and clothes giveaway, and deciding on cremation, he also wanted to do some spiritual studying so he could greet God having done his homework.

As if the Bible, the Torah, the Koran, the Tibetan and Egyptian Books of the Dead were required reading to pass the grade, he pored over these pages of ancient texts and memorized the high points. The last book on his list was the Bhagavada Gita. He read it but didn't get it. Too many gods and goddesses.

He was told by someone that he ought to read the biography of Gandhi instead, because Gandhi was a Janist and pretty well embodied the spirit of the Hindu scriptures. It was while reading this biography that everything changed for Dodge. This book became his real salvation. Actually it wasn't the book itself but a fact about Gandhi that it revealed. If Dodge hadn't found out this fact, this secret, he would have died within the month. He had almost lost it all, his hope, his pride, his sense of humor, and his life, but he instead fell right into a pit of miracles.

To his wild delight, Dodge discovered that Gandhi, to maintain optimum health, drank his own urine every day. He discovered that many people, prime ministers and religious leaders in India, did likewise. Then he found out that lots of healthy people all over the world, including people in the United States, were drinking their own urine. It was a homeopathic remedy; it worked the same way vaccines work.

Well, Dodge couldn't believe it. It was a miracle! It was exciting! Mind-boggling! A new adventure! It made such perfect sense. He was a new man immediately. The minute he read the passage on Gandhi's urine-drinking he grabbed his urinal bottle and downed it with gusto. He was back on his feet in three days. As long as he drank his own urine he was going to be well.

He threw away his prescription pills. He ripped up doctors' phone numbers. He tossed away the aluminum walker.

He was happy with his own urine. It tasted really great. And what a cheap cure! Free in fact! And he'd certainly never misplace his medicine! It was all right there in his handy bladder!

Years later, after the discovery of Gandhi's secret, Dodge was healthy and happy. He even discovered a medical facility, an institute in New York City that was exclusively for "Life Fluids" drinkers. They held meetings and he decided to attend.

It took a lot of courage to walk into that meeting room the first time. He had been terrified until he finally lifted his downcast eyes and looked around. Lo and behold, all his old buddies from the pee bars were there, smiling at him, happy to see him, clapping for him. He felt like he had somehow, suddenly returned home. His joy cup ran over. He was once again where he belonged . . . among the one percent.

DAVID WOJNAROWICZ

BEING QUEER IN AMERICA:
A Journal of Disintegration

one. I'm walking through these hallways where the windows break apart a slow dying sky and a quiet wind follows the heels of the kid as he suddenly steps through a door frame ten rooms down. A quiet and simple grace in his arms and legs as the doorways fold out to produce more doorways and it's all some barbershop vision of mirrors with the wall ending at the distance of sky: small sparks of aeroplanes in that late blue and yellow and these little black pills stirring like small bees in my belly. The kid passed me earlier in the street about a mile away by the black shiny fence of a church: wrought iron spikes topped with deadly blades part zulu. But now it's just the sun piercing the waters of a veridian sea; his eyes set in the pale white face, arms a pale shade of red—something monkey, something borneo. His eyes make him look like he's starving for food or just feeling lust or else he's got the look of one of those spiritual types that hover on street corners trying to waylay and sweet-talk some passive kid into a lifetime of psychic control.

If viewed from miles above, this place would just appear to be a small boxlike structure like thousands of others set down along the lines of the rivers in the world; the only difference being that in this one the face of the kid starts moving up the wall past a window framing the perfect hazy coastline with teeth of red factories and an incidental gas-tank explosion that sends flowers of black smoke reeling up into the dusk. I can feel his lips against mine from across the room, tasting reefer or milk on them as he disappears through a square hole in the ceiling. I watch as his legs and feet leave the rungs of the metal ladder following his hips through that dark space, the soles of his sneakers floating effortlessly in the opening for a second, then shifting out of view. I follow his motions, pulling myself up two rungs at a time, and as my head clears the ceiling I see him recede farther back in the attic crawlspace. The horizontal red lines of his shirt become dark and indistinct, just the pale rose of his arms still luminous. He turns and leans up against the wall at a point where a crack in the roof lets light pass through, illuminating the wall and his head like some old russian icon of a saint in mausoleum darkness. Like him I have to crouch in order to move through the narrow space, walking along the tops of spaced beams like a horizontal ladder so as not to tip and crash through the rotting tin ceiling. I bump my head a couple of times on unseen pipes and finally reach him. His hands slide from his pockets and over the front of my trousers, moving back and forth until there is swelling. My hands drift over and repeated the actions over his crotch and like water falls from the sky I lean in close and slide down and unsnap his jeans button by button using only my teeth. He is wearing no underwear and I peel back the flaps of his trousers, his dick falling neatly out to rest on my lips. It is uncircumcised, slim and warm. I pass my face underneath it, wetting it slightly, teasingly, finally taking it into my mouth and sliding my hands upward beneath his shirt; the lines of it rippling like water and I feel the downy sensation of hair beneath my palms. His chest is hard: rippling stomach, the curve of it in dim light, the brown heat of his belly against my forehead. His hands slip softly down my collar and knead the muscles of my back, my neck and finally he make a rushing sound with his breath and he comes. I can feel it jetting in warm streams hitting the back of my throat: warm liquid sensation. Feels good. Nothing but the energy in his hands speaking with me.

three.   I walked for hours through the streets after he died, through the gathering darkness and traffic, down into the dying section of town where bodies litter the curbsides and dogs tear apart the stinking garbage by the doorways. There was a green swell to the clouds above the buildings like a green metal retrieved from the river years ago and notions of time were retracting and extending and somewhere in the midst of this I had to take a piss. I kicked around an alleyway among the piles of dead rotting fish, buzzing flies, piles of clothing and fluttering newspapers of the past with photographs of presidents and their waving wives haloed in camera flashes and suddenly in the stench and piling of decaying fish I realized I was staring at a human hand, with the fat pale shape and color of a cherub's hand. It stirred to life and where previously there had been discarded men's suits and playing cards, a fat white man naked down to his waist suddenly materialized and sat up angrily. He had an enormous, pale belly on which was incised a terrible wound from which small white worms tumbled as he gesticulated like a marionette, shrieking: DO YOU HAVE PERMISSION FROM THE OWNER OF THE ALLEY TO BE HERE?

I turned and left, walking back into the gray haze of traffic and exhaust, past a skinny prostitute doing the junkie walk bent over at the waist with knuckles dragging the sidewalk. She had some kind of disease on her legs: large bloodless wounds which she attempted to disguise with makeup. Whenever she heard the sound of a car slowing down near the curb, thinking it was a potential customer, she would painfully lift her body up to reveal a delirious smile and dead eyes and a weak flailing of her arms as a sign of greeting. Kids ran back and forth on the sidewalk dragging a small kitten by a rope and a bunch of winos descended like buzzards onto the waves of cars stopped at the nearest traffic light.

My arms sometimes feel twelve feet long and I get consumed by the emptiness and void surrounding and lying beneath each and every action I witness of others and myself. Each little gesture in the movements of the planet in its canyons and arroyos, in its suburbs and cities, in the motions of wind and light, each little action continuing, helping to continue the slow death of ourselves, the slow motion approach of the unveiling of our order and disorder in its ultimate climax beginning with a spark so subtle and beautiful that to trust it is to trust our own stupidity; it sparks in the inversion of wind and then flowers out momentarily in black petals of smoke and light and then extends vertically in an enlargement of a minute vision. In the very center, if one could withstand the light, it would appear to be octopal in its appendages. Wormlike tentacles thousands of feet long vibrate stroboscopically in the bluish mist that exudes from its center. The center is something outside of what we know as visual, more a sensation: a huge fat clockwork of civilizations; the whole onward crush of the world as we know it; all the walking swastikas yap-yapping cartoon video death language; a malfunctioning cannonball filled with bone and gristle and gear wheels and knives and bullets and animals rotting with skeletal remains and pistons and smokestacks pump-pumping cinders and lightning and shreds of flesh, spewing language and motions and shit and entrails in its wake. It's all swirling in every direction simultaneously so that it's going neither forward nor backward, not from side to side, embracing stasis beyond the ordinary sense of stillness one witnesses in death, in a decaying corpse that lasts millions of years in comparison to the sense of time this thing operates within. This is the version I see beneath the tiniest gesture of wiping one's lips after a meal or observing a traffic light.

six. In the skidrow section of town, the only movement in the streets was the automobiles cruising along the curbside and river parking lot. In the dusk they were like aquariums on wheels: amphibious stares of strangers pressed behind glasses. Tall granite buildings with tiny windows speckled with fluorescent lights; gray vague shapes in the dripping alleyways and shit and garbage rattling in the wind along the flooded gutters, splashes of red and green neons sliding across the wet pavements. A skinny bum with red bare feet—once somebody's little baby—crawled into a box that once contained a refrigerator nestled in the weeds of an empty parking lot. A small black dog hurtles through the wet evening air amid a squeal of tires and thumping of glass and all civilization is at the wheel.

I pushed through the heavy glass doors and entered the place as a thin pale teenager seated at the elevated desk was yelling at the men in the back to put quarters into the machines or leave. I gave him a couple of dollars and he pumped out eight quarters from a chrome gadget on the desk. I passed through a room of enormous rubber dicks and fuck magazines and entered a moist and dark hallway. A couple of black drag queens with too much lipstick hovered in the shadows of a malfunctioning pinball machine, its flippers clacking and thrumming endlessly while the scoreboard revolved and whirred. A fat man with skin the color of liver sat in a booth with the door open, his mouth gaping and his tiny, perfect white hands fluttering around his open zipper.

He was the kind of guy I'd rob banks for, leaning against a stone wall, everyone else in the crowded street disappeared. He leaned in front of me rubbed my chest and belly like he'd known me for years—some distant relative—and I left reason behind in one of those moments where all sense of living takes a slow quiet dive into mystery and possibilities. I needed to be shook. I'd forgotten who I was and anything was welcome including the rough tight line of his neck turning in a warm shirt collar. He gave a drunken half-smile and stepped inside the alleyway and began climbing the fifteen-foot high mountain of spare tires. This was next to some gas station. I was fifteen and hungry.

I saw a guy in an old black leather jacket and a fishing cap half standing in the doorway of an open booth. The orange interior walls were illuminated by the metallic blue of a video monitor; over his shoulder, a sadist on a motorcycle was shoving his boots into the belly of an obviously drugged adolescent who lay naked on the gravel road. Halfway up the right wall of the booth was a large dick pushed through a hole, suspended and throbbing; it looked like it'd been hung up there like an unwanted gift.

I got to the top of the mountain, both of us in the cool evening wind, each footstep more like a bounce on top of all that rubber. Sounds of faraway voices and traffic circling into the alley, his cold hands started with my shirt buttons, my tongue starting with his neck and then sliding up to his mouth. Next to his left ear an enormous and luminous white ship plowed through the waters of the river.

A couple of quarters fished from his pockets turned on the video monitor and he flicked the stations until there was a blue image of a man's head floating across the screen. It was a forest at night and the video was badly transferred so that everything in it was translated into different shades of cobalt. An overly sensitive microphone was being used so the entire soundtrack was crickets. A blue cowboy removing his blue plaid shirt with muscled blue arms, leaning down in a blue naked haze to lick the belly of a blue shirtless bunkmate. Crickets. A close-up of an amazing blue eye floating in a blue field cut to a blue tongue coasting along the endless surface of rough blue flesh. Crickets. Blue trees at night with a luminous blue haze of light casting about their leaves. Crickets. A blue dick floating across dark blue shadows and burying itself into a waiting blue mouth. Crickets.

The sound of carwheels slicing through puddles on the highway: Ah man says he is lowering himself onto my back one of his arms muscled and furry wrapping itself under

my jaw and against the side of my face yer my babe ohh
yer my babe whispering in my ear lips brushing lightly each
sound a warm burst of breath ah man . . . yer my babe with
that roping-the-steer cowboy voice I can hear the distances
in that voice and smell the gathering sweat on the surface
of the tires yer my babe ahh and I'm already falling cowboy-
off-the-cliff like and he's moving his warm belly sliding it
against my back taking the nape of my neck in his cold white
teeth and turning my head slightly opening my eyes without
my glasses and through the luminous blaze of sudden sunlight
fall these shadows—the outline of thousands of leaves connected to branches that dip and bend in the wind.

A pair of empty cowboy boots sailing slow motion across
dark blue space and bouncing lazily against a bunkhouse
wall and then settling slowly into a series of geometric blue
shadows. Crickets. Blue cowboy bodies amputating from
blue darkness into the pale light. Crickets. Light blue semen
uncoiling across a blue torso in some small fever.

seven.   He's got me down on my knees and I can't even
focus on anything I have no time to understand the position
of my body or the direction of my face I see a pair of legs
in rough corduroy and the color of the pants is brown and
surrounded by darkness and there's a sense of other people
there and yet I can't hear them breathe or hear their feet or
anything and his hand suddenly comes up against the back
to my head and he's got his fingers locked in my hair and
he's shoving my face forward and twisting my head almost
gently but very violent in that gentleness and I got only half
a breath in my lungs the smell of piss on the floorboards
and this fleshy bulge in his pants getting harder and harder
as my face is forced against the front of his pants the zipper
tears my lips I feel them getting bruised and all the while
he's stroking my face and tightening his fingers around the
locks of my hair and I can't focus my eyes my head being
pushed and pulled and twisted and caressed and it's as if I
have no hands I know I got hands I had hands a half hour

ago I remember lighting a cigarette with them lighting a match and I remember how warm the flame was when I lifted it toward my face and my knees are hurting cause they banged on the floor when he dragged me down the cellar stairs I remember a door in the darkness and the breath of a dog his dog as it licked my hands when I reached out to stop my headlong descent its tongue licking out at my fingers and my face slams down and there's this electric blam inside my head and it's as if my eyes suddenly opened on the large sun and then went black with the switch thrown down and I'm shocked and embarrassed and his arms swing down he's lifting me up saying: lookin for me? and he buries his face in my neck and I feel the saliva running down into the curve of my neck and my arms are hanging loose and I can see a ceiling and a dim bulb tossing back and forth and suddenly I'm on my knees again and my face is getting mashed into his belly and sliding down across rough cloth and zippers and there's this sweet musty smell and his dick is slapping across my eyes and rubbing over my cheeks and bloody lips and suddenly it's inside my mouth and the hands twisted up in my hair and cradling my skull shove me forward and I feel this dick hit the back of my throat and I feel pain for the first time like the open pants are in focus and he's pulled his dick out of my mouth and I'm choking and he's running one hand over my face putting his fingers in my ears in my mouth dragging down my lower jaw and forcing his dick in between the fingers and the saliva and blood and shoving shoving in and out and pulling on my hair and everything goes out of focus my eyes moving around blindly the smell of basement water and sewage and mustiness and dirt and he's slapping my face like he wants to wake me up and I realize I'm crying and he tells me that he loves me and he lifts me up and puts his lips over mine and sticks his tongue in my mouth and buries his rough face down in my collar and licks and drags his tongue over my shoulder and neck and his hands are up inside my shirt and he's rubbing them back and forth across my belly and sides taking quick handfuls of flesh and twisting and rubbing and then they're inside my pants and he suddenly rips apart the opening of my pants I hear metal buttons hitting the floor and he punches me in the side of the head at the same time pulling my hair and pulling me back down to the floor and I'm on my belly I feel cold rough stone scratching my skin and he kneels down suddenly into the center of my back and it hurts and I try to yell but he's shoving my underwear into my mouth and I'm suddenly hit with such a feeling of intense claustrophobia and fear that it's hours before I realize that my hands and legs are tied together and that I'm lying on my side and the rag in my mouth is soaking wet and making small bubbling sounds each time I breathe.

ten. I walk this hallway twenty-seven times and all I can see are the cool white walls. A hand rubbing slowly across a face, but my hands are empty. Walking back and forth from room to room trailing bluish shadows I feel weak: something emotional and wild forming a crazy knot in the deep part of my stomach. On the next trip from the front of the apartment to the back, I end up in the kitchen, turn once again and suddenly sink down to the floor in a crouching position against the wall and side of the stove in a blaze of wintery sunlight. It's blinding me as my fingers trace small circles through the hair on the sides of my temples, and I've had little sleep having woken up a number of times slightly shocked at the sense of another guy's warm skin and my hands, independent of me in sleep, were tracing the lines of his arms and belly and hips and side. How the world is so much like dreamsleep with my glasses hidden somewhere along the windowsill above the bed; there's a slow stir of measured breath from next to me and through the six A.M. windowpanes I see what appears to be a dim forest of trees in the distance, leafless and shivering, but it's just some old summer plants in a window box gone to sleep for the season. I think of these trees and how they look like the winter forests of my childhood and how they were always places of refuge: endless hours spent among them creating small myths of myself alone or living in hollowed-out trees or sleeping in nests twenty times larger than crow's nests made of sticks instead of twigs. I realized then how I always tend to mythologize the people, things, landscapes I love, always wanting them to somehow extend forever through time and motion. It's a similar sense I have for lovers, wanting somehow to have some degree of permanence in my contact with them but it never really goes that way. So here I am heading out into the cold winds of the canyon streets, walking down and across Avenue C toward my home with the smell and taste of him wrapped around my neck and jaw like a scarf. It follows me in and out of restaurants and past cops and past morning children and past bakery windows filled with brides and grooms on rows of wedding cakes and across fields of brick and mortar. Small traces of memory fold and slip back to where he and I are sitting in his place late evening playing games of poker. I had never really played before in my life and suddenly after losing a sock and a shirt I became an expert. We're laughing about it and I don't stop for the smaller articles of clothing. I tell him I have to get it while I can, having won my first game and I motion toward his pants and in the evening stillness there's a slight rustle of clothing. Coins spill freely to the ground and my hands are animated and drifting soundlessly up his calves, up his thighs and he tells me he learned this game years ago with some kid across the street after school in some town outside atlantic city. When their clothes were gone the loser had to suck the other guy's dick, only they put saran wrap around each other's dick after all you couldn't possibly touch your tongue to flesh.

. . . Through his memories I recall hours on end sitting in the weeds in the backyard next to the lawn chair where my uncle lay in shorts and a wedding ring, his body hardened and brown from days of skin-diving in far away oceans filled with the mysterious fish and creatures he described. I stared and stared and sometimes played with his arms for hours and I remember feeling a slight dizziness that years later I came to see first as a curse and then as a tool: a wedge that I might successfully drive between me and a world that was rapidly becoming more and more insane.

eleven.   A number of months ago I read in the newspaper that there was a supreme court ruling which states that homosexuals in america have no constitutional rights against the government's invasion of their privacy. The paper stated that homosexuality is traditionally condemned in america and only people who are heterosexual or married or who have families can expect these constitutional rights. There were no editorials. Nothing. Just flat cold type in the morning paper informing people of this. In most areas of the u.s.a. it is possible to murder a man and when one is brought to trial one has only to say that the victim was a queer and that he tried to touch you and the courts will set you free. When I read the newspaper article I felt something stirring in my hand; I felt a sensation like seeing oneself from miles above the earth or like looking at one's reflection in a mirror through the wrong end of a telescope. Realizing that I have nothing left to lose in my actions I let my hands become weapons, my teeth become weapons, every bone and muscle and fiber and ounce of blood become weapons, and I feel prepared for the rest of my life.

In my dreams I crawl across freshly clipped front lawns, past statues and dogs and cars containing your guardians. I enter your houses through the smallest cracks in the bricks that keep you feeling comfortable and safe. I cross your living rooms and go up your staircases and into your bedrooms where you lie sleeping. I wake you up and tell you a story about when I was ten years old and walking around Times Square looking for the weight of some man to lie across me to replace the nonexistent hugs and kisses from my mom and dad, I got picked up by some guy who took me to a remote area of the waterfront in his car and proceeded to beat the shit out of me because he was so afraid of the impulses of heat stirring in his belly. I would have strangled him but my hands were too small to fit around his neck. I will wake you up and welcome you to your bad dream.

KAREN FINLEY

IT'S ONLY ART

I WENT INTO A museum but they had taken down all the art. Only the empty frames were left. Pieces of masking tape were up with the names of the paintings and the artists and stating why they were removed. The guards had nothing to guard. The white walls yellowed. Toilets were locked up in museums because people think someone peeing is art. Someone might think that pee flushing down that toilet is art. Someone might think that the act of peeing is a work of art. And the government pays for that pee flushing down that toilet. There were many bladder infections among those who inspected the museum making sure that there was no offensive art. They might lose their jobs. It's a good life when no one thinks that you ever piss or shit.

In the empty frames were the reasons why art was con-
fiscated.
Jaspar Johns—for desecrating the flag.
Michaelangelo—for being a homosexual.
Mary Cassatt—for painting nude children.
Van Gogh—for contributing to psychedelia.

Georgia O'Keefe—for painting cow skulls (the dairy industry complained).

Picasso—for urinating, apparently, on his sculptures, with the help of his children, to achieve the desired patina effect.

Edward Hopper—for repressed lust.

Jeff Koons—for offending Michael Jackson.

All ceramicists were banned because working with clay was too much like playing with your own shit.

All glassblowing became extinct because it was too much like giving a blow job.

All art from cultures that didn't believe in one male god was banned for being blasphemous.

We looked for the show of early American quilts, but it had been taken down. One guard said that a period stain was found on one, another guard said he found an ejaculation stain on a quilt from Virginia. In fact, they closed all of the original thirteen states. You can imagine what happened under those quilts at night!

Since the Confiscation of Art occurred, an Art Propaganda Army was started by the government. Last month the national assignment for the army artists was to make Dan Quayle look smart. The assignment for the army writers was to make the Stealth bomber as important as the microwave oven. Musicians were asked to write a tune, that the HUD scandal was no big deal, like taking sugar packets from a café. Dancers were to choreograph a dance showing that the Iran-Contra affair was as harmless as your dog going into your neighbor's yard. And filmmakers were told to make films about homelessness, poverty and AIDS, saying that God has a plan for us all.

But no art came out.

No art was made.

Newspapers became thin and disappeared because there was no more criticism. There was nothing to gossip about.

Schools closed because learning got in the way of patriotism. No one could experiment, for that was the way of the devil.

There was no theory. No academia. No debate teams. No "Jeopardy."

Everyone became old overnight. There was no more reason for anything. Everything became old and gray. Everyone had blue-gray skin like the color of bones, unfriendly seas and navy bean soup. And then the Punishers, the Executioners, the Judges of creativity grew weary, for there was no creativity left to condemn. So they snorted and they squawked, but they held in their boredom. All that was printed in newspapers, journals and magazines was the phrase "I don't know."

All actresses and actors were gone from TV except Charlton Heston. Charlton did TV shows twenty-four hours a day (with occasional cameo appearances by Anita Bryant).

One day Jesse Helms was having some guests over from Europe. A dignitary, a land developer and a king. Mrs. Helms asked them where they'd like to go in America. The king said, "Disneyland."

Mr. Helms said, "Oh, that was closed down when we saw Disney's film *Fantasia*."

So the guests said, "Nathan's Hot Dogs in Coney Island."

Mr. Helms answered, "Sorry, but hot dogs are too phallic. In this country we don't eat anything that's longer than it's wide. Nathan's is history. In this country we don't even eat spaghetti. Bananas aren't imported. Tampon instructions are not allowed."

"Well," the guests said, "we'd like to go to the Museum of Modern Art, and if we can't go there, then why come to America?"

Mr. Helms was stuck. He wanted everyone to think he was cool, having Europeans visit him. Then he had an idea. He'd make the art himself to put back into the empty museums. He'd get George Bush and William Buckley and Donald Wildmon and Dana Rohrabacher and Tipper Gore and other conservative allies to come over and make some art on the White House lawn. So he called all of his cronies to come on down and make some art. And everyone came because it was better than watching Charlton Heston on TV.

Mr. and Mrs. Helms looked all over for art supplies. They came up with old wallpaper, scissors and house paint and laid it all out for their friends to express themselves.

When the friends arrived they were scared to make art because they never had before. Never even used a crayon. But then a child picked up a crayon and drew a picture of her cat having babies. Then she drew a picture of her father hitting her. Then a picture of her alone and bruised. The mother looked at the picture and cried and told the daughter she didn't know that had happened to her. The child screamed out "DRAW YOUR DREAMS! DRAW YOUR NIGHTMARES! DRAW YOUR FEARS! DRAW YOUR REALITIES!"

Everyone started making pictures of houses on fire, of monsters and trees becoming penises, pictures of making love with someone of the same sex, of being naked on street corners, of pain and dirty words and things you never admitted in real life.

For thirteen days and nights everyone drew and drew nonstop. Some started telling stories, writing poems. Neighbors saw the artmaking and joined in. Somehow pretend was back in. Somehow expression sprang up from nowhere.

But then the Confiscation Police arrived and they took everyone away. (The father of the child who drew the father hitting the child complained.) Everyone was arrested. They even arrested Jesse Helms, for he was painting his soul out, which was HATE AND ENVY AND CRIME AND DARKNESS AND PAIN. They threw him into the slammer. He was tried for treason and lost. And on his day of execution his last words were: "IT WAS ONLY ART."

Cookie Mueller with her husband, Vittorio. Nan Goldin, 1989.
Courtesy of Pace/MacGill.

ABOUT THE AUTHORS

Kathy Acker is the author of *Empire of the Senseless, Great Expectations, Blood and Guts in High School, Don Quixote,* and *Literal Madness,* which consists of three short novels. She lives in San Francisco.

Dorothy Allison is the author of *The Women Who Hate Me,* a book of poetry; *Trash,* a collection of short stories honored by two Lambda Literary Awards; and a forthcoming novel, *A Bastard Out of Carolina.* She lives in San Francisco.

Dodie Bellamy is the author of *Feminine Hijinx.* She lives in San Francisco with her husband, writer Kevin Killian.

Kate Bornstein is a transsexual lesbian playwright and activist. Her play *Hidden: A Gender* has been performed on both U.S. coasts, with an upcoming European tour. She is currently working on a new musical, *The Three Dollar Bill Opera.* She lives in San Francisco.

William S. Burroughs is the author of the classics *Junky* and *Naked Lunch,* as well as many other works. He is a member of the American Academy of Arts and Letters. He divides his time between New York City and Lawrence, Kansas.

Pat Califia is the author of *Sapphistry,* a sex-education text for lesbians; *Macho Sluts,* a collection of short erotic fiction; and *Doc and Fluff,* a novel. She has written an advice column for the *Advocate* since 1981.

Wanda Coleman is a Los Angeles–based writer and the working mother of three children. Her poems and stories have appeared in numerous magazines, including *Callaloo, Caliban,* and *Black American Literature Forum.* Her books include *A War of Eyes and Other Stories, Dicksboro Hotel,* and *African Sleeping Sickness.*

Dennis Cooper is the author of several volumes of poetry, one of which, *The Tenderness of the Wolves,* was nominated for the Los Angeles Times Book Award for Poetry in 1984. He is the author of *Closer,* which won the 1990 Ferro-Grumley Award for Gay Fiction; *Frisk,* a novel; and *Wrong,* a collection of short fiction.

Jane DeLynn is the author of *Don Juan in the Village, Real Estate, In Thrall,* and *Some Do.* Her work has appeared in the *New York Times Magazine, Seven Days,* and *Christopher Street.*

Karen Finley is a performance artist, writer, and visual artist. She has recorded several albums and appeared in many films. She is the author of *Shock Treatment,* a book of monologues, essays and poems.

Bob Flanagan is the author of *Slave Sonnets, The Wedding of Everything,* and *Fuck Journal.* He lives in Los Angeles.

Mary Gaitskill is the author of a critically acclaimed volume of short stories, *Bad Behavior,* and a novel, *Two Girls Fat and Thin.* She divides her time between New York City and San Francisco.

Robert Glück is the Director of the Poetry Center at San

Francisco State University. His books include *Jack the Modernist,* a novel; *Reader,* a collection of poems and short prose; and *Elements of a Coffee Service,* a book of stories.

Hattie Gossett is a writer, performance artist, and lecturer. She is the author of *presenting . . . sister no blues,* a collection of prose poetry. *bras and rubbers in the gutters* was written as part of a performance series curated by clovrrr chango.

Essex Hemphill is the author of two books of poetry, *Earth Life* and *Conditions.* His work is featured in the Black gay films *Looking for Langston* and *Tongues Untied.* He is the editor of the anthology *Brother to Brother: New Writings by Black Gay Men.*

Gary Indiana is the author of *White Trash Boulevard, Scar Tissue,* a collection of short stories, and *Horse Crazy,* a novel. He lives in New York City.

Michael Lassell is the author of *Decade Dance* and *Poems for Lost and Un-Lost Boys.* His fiction and poetry have appeared in many publications, including *Gay and Lesbian Poetry in Our Time, Poets For Life,* and *Men on Men III.* He lives in New York City.

Cookie Mueller is the author of *How to Get Rid of Pimples, Walking Through Clear Water in a Pool Painted Black,* and *Fan Mail, Frank Letters and Crank Calls.* She was the art columnist for *Details* magazine for many years. She died of AIDS in 1989.

Manuel Ramos Otero is the author of many books of fiction and poetry, including *Página en blanco y staccato* and *Invitación al polvo.* He is the editor of *Tales from an Urban Landscape: An Anthology of Contemporary Fiction from Puerto Rico.* Ramos Otero was born in Puerto Rico and now lives in New York City, where he is a professor of Caribbean and Latin American Literature at Lehman College of the City University of New York.

John Preston is the author of numerous books including *Franny: The Queen of Provincetown*. He edited the anthology *Personal Dispatches: Writers Confront AIDS*. His essays and reviews have appeared in a range of periodicals, including the *Advocate, Drummer, Harper's,* and *Semiotext(e)*. He serves as the writer-in-residence at the AIDS Project in Portland, Maine, where he lives.

Terence Sellers is the author of *The Correct Sadist* and *The Obsession*. She is working on a novel, *One Decadent Life,* and on *The Second Book of the Correct Sadist*. She divides her time between New York City and New Mexico.

Ana Maria Simo is a playwright living on New York City's Lower East Side. *How to Kill Her* is her first novel; it is also the title of her first film, a short feature produced with filmmaker Ela Troyano. She is currently working on a feature-length screenplay also based on the novel.

Lynne Tillman is a writer and filmmaker. She is a contributing editor of *BOMB* magazine, and the author of *Haunted Houses, Motion Sickness,* and *Absence Makes the Heart*. She lives in New York City.

David Trinidad is the author of several books of poetry, including *November, Three Stories,* and *Monday, Monday*. His poetry has appeared in the *Paris Review, New American Writing, BOMB,* and the anthology *American Poetry Since 1970: Up Late*. Trinidad is originally from Los Angeles and now lives in New York City, where he teaches at The Writer's Voice/63rd Street YMCA and at Brooklyn College.

David Wojnarowicz has exhibited his artwork in galleries and museums worldwide. His work has been included in the Whitney Biennial. He is also the author of three books, including *Close to the Knives: A Memoir of Disintegration*.

ABOUT THE EDITORS

Amy Scholder is an editor at City Lights Publishers. She has served on the Board of Directors for the Words Project for AIDS and as a founding organizer for OutWrite: The National Lesbian & Gay Writers Conference. She has curated many public readings in San Francisco and Los Angeles. Raised in Los Angeles, she now lives in San Francisco.

Ira Silverberg is a literary agent and publicist. He is on the board of directors of *BOMB* magazine, the Words Project for AIDS, and the AIDS Treatment Project, where he established the Carl Apfelschnitt Memorial Fund for Poets and Artists with AIDS. He also works with the PEN Benefit Committee for Writers and Editors with AIDS, Giorno Poetry Systems, and the Kitchen, a performance space in New York City where he curates a reading series.

Plume

THE FINEST IN SHORT FICTION